ONE SPARK OF MAGIC

by

Iris Bolling

Printed in the United States of America

ISBN- 978-0-9913426-8-6

Library of Congress Control Number: 2016921188

SIRI AUSTIN ENTERTAINMENT LLC
RICHMOND, VIRGINIA
www.siriaustin.com
www.irisbolling.net

Books By Iris Bolling

The Heart Series
Once You've Touched The Heart
The Heart of Him
Look Into My Heart
A Heart Divided
A Lost Heart
The Heart

Night of Seduction Series
Night of Seduction/Heaven's Gate
The Pendleton Rule

Gems and Gents Series
Teach Me
The Book of Joshua I – Trust
The Book of Joshua II – Believe
A Lassiter's Christmas
Ruby...Red Slippers & All
The Book of Adam – Hypnotic

Brooks Family Values Series
Sinergy
Fatal Mistake
Propensity For Love

CHAPTER ONE

It was inconceivable to believe he was being played. Yet, that was exactly what Jarrett Bryson was thinking as he boarded a flight to Richmond, Virginia. His agent had stated it was imperative that they speak face to face. The call had him wondering what the front office of the Brooklyn Knights Baseball Team had up their sleeves.

"Welcome aboard Mr. Bryson," the flight attendant greeted with a flirtatious smile.

"Thank you," Jarrett replied as he took one of the four seats in first class.

"Would you like a glass of champagne, Chardonnay, Remy on the rocks, or something else?" The attendant asked in a voice that offered more than what was on the menu.

Jarrett looked up, recognizing the unspoken offer. The attendant stepped closer making certain the offer was understood. This was the norm for Jarrett. As one of the top shortstops in major league baseball, offers from the female persuasion were an every hour occurrence.

At twenty-nine, he was considered a veteran of the sport with at least another ten good years ahead of him. His last contract, a cool 123 million, was small compared to the anticipated extension being negotiated. Additionally, his endorsement deals tripled his income giving him unprecedented media exposure. He had graced the cover of Sports Illustrated several times over with numerous covers for GQ and Men to Men. Not to mention the gossip magazines that made major funds from chronologically accounting who he was dating, proven or unproven. Women dreamed of him with his rugged good looks, athletically toned body, and somewhat reserved personality. Most women did all they could to carry out those dreams, whenever the opportunity arose. It seemed the attendant was taking her place in the batter's box.

"Nothing at this time," Jarrett replied displaying his megawatt smile. Some speculated the smile was insured with a million dollar policy. It was actually ten, however, only Jarrett and his agent knew for sure.

"If you desire anything...anything at all, my name is Mona Lisa. You're the only passenger with us today in first class. We have the section to ourselves. It will be a pleasure to serve you. Don't hesitate to call."

"Thank you."

Mona Lisa turned and made her way towards the galley. He watched her exaggerated body movements as any male would.

"I will not hesitate at all." He grinned as he ran his hands down his face. There was nothing like a woman with the confidence to go after what she wanted. However, Jarrett learned early in his career to be very selective when it came to women. Most were after fame and fortune, or worse, a baby daddy and marriage. Jarrett wasn't opposed to marriage. It was something he just wanted to do once. Like his parents, he wanted a marriage with love as its foundation. To date, no woman had peaked his interest. Until one did, women were a casual pastime for him and nothing more.

After securing his overnight bag in the overhead compartment, Jarrett took a seat, relaxed his six-two frame by stretching his legs out, crossing them at the ankles. Pulling out his phone, he read the text he'd received from Nick Brooks, his agent. Nick in addition to the face to face, had requested his help with a new client, Jason Whitfield, a power forward who claimed the number one spot in the NBA Draft. Under normal circumstances, the agency would have sent the company jet for him, but it was being used to deliver Whitfield. Jarrett didn't mind flying commercial for the hour it would take to fly from New York to Virginia. It gave him the rare opportunity to meet fans face to face. Contrary to popular belief he wasn't the Prima Donna of sports that the media made him out to be.

"Excuse the delay Mr. Bryson. It seems we have another passenger joining us in first class," Mona Lisa stated in a professional but tense voice. "Once she boards, we will be on our way."

"It's not a problem."

"It's just inconsiderate to the other passengers. Usually it's someone that thinks they own the world and wants everyone to walk to the beat of his, or in this case, her drum. Imagine holding up a plane of people just for one person."

"It's probably something last minute that couldn't be helped," Jarrett offered, not necessarily interested in the commentary.

The statement generated a smile from his admirer. "That's very gracious of you. And you may be right." Mona Lisa walked back towards the galley then turned back and stated, "I'll have a layover in Richmond if you need some company."

Jarrett smiled. "I'll keep that in mind."

Mona Lisa walked away and Jarrett went back to his messages. The next message from Nick concerned him. It seems his team owners did not wish to negotiate a new contract until the end of the season. It was September. Jarrett had delivered home runs and batted in averages that had delivered them to the number one spot in their division. All but guaranteeing them a spot in the playoffs. His numbers had slumped a little after the All-Star Game. He couldn't put his finger on why. Putting in extra time working out or in the batting cage had occupied his mind instead of trying to figure out what was behind his slump. Even with the slump, he was still leading the field in pertinent areas.

While reading the message, a slight tremble began in his stomach. It was the feeling of nervous energy Jarrett usually experienced when at the plate, with an opportunity to advance his team to the playoffs. Since neither was the case, he ignored it, and continued reading. A moment later he thought he detected the sensual scent of fresh jasmine. It reminded him of a spring day in a field of flowers, almost forcing him to look up, but he didn't.

"Good morning. Please accept my apology for the delay."

Jarrett had ignored the punch in the gut caused by the sensual smell, but his senses could not ignore the musical sound of the voice. He looked up just as Mona Lisa walked by to greet the owner of the voice. The way Mona Lisa's body tensed from the back, clearly indicated the person causing the delay was not welcome.

"You're here now. Let's get you seated and prepare for takeoff."

"Yes, of course," the woman replied as she hurriedly took the window seat across the aisle from Jarrett.

With Mona Lisa standing between them, Jarrett could not see the woman, but her thick luxurious black hair swirled just above her shoulders as she settled in and buckled her seat belt.

"May I take your coat?" Mona Lisa offered.

"No, I'll keep that. I've delayed you long enough."

"Would you like any refreshments?" Mona Lisa asked curtly.

"No, thank you. Please don't go through any bother on my part."

"No bother. My name is Mona Lisa if you need anything."

"What a beautiful name."

"Thank you."

The next few moments seemed to go in slow motion, as Mona Lisa turned to him, smiled, then walked back towards the galley. As she stepped away the new passenger came into view. The woman was breathtakingly beautiful. Exotic, expressive eyes, a small pert nose, smooth, dark sable skin and the sweetest looking lips he had ever seen. The woman never looked across the aisle where he sat for she was busy putting a headband on her short wavy cut, pulling her hair away from her face. He almost wished she had left it down until she looked up, taking in her surroundings, and her gaze fell on him. He saw, more than heard, her sharp intake of breath when she saw him. The flush of embarrassment was instantaneous.

"Hello." she said. "I apologize for not speaking when I first arrived, but as you can see I was a little late. And, well, I think the flight attendant is a little upset with me." She ended with a sigh. "I do understand her reasons. I so hate when people are late."

Mesmerized by her looks and the way her voice touched him, it took Jarrett a moment to realize she had stopped talking.

"Hello to you. I'm sure it was unintentional."

"Oh it was," she replied so sincerely Jarrett had to smile. "My Grand'Mere called early this morning and said she had a dream and I needed to come home right away." She rushed to offer, "And when my Grand'Mere says move you don't ask questions, you just move."

Jarrett broke out in a huge grin at her statement. "I have a grandmother like that."

"Then you know what I mean." She nodded with laughter. Warmth, unlike anything Jarrett had experienced before, came over him. "She said, your plane leaves in two hours, and I was half asleep," she said expressively. "Then to step outside in the rather cool September air, well I don't have to tell you, but that certainly awakened my senses."

"Ms. Cartwright," Mona Lisa called out as she walked over and spoke quietly in her ear. "People in first class enjoy their privacy and do not like being disturbed."

"Oh." She leaned forward to look around Mona Lisa to speak to Jarrett. "I do apologize." She then looked up at Mona Lisa to explain further, "I may not be clear on the proper etiquette of flying. I will not disturb..." She hesitated then looked at Jarrett. "I'm sorry, I don't know your name."

Jarrett almost laughed. The thought of a woman not recognizing him was unusual. But from the questioning look on her face, he believed she didn't.

"His name is Jarrett Bryson," Mona Lisa said before he could respond. "And he should not be disturbed by your chatter."

The woman looked back over at him, then gasped. "Are you sure?" She frowned.

Jarrett's eyebrow rose at her response. Mona Lisa testily replied, "Yes, of course I'm sure."

The woman turned back to him. "I'm sorry Mr. Bryson. I will not disturb you again." She looked up at Mona Lisa. "I'm sorry."

Mona Lisa turned to Jarrett. "If you wish I can have her seat changed."

Jarrett immediately shook his head. "She is not disturbing me." You are, he wanted to say, but didn't. The jealousy stemming from the possibility of a little competition was evident in the attendant's actions.

Mona Lisa turned back to the woman. "This is your only warning," she said, then walked away.

Looking completely dejected, the woman turned and looked out the window. Missing the carefree atmosphere she'd brought on board, Jarrett searched his mind for something to say to the woman. Why he felt he needed to make her feel better he didn't know, but he had to. Struggling to come up with something was odd. He was never speechless with women. Words always flowed freely. However, with this woman, he wasn't trying to hit on her, he just wanted to see her light up the silent cabin with her aura. Then it hit him.

"You wouldn't happen to be related to Ben, Hoss and Little Joe would you?"

She turned to him with the biggest smile and the gleam back in her dark brown eyes. For a moment she did not say anything, she just smiled at him, and he was content to sit there and bask in the vision. Then they both broke out in complete laughter as the plane began to take off.

Brushing away the one strand of hair that had fallen out of place, she sobered. "My father says I've never met a stranger because I talk to just about everyone I meet as if I know them. That's why I stay in trouble all the time." She shyly looked towards Mona Lisa. "I don't think she likes me very much. Although I can't imagine why, I never met her before."

Jarrett knew exactly why. Other women would fade in a room with this woman. "Would your father's name happen to be Ben?"

Beaming again, the woman tilted her head to the side. "No, his name is Horace Cartwright. Make that Judge Cartwright."

Jarrett thought for a minute, he recognized the name. "Justice Cartwright?"

"Yes, do you know my father?"

Jarrett nodded. "I met him at a game once."

"You remember that?" Her eyes beamed. "I have heard the story about that game a number of times. He's going to be thrilled to know you remember it as well." She looked away. "I'm sorry I didn't recognize you before, I'm not a Knights' fan. I like Atlanta."

Jarrett clutched his chest as if he had been injured.

"Stabbed right in the heart." He smiled. Removing his seatbelt, he stood and extended his hand. "Jarrett Bryson... officially."

She placed her hand in his. "Paige Cartwright... officially."

Jarrett looked down at the small hand inside his and marveled at the sense of calm that infused his body. He reluctantly released her hand and retook his seat.

"It's nice to officially meet you Ms. Cartwright."

"The pleasure is mine."

Jarrett rested his elbow on the seat handle, placing his chin in his hand and turned to her. "So, Ms. Cartwright what do you do?"

"I'm a dancer."

"In New York?"

"Yes, but my company does tours all over the world. It's so fascinating meeting people from all cultures and walks of life. Don't you think so? I mean you travel all the time. Don't you enjoy meeting people and hearing their stories?"

Nodding his head, Jarrett had to agree, he did like that aspect of his job.

"I think it's wonderful to get to travel, meet people, see the world and get paid, all for doing something you love to do. Don't you?"

For a while Jarrett just sat there thinking about her statement. She was right. He was fortunate to go out every day and do what he loved to do, play baseball. Not many people could make that claim.

"I'm sorry. Sometimes I talk too much."

Jarrett shook his head. "No, it's not that." He sat up. "Your question made me think of a situation I'm dealing with."

"The contract negotiations?"

"Yes." He stretched out his legs and crossed them at the ankles, again. "You're right. We are fortunate."

"Sometimes, contracts and legal issues muddy up the waters. The truth of the matter is you love to play baseball. Don't worry about the legal stuff or next year. Take the moment that God has given you now and enjoy it. We never know when or if it will be taken away. That's the advice my Grand'Mere gave me."

Jarrett smiled. "Your Grand'Mere sounds like a very wise woman."

If the look on her face was any indication, that comment made her day.

"She is...she really is."

Paige looked at the man that every woman in New York and beyond, wanted to get next to and who every man wanted to be. He seemed normal, not god like as she thought he would be, based on all the hype in the news surrounding his new contract negotiations. He was a handsome devil, as her Grand'Mere would say. Yes indeed, quite pleasing to the eyes and from their brief talk, she could tell there was a lot more to him than the newscasters reported.

There was something intriguing about Jarrett Bryson. Yet, there was something else. He seemed to be at a crossroads in his life and was in need of guidance. He really needed a sit down with her Grand'Mere, she thought. When he took her hand earlier, for a moment...just a moment, she felt connected to him, and sensed he was searching...for something. Whatever it was, he needed her to help him find it. She wondered if that was the reason Grand'Mere insisted she come home immediately. Was she supposed to meet this man on this day, to help him in some way? Before she could get her answers, he removed his hand and his shields went up.

"You know," she saw him look over at her as she spoke, "my Grand'Mere taught me something else."

"What was that?" he asked genuinely interested.

"To love is to listen," she said bouncing her head up and down. "Yes, it's true. The key to showing people how much you love them is listening. I know it may not seem so, but I'm better at listening than I am at talking."

He laughed and she easily laughed along. '

Looking at her sideways he gave her a crooked smile. "You're not from New York, are you?"

"No." She waved his notion off. "Is anyone ever really from New York? It's like the breeding ground for all who have dreams. We flock to New York, fall in love with the city and stay."

Intrigued by her whimsical look at life, he smiled.

"Does that include you?"

"Oh yes, to my father's dismay. His wish is that I follow in my parent's footsteps, become an attorney and join the law firm. I promised him if my career does not take off by my twenty-fifth birthday I'll give it a try."

"When is that?"

She sighed, "December 25th."

"That's only a few months away. Will you be able to let the dream go?"

Tilting her head she smirked. "Dancing is in my blood as deep as the law." She shook her head. "I just don't know."

The uncertainty showed in her eyes. *Everything showed in her eyes.* The thought tickled him inside for some reason. She could never play poker. Even now he could see when her thoughts changed from her to him.

"God must be shining down on me today to have placed you here. Before you came on board I was in a bit of a funk over things with my contract. I'll have to make the same decision as you after this season." He frowned. "If we ever sign one." He looked up at her and smiled. "Now, I believe my time and energy would be better spent just enjoying the opportunity to play."

"I think that's wise. However, you may want to work a little on swinging at that first pitch." Shaking her head she continued to speak. "Percentages are not your friend at the moment. That first pitch is destroying your numbers. Every pitcher in the league knows you are going to swing at it, so they don't bother to give you anything you can really hit. Sit back on the first pitch a few times and see what they start sending your way. That alone will raise your batting average and if the Knights don't re-sign you, the heck with them. It will be their loss. Any team will pay you double to have that pretty face and monster body in their uniform."

Jarrett wasn't sure if he was offended or intrigued by her suggestion. He raised an eyebrow at her.

A shocked look appeared on her face. Her hands flew to her mouth. "I did it again." Her eyes grew large pleading for forgiveness. "I'm sorry. I have a bad habit of speaking what's on my mind before thinking. I did not mean to offend you."

She looked as if she was about to cry.

"No offense taken," Jarrett replied as he sat back. His batting coach had been on him about the same thing. That first pitch was a curse to him and he knew it. His eyes watched her fidget as if she was trying to determine if she should continue to talk or not. The truth of the matter was he liked hearing her voice. "I've heard it before, just not as nicely."

Paige stared into his eyes before she spoke. Tilting her head to the side she asked, "May I ask you a question?"

He wondered if he could stop her. Smiling inwardly, he said, "Sure."

"If the Knights only paid you one dollar, would you love the game any less?"

Without hesitation he replied, "No."

"Well, there you go."

CHAPTER TWO

The moment Jarrett stepped out of the sedan he was greeted by his agent and friend, Nicolas Brooks and was escorted from the garage of the downtown office building into a private elevator.

"How was your flight?" Nick asked as he extended his hand.

"Interesting." Jarrett smiled.

Nick gave him a suspicious look. The pleasant mood was not what he expected. Jarrett was a pretty nice guy, but he was sure the email he'd forwarded from the Brooklyn Knights' front office would have generated a different response.

The men walked through the lobby to stares from men and women. One or two asked for autographs before Nick guided Jarrett into another the private elevator.

As the doors closed, Nick turned to Jarrett. "I appreciate you making this trip. The last email indicated the negotiations are on hold. We have a few ways to bring them back to the table. Later, we really need you to sit down with Jason Whitfield. He's a new acquisition for Pendleton - Brooks. He's young, arrogant and prone to hanging with the wrong crowd."

"Sounds about right for a nineteen year old who just signed a multimillion dollar contract." Jarrett smirked. "What can I do to help?"

"Calm his ass down," Nick replied.

Jarrett laughed, "What makes you think I can do that? I don't even know the kid."

"He's a fan," Nick stated just as the elevator doors opened, "a huge fan of yours."

"Hello, Stacy." Jarrett smiled at the receptionist just as they stepped off the elevator. "I see they kept the prettiest woman at the front door."

"Flattery will get you everywhere with me, Jarrett. May I take your coat?"

"Will you stop flirting with the women in my office?" Nick grinned.

"Yes, when you get some that are not so easy on the eyes. Hello, Vicki. You're still looking good." Jarrett kissed the woman on her cheek.

"I know." She winked. "You look better."

As they reached Nick's office, Jarrett walked around the big oak desk in front of the door and picked up the woman standing behind it, gave her a huge bear hug, then kissed her on the cheek.

"Hello, Mrs. Holmes." He sat the woman back down on her feet. "Did you get that divorce yet?"

The fifty-two year old sleek looking grandmother laughed. "You can't handle me, Jarrett. I thought we established that at the Carlyle."

Nick shook his head. "I don't even want to know what that was about."

As they walked into the office, the interior was a depiction of the success of the agency and the taste of the occupant. Across the room, a large, tinted glass and chrome desk sat, diagonally, in front of a room of windows. A large glass conference table with eight chairs was to the right of the room and was the place where several high dollar contract negotiations took place. To the left was the relaxation area, which included a bar, and entertainment center flush against the wall. A large flat screen television in the center of the entertainment area, a sofa that looked as if it could seat eight, and four lounge chairs that surrounded an oval shaped glass table, completed the office.

"Have a seat." Nick pointed to the sofa as he walked over to the bar, pulling out two bottles of water, flipping one to Jarrett as he took a seat in a lounge chair. "Sorry about the commercial flight."

Jarrett stretched his legs out, crossing them at the ankles. "I rather enjoyed it." He grinned. Nick looked at him sideways, as Jarrett changed the subject. "What's the kid's story?"

"Oldest child to parents of three, with the weight of their future on his shoulders," Nick summarized. "Too much pressure for a young man just starting out."

"Family depending on him to lift them up," Jarrett stated more than asked.

Nick nodded. "This kid has one of the sweetest three-point shots I've ever seen, from any position on the court."

"I've seen him play." Jarrett sat the now empty bottle on the table. "So what's the issue?"

Nick sat up as he spoke. "His posse of twenty."

Jarrett began laughing.

"I'm serious. The Ruler speaks for him, Jason only speaks when necessary. Red walks in front of him to clear his path, and De-lite tests his food before he eats."

Laughing harder, Jarrett asked, "Which one wipes his butt?"

"I believe that would be Lil T," Nick laughed. "He gets all the dirty jobs."

Jarrett laughed more.

"I'm serious man." Nick had to chuckle. "My partner turned this kid over to me. I have to get Jason under control or we are going to lose him. The media is already following him around predicting he will have a gun charge or something before he sets foot on the hardwood."

A knock sounded at the office door.

"Mr. Brooks." Mrs. Holmes entered the room. "It seems Mr. Whitfield did not arrive on the plane."

Nick turned in the seat he was occupying to look at his secretary. "What do you mean, he wasn't on the plane."

"Well, it seems he sent his posse ahead of him."

Before she could explain further, the man known as The Ruler stepped inside the office dressed in what Nick knew to be a three-thousand dollar suit, that he was sure came from Jason's bonus check.

"Man, you need to get a bigger plane if you are going to handle Jason's affairs. We roll twenty deep. It will take three trips to get all of us here using an eight seater jet."

Nick stood, not believing what he'd just heard. "Where is Jason?"

"He sent us first, said for you to send the jet back for the rest of them."

Nick looked from The Ruler to Jarrett. It was clear the man he had called a friend for a few years, was doing his best not to laugh. Turning back to The Ruler he spoke. "Mrs. Holmes, would you please show The Ruler," his voice dipped, "and his associates to the conference room. I'll be with you in a moment."

"A'ight, man, but we don't have all day. We supposed to go clubbing tonight."

"I'll keep that in mind," Nick said as he and Mrs. Holmes shared a look while she closed the office door.

He just couldn't hold it any longer. Jarrett threw his head back roaring in laughter. Nick just stood there with his hands on his hips shaking his head.

"Don't laugh. You want to give me some advice here? You see what I'm dealing with."

Jarrett sat forward and just shook his head. "Whew. I'm sorry, man, but you know that was funny as hell."

Nick just looked at his friend, then he had to let the exasperated laugh out. "This is what I've been trying to tell you. Man, you are the captain of your team. How would you handle something like this?"

"Seriously?"

"Yes, man, seriously, what would you do?"

Jarrett sobered, then thought for a minute. "I would nip it. The posse would find a way to get home on their own. I would take the jet back to Jason's home, lay down the law and tell him to take it or leave it."

"I can't leave the people stranded."

"You didn't ask them to come; Jason did. It will be his dime to get them home."

"He's going to be pissed."

"Well, there you go." Jarrett stood and walked out of the room.

Nick watched him leave, then yelled, "What in the hell is that supposed to mean?"

* * * * *

In Boston, General Manager Kurt Stack sat in his leather chair at the plush corporate offices of the

Dragons, watching a practice film of the Knights with his team Manager Ben Stanley. Picking up the remote, he clicked the button turning the film off, then leaned back in his chair.

Sensing the mood in the room, Ben spoke. "He's still swinging at the first pitch. That is going to go well with our pitching staff."

"And what do you suggest for the other 600 times he comes up to bat?" Kurt dropped the remote on the desk resulting in a loud clunk.

"He's just one man."

"With a hell of a supporting cast." Kurt stood in a fit of disgust.

"We have a damn good team this year, Kurt. Looks like we are going to be in the playoffs; hell at the rate we are going we could go all the way to the World Series in October."

"Yes, we have a good team. The only problem is we are number two behind the Knights. Looks to me, the Knights have a better chance than we do."

"Only if Bryson remains healthy."

Kurt turned with a pointed stare. "You just hit the nail on the head. If Bryson goes down, his supporting cast will wither away just like the triple A team they are." He walked over and sat in the chair across from Ben. "The organization's survival depends on this season. Between the players' contracts and overhead, we are seriously over extended. We need a winning season."

"We are going to be in the post-season, Kurt. I'll bet my job on it."

"That's exactly what's on the line here, Ben, your job and mine. We need to make the World Series. Nothing less will do." He stood and towered over Ben. "Harding needed a winning season and took steps to ensure it happened."

Ben frowned up at Kurt. "Harding? Are you freaking kidding me? You're talking about ruining the career of a hero in this game. You don't mean that Kurt."

"Kerrigan came back," Kurt stated then walked away.

Ben watched as he sat back behind his desk, picked up the remote control, pushed the button and continued to watch the footage.

"The only thing standing in the way of the Dragons making it to the World Series is the Knights. The heart of the Knights is Jarrett Bryson. Cut out the heart and the Knights will fall."

CHAPTER THREE

"Welcome home Ms. Paige." Leona Carter, the caretaker of the Cartwright family spoke. "It's good to have you home, child," she said as she took Paige's overnight bag and purse.

"Thank you, Leona." Paige kissed the elderly woman on her cheek as she talked. "How's Mr. Carter and the grandchildren? Is Ellen engaged yet? What about Jacob, how is he?"

"Child, slow down. Your mouth is going a mile a minute." Leona laughed as she followed Paige to the kitchen. "You have to give this old lady time to catch up with you."

Paige laughed as she entered the kitchen. She flopped down on a seat at the granite breakfast bar that seated at least six.

"Where's Mother? Is Dad at work?"

"Where do you want me to start with your hundred questions a minute?"

"Sorry, Leona. How are you?"

"I'm doing just fine. Now, how are you and what are you doing home? We didn't expect to see you until the holidays."

"I know, but Grand'Mere called and insisted I come this morning. I think I know why. I met this man on the way home and I'm sure he's the reason she wanted me on that plane. You know how she is with her dreams. In this case, I think she may have bitten off more than she or I can chew. This man has a wonderful aura around him." She hesitated, placing her hands on her hips as if in thought. "I also sensed a little sadness. I'll have to find a way to fix that, you know."

"No honey, but then again, I never know what you are talking about. Only your Grand'Mere can decipher your ramblings when you get like this."

"Paige!"

"Mother!" Paige jumped up from her seat, ran into the foyer and straight into her mother's open arms.

Hugging her daughter, Eleanor Cartwright, beamed.

"Let me look at you." She held her at arms' length. "You are still the prettiest little girl in the world." She pulled her back into a big hug. "I've missed you so much. What are you doing home? I was so surprised when Leona called to say you were on your way from the airport." She kissed her daughter's cheek.

"I've missed you too. I have so much to tell you." The two walked arm in arm into the kitchen where they knew Leona would have two cups of hot tea waiting on the breakfast bar for them.

Instead of mother and daughter, they sounded and looked like two girlfriends seeing each other for the first time in years. Actually, it had only been a few months and they talked every day. Leona shook her head, loving the burst of energy that naturally accompanied Paige whenever she walked through the door. It was the same as the day she was born.

Horace and Eleanor Cartwright married the day after they graduated from law school. Most thought the marriage was doomed from the start, Eleanor being one of the well-off Hyltons and Horace being from a not so influential family. The speculation grew more after eight years of marriage and no children had been produced from the union. Everyone thought Ophelia S. Hylton was going to have the marriage annulled, but Horace stood up to her. Told her no one was taking Eleanor away from him, he didn't care how much money she had. That was a hot night, and the night Leona believes Paige was conceived. A little over nine months later, Eleanor was spending Christmas Eve with her mother, when she went into labor. She never made it to the hospital, for the bundle of joy popped out, right into her grandmother's arms at 12:01 am Christmas day. From that moment on, that child had been the apple of her Grand'Mere's eye. Hence, the double celebration every Christmas morning. It was hard to say who loved the child more-Ophelia, Eleanor, Horace or Leona.

Looking at the clock on the wall, Leona estimated it would be about fifteen minutes before Judge Cartwright would come running through the door. The front doors opened with a bang. Leona had miscalculated the time.

"Paige." The deep voice rocked the house. "Paige."

"Darling." Eleanor walked from the kitchen with a questioning look on her face. "Why are you yelling for Paige?"

"Leona said she was home," he said, a frown marring his face. "She's not home?"

Paige came up from behind, threw her arms around her father's neck and jumped on his back.

"Hello Daddy," she said as she kissed him on his cheek.

The six-four, two hundred twenty-five pound man turned with the most brilliant smile on his face.

"Paige."

He turned and swung his twenty-four year old daughter around as if she was still six years old with ponytails swinging. He wrapped her in a bear hug as his wife joined them.

"Welcome home, sweetheart." He looked from his wife to his daughter. "I don't know who's the prettiest, my daughter or my wife."

"Aww, you sweet talker you." Eleanor kissed her husband.

"She said yes years ago, Daddy. You don't have to sweet talk her anymore."

The three walked into the kitchen arm in arm.

"Yes, Sweet-pea, I do, if I want to keep her." He looked at Leona. "Is she here yet?" Horace asked as they all sat down at the bar.

"No." Eleanor tapped her husband on the shoulder. "Behave. Mother is the reason your daughter is home. Be thankful," she said as she walked behind the bar and over to the stove to help Leona with lunch.

"Daddy, why do you give Grand'Mere such a hard time? I swear you two act like ex-lovers or something."

"Ha, your grandfather was the only man who would have her," Horace replied. "She can't be called grandmother, like anyone else. Nooooo, she has to be the Grand'Mere. Just like those old mares she has in her barn."

"That's my mother you're talking about Horace." Eleanor knew the history between her husband and mother. She also knew Horace would move heaven and earth for her mother simply because he loved her. She also knew the same to be true with her mother.

"Mother's right, Daddy." Paige smiled at her father. "You love Grand'Mere as much as I do. After all, she did call and ask...no insisted that I come home this morning. She said this afternoon would be too late."

"Too late for what?" Horace and Eleanor turned to her at the same time and asked.

Paige shrugged her shoulders. "I'm not sure, but I think she wanted me to meet a man."

"What man?" Horace frowned.

"I can't say yet. However, as soon as my suspicions are confirmed, I'll tell you about him."

Leona and Eleanor shared a look.

"What exactly did your grandmother say when she called?"

Paige closed her eyes and repeated the conversation with her grandmother.

"Verbatim, her words were, 'Good morning, baby girl. A journey begins with an understanding and acceptance of your past. You, my dear granddaughter, are destined for great love. It is time for your journey to begin. There is a ticket waiting for you at United Air Lines for a flight that leaves in two hours. Pack your bags and be on that flight before it's too late.'"

Horace looked at his daughter with the dreamy look on her sweet face, then at his wife.

"Sweetheart, I'm telling you, your mother..." He took his finger and circled it around his temple.

"My mother is not crazy," Eleanor laughed. "She said something similar to me the night before I met you. There may be some stock in what she said." Eleanor turned to her daughter. "What happened when you boarded the plane?"

"Who did you meet?" Leona smiled.

Horace glanced at his housekeeper. "Leona?" Then he looked at his wife. "You are not seriously considering your mother has psychic powers now."

"Yes, darling I am." She took a seat next to her daughter and sat her teacup on the bar. "Who did you meet?"

Paige spoke enthusiastically, "A man who makes my heart smile." She took her mother's hand and laughed. "I could just listen to him or not. Just sitting in his presence would be okay with me."

"Who is he?" Horace had an edge to his voice.

"Don't worry, Daddy, it is inconceivable that this man would ever be interested in me. He is literally the king of the knights." She laughed at her play on words.

"And you, my darling granddaughter, will be his queen," Ophelia Hylton said with the air of superiority befitting her.

Walking in dressed in her signature two-piece suit and pearls, with a purse that cost more than the size twelve custom fit shoes Horace was wearing, she looked around the room.

"Hello, my daughter, Leona, and you too, Harold."

"My name is Horace. You would think after thirty-two years of marriage to your daughter you would remember that. Oh, I forgot, you are up in age." Even though to look at her you would never think she was a day over fifty instead of eighty-one.

"There is a chill in the air. Must be the September weather," Ophelia stated. "Or it may be the arctic air coming from your mouth, Harold."

"Hello, Mother." Eleanor stood and kissed her mother's cheek as she frowned at her husband.

"Good afternoon, Mrs. Hylton. How are you?" Leona laughed at the 'what did I do' expression on Horace face.

"Hello, Grand'Mere." Paige hugged her tightly. "I'm here."

Ophelia looked at her granddaughter and all she could ever do was smile. She loved that child more than life itself. Looking into her granddaughter's eyes she found what she was looking for.

"You met him." She took Paige's hands in hers. "Your journey begins."

Horace stood at the end of the breakfast bar watching three grown women standing around the room smiling with knowing eyes.

"What damn journey?"

CHAPTER FOUR

The Knights stadium was packed. Fifty-thousand fans on their feet stomping, clapping, sending cat calls, some praying that their Mr. Clutch, as they called Jarrett, would bring home the players that were loaded around the bases. It was the game that could clinch their spot in the playoffs. Bottom of the ninth, two outs, full count and the Knights were tied, five to five with the Dragons.

"If anyone can bring them home, Mr. Clutch can. He's proved it time and time again," the announcer said.

"That was before the Knights stalled his contract negotiations," the analyst stated. "There may be some bad blood brewing."

"For some others, I would agree; not Bryson. He loves the game. It's all about the game. A win tonight can guarantee the Knights a playoff spot. If the Dragons hold on to their lead, a win gets them one step closer to the playoffs."

"It's the Dragons' bad luck that Bryson made it to the plate. Here comes the pitch...the swing. Whoa.... it's going....going, it went foul." The crowd groaned, as did the announcer.

"You get the feeling he's teasing the Dragons, drawing out this at bat?" The men in the booth laughed.

Jarrett stepped back into the batter's box. Blowing the air from his cheeks as he tried to calm his nerves.

The clinch game of the season, on their home field, came down to him. He took a look at the pitcher. He's going to send his sinker to the right. Try to jam me at the plate. The brass is going to base my new contract on this season. Not what I've done in the past. Three championship rings and they want to screw me. Swing.

Crack, the ball went foul again.

Damn.

Jarrett stepped outside of the box again, looked out to the furthest point on the field - four hundred eighty feet.

Why do I put myself through this turmoil? Because I love the game. If they paid you one dollar would you love the game any less?

The question played in his mind several times, over the last two weeks. Paige Cartwright's smiling face tilted to the side, always followed the thought.

He looked at the ground, tapped the end of the bat on the plate, stepped back into the batter's box, raised the bat and waited.

It was a fastball, right across the plate. Jarrett's swing was precision...the power...unyielding...the hit, right over the four hundred and eighty foot mark into the stands.

Jarrett dropped the bat smacking his hands together.

"I love this game," he chanted as he made his rounds through the bases.

The announcer was yelling, "Grand-Slam...Grand Slam. Jarrett Bryson has clinched the playoffs for the Knights like a man possessed. The crowd is in a frenzy. The entire dugout has emptied out onto the field."

His teammates stood at home plate waiting for Jarrett to touch the plate, clinching their spot in the playoffs.

"You hit the hell out of that ball man," Sergio Martinez, the catcher laughed as he gave Jarrett a high five.

"Clinch game, grand-slam. Was Miller's face on the ball when you hit it?" Ron Mackenzie, the third basemen and Jarrett's best friend joked.

Jarrett grinned. "I was thinking about a woman."

"You need to keep her around, if you're going to be hitting grand-slams like that," Jake Weingart, the first baseman, added as the men lined up to shake hands.

Ron gave him a look. "What woman? You haven't said anything to me about a woman."

"Jarrett!" Casey Lane, the clubhouse reporter grabbed his arm as they headed off the field. "Five minutes."

At least ten cameras and microphones were surrounding him. After this, he knew another twenty or so would be in the clubhouse, then there was the post-game interview and celebration. This was part of the job. He'd known this season was going to be intense with the negotiations looming in the air. As long as things stayed positive and in house, all should go well.

"Jarrett, how did it feel a double, a triple and a grand slam clinching the playoffs for the season?

Looks like you are sending a message to the front office?"

Ignoring the jab, Jarrett responded, "It felt good. The team has worked hard all season and we expected great results."

"Are you concerned with the lack of talks from the front office?"

"No, I'm concerned with winning games."

"You seemed nervous at the plate for a moment, then the expression on your face changed. What was going through your mind when that pitch came across the plate?"

"I need to hit the ball."

The reporter laughed. "You did that. Hit it rather well. Are you finding ways to keep the distraction of the negotiations from interfering with the game?"

"My job is to win games. I leave everything else off the field. Thanks for the interview."

"Congratulations on making the playoffs."

With that he walked off the field, down the steps and through the tunnel, into the locker room. There was another group of reporters waiting. Jarrett made a beeline to his locker, pulled his sweaty shirt over his head, then turned to the camera and hordes of microphones that were shoved into his face.

It's going to be a long playoff season went through his mind.

An hour later, he had finally showered, met with the press in the post-game interviews and was now on his way to Chalet's, a club where the players hung out after the game. Sergio and Ron were already in the place, scoping out the women, when Jarrett arrived. Walking through the private entrance located on the backside of the club, he could hear the music pumping, the raised voices and the clatter of glasses. Before he took a second step into the club, he was surrounded by three women all vying for his attention.

"Good evening, ladies."

"Jarrett, I wasn't sure you were coming tonight." Jacki' who was Jacquelyn Reed from around the corner, who had added a little butt, reduced the size of her nose and had hair hanging down her back. Oh, and of course the body to kill for. He was about the only one from the team that had continuously passed on her advances. "You buying me a drink tonight?"

"Sure, drinks for all the pretty ladies." He smiled at each of them. "Where's Sergio?"

"The usual spot," Jacki' replied, disappointed again at his snub.

"Thanks Jacki', I need to catch up with the boys." He kissed her on the cheek and looked her up and down. "You are still hitting on all cylinders." He winked as he walked off.

"Great game tonight, Jarrett," he heard as he walked through the crowd.

"You brought them home tonight Jarrett," another man said as he shook his hand.

"Grand slam, whoa." Another man chest bumped him.

Finally making it to the booth he always shared with his teammates, Sergio held a beer out for him.

"The press finally let you go," he said with the accent from his homeland, the Dominican Republic.

Jarrett took a swig of his beer and shook his head. "I have no idea how I make it through the season with the same damn question over and over. How many times do I have to say it? I'm not discussing the negotiations in public."

"Man, they are going to be on you until either you give them something, or the front office does," Ron replied. "And don't think it's going to stop now that we are in the playoffs."

"No, my man." Pedro, who played for the Dragons, but was a good friend, nodded his head in agreement. "Prepare yourself, my man, until the front office signs the deal the media is not going to let up."

"I'm not dealing with them. I'll answer questions regarding the game and that's it."

"You've been in this league for years. We don't have to tell you how to handle yourself with the media," Ron cautioned. "Just know, this year you've been a beast at the plate."

"Speaking of beast." Sergio pointed then nudged Ron. "Here comes your wife."

The men at the table looked in the direction he was pointing and there was a collective moan.

"Damn." Ron shook his head and looked at Jarrett, "I'm sorry man."

Jarrett exhaled as he watched Ron's wife, Suzette Mackenzie, the 'want to be' superstar walking towards them. She wasn't alone. Lacy Dupree, Jarrett's most recent ex-girlfriend was with her. There were no hard feelings on Jarrett's part, however, Lacy had been under the impression that things were a lot more serious than things were. To that end she was having a little trouble letting go.

Both women were beautiful in a showroom kind of way, wearing the typical short black dress, revealing cleavage, legs and just about everything else. While Suzette was out there, 'bam' in your face, Lacy was a little less flamboyant and carried herself with a little more grace. They took very good care of themselves to ensure they stayed that way. At least with Lacy, she had good reason to spend the thousands monthly to keep her looks intact. She was a budding actress, who was actually pretty good. She had an impressive resume' building and Jarrett expected once she got the right role, Lacy would be on the big screen. He hoped it happened for her soon, that way her attention could be on something other than him.

"Hello, darling." Suzette bent over to kiss her husband. "Lacy and I decided to step out for the evening."

"Hi, Jarrett." Lacy smiled.

"Hello, Lacy," Jarrett replied then glanced around the room.

"Doesn't Lacy look good tonight, Jarrett? She's wearing the hell out of that dress," Suzette goaded with her Jersey accent.

"Yes, she does," Jarrett, agreed. "I've got to run. It's good seeing you, Suzette. Take care, Lacy," he said as he stood.

"Jarrett, I was wondering if you could do me a favor." Suzette followed him from the booth. "Lacy rode with me tonight and I'm not ready to leave yet. Would you be a dear and run her home? Please Jarrett? I haven't been out of the house in ages and the kids are running me into the ground. It's my first night out and I want to party." She shimmied her breasts at him, and smiled.

"I'll make sure she gets home." He turned back to the table. "Lacy, you need a ride?"

Lacy looked from Suzette to Jarrett. "If you don't mind."

"No, I don't mind. I'll make sure you get home safe." He took Lacy by the hand. "Not too late tonight fellows, we have practice in the morning."

"Night, Cap." Sergio held up his beer.

As Jarrett and Lacy moved through the crowd, there were cameras everywhere. A few flashes came his way, but he kept moving through the crowd. When they reached the private entrance, Jarrett whispered to the parking attendant, then turned to Lacy.

"My car service will be here in a minute to take you home. I'll stay until they arrive."

A disappointed Lacy looked away.

"I didn't plan this Jarrett. Suzette called and said she wanted to get out."

"I'm sure you had no idea she was coming to the club or that I would be here with Ron and Sergio as we usually are after just about every game."

She shrugged her shoulders. "I didn't mind the possibility of seeing you again."

He nodded.

She brushed her brunette hair over her shoulders. "Do you have plans for the evening?"

"No," Jarrett replied, "I'm just going home."

"I don't have any plans either. Would you like some company?"

Jarrett stood there in his grey tailor made suit, white dress shirt and his Italian loafers, looking like the million-dollar man he was, and shook his head.

"I don't think that would do either of us any good." He gave a small smile to the woman he'd enjoyed being with more than most, but knew he could not give her what she wanted. "You know why we can't be together. You want a ring, the papers, the house and the picket fence. I don't see that happening."

She reached out, placing her hands on the lapel of his suit and looked up at him. "We could just enjoy each other like we used to, until that comes."

Taking her hands in his, he gently removed them from his chest. Holding them away from his body, he shook his head.

"As I said before, Lacy, I don't see that in the future for us." His car pulled into the tunnel area of the parking deck. "The car's here." He kissed her on the cheek as the car pulled along the curb. Reaching over, he opened the back door and closed it after securing her inside.

He watched as the car pulled away with her in the backseat and her head hanging low. It hurt him to see her like that, but he knew this was best. The white house with the picket fence with Lacy wasn't something he saw in his future. As he stepped off the curb, heading towards his car, the vision of Paige Cartwright came to mind and he smiled.

"Well, there you go." He laughed as he got into his car, but had no idea why.

Jarrett walked into his two-bedroom, forty-seven hundred square feet penthouse that had magnificent views of Central Park, the city skyline and the Hudson River from every room. The En Suite bathroom had a Japanese soaking tub that he couldn't wait to experience tonight. The bamboo flooring throughout the tastefully decorated open foyer, living room and dining room, created an elegant feel without it being cosmetic. The automatic curtains opened when he walked through the door. The skyline view of the city lights always welcomed him home when he opened the door. He loved coming home. Clubbing was a fun way to release some of the stress of the day and hang out with his teammates, but coming home, well this was his sanctuary.

Dropping his keys in the tray on the credenza in the foyer, he walked into the kitchen, opened the refrigerator and pulled out a drink. One of the amenities of the building was the concierge service that kept the refrigerator stocked with fresh fruit and vegetables, hot meals in the warmer on home game nights and a supply of various beverages. Pulling the meal from the warmer, he removed the cover to find roasted chicken and a melody of mixed vegetables. He sat at the table then clicked the remote to turn on the television. ESPN was showing highlights from the game. He switched the channel, preferring not to listen to the hype, sooner or later he would start believing it and that would stop him from doing his best. At least that was his philosophy. His phone rang just as he began eating.

"Hey, Pop. What's up?" he answered.

"Just checking on you, son. You played a good game tonight."

His parents never failed to tell him that, just as they never failed to tell him when he was not giving one hundred percent.

"Your mother wants to know if you have eaten dinner and if it included vegetables?"

Jarrett could only laugh. "She would ask that."

His parents, Frank and Connie, still lived in Marietta, Georgia where he grew up. They weren't rich, but they weren't bad off either. His father was a financial advisor, which provided well for him and his two sisters. They were fortunate to have had a stay at home mom who had seen to their every need. However, he and his sisters, Faith and Autumn, were raised in a strict environment. Only their best was expected from them. If their best was a C in math, then that was fine, but slouching was not allowed in their household. Bryson's, as his father was called by many, baritone laughter came through the line. "You know I had to ask or your mother would be calling you next. You're not out with the boys celebrating?"

"I was out for a minute, but Lacy showed up and I thought it was best that I leave."

"She's still trying to hold on, son. Be careful with that one."

"I'm keeping my distance, Pop."

"Finding that right one is never easy and it's more difficult in your profession. You are surrounded by people trying to be something that they are not. Be patient. Wait for that one who makes you smile just thinking of her. Now tell me, how did that grand-slam feel?"

The nightly conversation lasted for another thirty minutes while Jarrett ate his dinner. Afterwards, he jumped in his Japanese tub, soaked the stress of the day away, and then climbed into bed. The view of the city encased two walls of the room. Pushing the button on the nightstand next to the bed, the drapes in the room closed out the city lights. As Jarrett closed his eyes, the smiling face of Paige Cartwright invaded his mind.

CHAPTER FIVE

"Do you ever sleep?" a sleepy eyed Victoria Gaye asked from the doorway in the room of the condo that she and her roommate used as a dance studio. Paige was working out on the fixed barre with mirrors mounted behind it. Windows on the other side of the room displayed a view of the skyline. The sound of Parliament Funkadelic's *Bring the Funk* could be heard in the background.

"It's not even six o'clock in the morning and you're working out with Dr. Funkenstien?"

"I like the P-Funk." Paige laughed with a leg stretched along the barre as she elegantly stretched the top portion of her body to the beat of the music.

"You are the principal in a ballet, not a hip hop video."

"I'm going to bust a move in a minute." She laughed. "You want to join me?"

"Hell no. I'm going back to bed." Victoria turned to walk out of the room. "We have a performance tonight. You should be resting."

Paige did a jete across the room, grabbed Victoria around the waist, twirling her once.

The ballerinas automatically went into a sequence of pirouettes. The two spun around the room as if they were one. When the music changed, Victoria broke out into the Walk It Out hip-hop move. From there they broke into the Soulja Boy, the Stinky Leg, finally breaking into the Wobble before they fell out in a frenzy of laughter. By the time they finished dancing, they had put in a forty-minute workout.

"You have entirely too much energy for this early in the morning," Victoria said as she stood to walk out of the room.

"Go hard or go home," Paige laughed.

"I'm taking a shower, you go hard on breakfast duty."

"You got it."

Twenty minutes later Victoria walked into the kitchen to find Paige, showered and flipping an omelet onto a plate.

"I can't believe you have me up this early." She took a seat at the table which was in the corner of the kitchen. There was a view of Central Park below.

"A good morning workout and a nutritious breakfast give you the stamina to work through the day. At least that's what my Grand'Mere says," Paige said as she sat in the chair on the other side of the table.

Looking at the table filled with fresh fruit, yogurt and juice, Victoria shook her head. "You and your Grand'mere are going to be the death of me. I didn't get in until after two in the morning and didn't get to sleep until four then you woke me up at six."

"I'm sorry." Paige frowned, "I didn't mean to wake you up."

"Oh take that frown off your face and stop saying I'm sorry all the time. You didn't really wake me up. I was joking." She hesitated.

"Who was it this time?" Paige laughed at the expression on Victoria's face as she thought. "You don't even know his name."

"Yes, I do." Victoria took a sip of her juice. "His first name was 'fine as hell', and his last name was 'can work a body overtime'. That was his name," she laughed.

"You are too much. I wish I was more like you." Paige shrugged her shoulder. "People love to hang out with you."

"You don't want to be like me. Stay just the way you are with that rosy outlook on life, that southern drawl and pleasing personality. Don't become a cynic like me."

"You're not a cynic, you just don't believe in things you can't touch or see. I believe everything is possible and can be felt in the heart or seen through another person's eyes."

"I know. You're a wimp and I'm surprised I haven't toughened you up over the last two years. Speaking of which, why did you let Jolene take your spot on the floor yesterday during the rehearsal? She is not the principal in this show, you are. Do not let her take your spotlight."

"She can't take what's mine, not if it's meant for me."

"Argh!" Victoria shook her head. "This is New York. The flashy get the spotlight, the meek get the chorus line."

"Talent and determination will prevail. That's what my Grand'Mere says and I believe it." Paige continued to eat.

"Really. What does your Grand'Mere say about this man in your life?"

A look of surprise crossed Paige's face. "What man?"

"I've been living with you for two years. In that time, I've had to deal with that damn good morning song of yours every day. For the last week, it's been pounding music accompanied by an hour-long workout. Either you're a health nut, which you are not, or you're trying to get a man out of your system."

"I'm not trying to get him out of my system. I just..." She hesitated as her head dropped down to her plate. "I just don't know what I should do next." As if talking to herself, she continued. "Should I contact him or should I continue to wait until he makes the first move. Or, maybe he's not the one." She shook her head. "That can't be, Grand'Mere is never wrong about something like this." She shrugged her shoulders. "I don't know."

"Was I supposed to be a part of that conversation?"

Paige shook her head. "I was just thinking out loud."

Victoria wanted to laugh, but she did not want to hurt her friend's feelings. She did not consider anyone in the industry a friend...everyone was competition, she learned that lesson long ago. But Paige was different. She was not out to take Broadway by storm, although she had the talent to do so. She only wanted to dance. To make matters worse, she was a genuinely nice person. She thought of others before herself, always had a pleasant disposition and never had a bad thing to say about anyone.

"Who is he?"

"Who's who?"

"What you're an owl now? You heard me, who is he?" Victoria took a bite of her omelet. The hesitation caused Victoria to think. "Hmm, from that reaction I would say it's someone whose name I would recognize. Is he in the business?"

Paige shook her head.

"Okay, someone whose name I would recognize but he is not in the business." She tilted her head to the side and held Paige's eyes. The merriment dancing in them was a clear indication that Paige was enjoying the guessing game. "Is he famous?"

Paige nodded her head, adding a slight smirk with a gleam in her eyes.

"You know I want to jump across the table and choke it out of you right now, don't you?"

Paige laughed. "You can't stand the guessing?" She put her fork down on her plate, looked up and sighed. "You can't say anything to anyone about this. Not even my parents. I haven't told them his name."

Victoria nodded. "Okay."

"Pinky swear."

"Oh for goodness sake. Who in the hell is he?"

"Pinky swear," Paige demanded.

Victoria exhaled. She circled her pinky finger around the one Paige extended across the table. "Pinky swear."

"His name is Jarrett Bryson."

"Ha, yeah you and every other woman in New York...hell the country," Victoria said as she yanked her finger away.

The look in Paige's eyes caused her to pause. "You're serious."

Paige picked up her fork, took a bite of her omelet and smiled, nodding her head.

"Whew." Victoria dropped her head, shook it then looked back at her friend. Paige was not a frivolous girl; yes she said girl because she was pretty sure her friend was not only still a virgin, but had not had a serious male-female relationship. Jarrett Bryson would break her heart and keep going.

"Jarrett Bryson is a womanizer. He loves them and leaves them Paige. He is not the type of man you should be involved with."

"I don't think he is a womanizer. I think he has dated his share of women. Whether he has loved any of them, I don't know. What I do know is that we have a connection. We talked as if we had known each other for years. When he touched me, my body, my mind, my very soul responded."

She placed her fork down, wiped her mouth with her napkin, then looked up at her friend.

"I know you think that I'm a naive, little country girl from Virginia, living in a big city that is going to eat me alive. You've told me that at least a thousand times in the last two years. Yet, I'm still standing, have the principal in our show and I'm still managing to live with you." She smiled. "I've got to have some balls somewhere." She sighed. "I know Jarrett's reputation. I also know how the press can and will sensationalize things. You do too. If I end up hurt, I'll get up, put on my big girl panties and cry all over your shoulder. I can let it go and be wondering for the rest of my life what did I miss. Or, I can go for it and deal with the outcome, whatever it may be. You've known me long enough to know, I'm not a runner."

Victoria held her friend's gaze. She sounded so mature and rational. And she was right, not about Bryson, but the fact that she would always wonder if she had run from this. As a friend she would support her and be there for her with a shoulder when he breaks her heart.

"So, when did you meet him and how long has it been since you heard from him?"

A smiling Paige sat up and told her friend about how she met Jarrett and the conversation they'd shared. Victoria had to admit it did sound like they'd made a connection and if Bryson was just after a lay, he probably would have at least called by now.

"Okay." She nodded. "It sounds like something could be there. But don't hold out hope that he's the one. In fact-" She stood and walked into the living room to retrieve her tablet. She pulled up a website, then handed the tablet to her. "Stay in the know."

Paige looked at the picture of Jarrett and a brunette holding hands at a nightclub.

"She's very pretty." She read the article. "An actress."

Seeing the questioning look on Paige's face bothered her.

"You're very pretty too," Victoria assured her. "But you have something else. You're real, and for a man like Bryson I'm sure that carries a lot more weight than just beauty. Besides, he's dated a lot of beautiful women and didn't marry any of them. That means you still have a shot."

Handing the tablet back, Paige shrugged. "I still believe he will call or something. He promised he would." Paige shook off the picture. "What time are you going to the center?"

"At eleven, when rehearsal starts. Why?"

"I want to go in around nine. I want to rehearse on the stage by myself before everyone arrives. I'll catch the subway in and leave Carlos here for you."

"Carlos is a driver, that's what your Grand'Mere pays him to do. Have him take you to the center and come back to get me around ten thirty."

Shaking her head, Paige smirked. "I don't want him to have to drive there twice. I don't mind catching the metro, I think it's fun."

"Oh Law." Victoria took her plate over to the sink, "Only a non-New Yorker would say anything so ridiculous. Look, your Grand'Mere pays for this condo, the driver, and all the other amenities in this place to keep you safe and comfortable. Hell, the only reason I'm here is because she didn't want you living in New York alone. I thank God for her over-protectiveness of you every day." She picked up the house phone and punched in a number. "If it wasn't for her, I'd still be living in a rat infested one bedroom and scraping to pull the rent together. Carlos, Ms. Cartwright will be going to the center around nine. Would you get the car ready? Thank you." She hung up the phone. "See, that wasn't hard. Now, I'm going back to bed."

"After you've just eaten a big breakfast?"

"Yes." Victoria looked over her shoulder. "Watch, I'll show you how it's done." She did a Jete down the hallway as Paige laughed.

CHAPTER SIX

"We're celebrating at Jake's restaurant Jarrett, you coming?" Ron called out in the locker room as the team dressed after their third straight win. "It's Saturday, we have the rest of the day and all night to get a little freak on."

"Don't you have a wife and two beautiful little girls waiting at home for you?" Jarrett frowned.

"Yes, but if I have to hear about this damn reality show from Suzette for another day I'm going to lose it."

"What reality show?" Jake asked.

"Val didn't talk to you about doing a reality TV show with Suzette and some of the other wives on the team?" Ron asked.

"Oh yeah, I remember her mentioning something about it and I said hell no. Haven't heard anything since."

"You should give some of that to Ron," Jarrett joked. "He can't say no to Suzette for anything."

"That is true. That little woman of yours wears the pants in your house." Sergio hit Ron on the back. Sometimes the catcher did not know his own strength, he damn near pushed Ron into the locker.

"Ah, but I control the bank accounts," Ron replied as he righted himself against the locker. "That's why she wants to do this show so bad, so she can have her own income. Make her own money."

"I don't think it's about the money with Suzette, she knows she can get whatever she wants from you," Jarrett said. "I think she just wants or needs her own identity. You know, show she's not just the great Mackenzie's wife."

"She knows she's more than that." Ron frowned.

"You and I know she is, but the public thinks she's just a pretty face from Jersey that caught herself a ball player. She wants to be seen as more."

"Well, I don't care if she does the show." Ron shrugged.

"I don't know, man." Jake shook his head. "Cameras twenty-four, seven can be hell on a relationship. Ask Jarrett."

"I'm not in a relationship," Jarrett replied.

"Does Lacy know that?" Jake raised an eyebrow.

"Yes, she does."

"Really?" Jake pulled out a tabloid. "I quote, 'Jarrett and I will always be close. We have a friendship outside of any relationship.' Unquote, and there's a nice picture of the two of you holding hands."

"Let me see that?" Jarrett reached for the paper.

Ron shook his head indicating not to show the paper to Jarrett, but it was too late, he had snatched the paper from Jake's hand and was reading it.

"That was from the other night when I put her in a car and sent her home."

"That's not what's portrayed in that article," Jake huffed.

Ron could have choked Jake.

"Technically, she didn't lie. You two do still have a friendship."

Jarrett gave Ron a look that indicated he should tread lightly.

"Look, I know Suzette and Lacy are friends and that puts you in a bad situation because you and I are friends. The thing with Lacy is over and it's not coming back. Closed subject." Jarrett slammed his locker door.

"I got it." Ron held out his hand in surrender. "We still boys?"

Jarrett slapped his hand twice in the air, twice down low then gave a fist pound. "Still boys." He laughed.

"So you hanging or are your folks in town?"

"No, they didn't make the trip. But I still have to pass, Sergio and I have plans."

Sergio didn't look up at hearing Jarrett's announcement. He had no idea what plans they had, but if Jarrett said they did, then they did.

"What time we meeting up, man?"

"Seven should be good. I'll pick you up on the way."

"Cool."

"If you're sure, we're out." Ron, Jake and a few other players left the locker room.

Sergio looked at Jarrett. "Dress code?"

Jarrett laughed. "Aren't you even going to ask?"

"What's to ask? You need a wingman. I'm there."

*****

"The ballet? Jake and Ron are at the bar having wings and beers and you bring me to a damn ballet. You're freaking kidding me," Sergio complained as he took his seat next to Jarrett.

"A little culture never hurt anyone Serg. Look at it as me broadening your horizons."

Sergio gave Jarrett the most incredulous look. "Be glad I love you like a brother from my other mother." Then he spilled out a chorus of what Jarrett was certain were curse words.

This is something he would have done solo in the past for he liked to keep his life as private as possible. With Paige Cartwright, his nerves seemed to be getting the best of him. He felt like a teenager with a schoolboy crush. They had exchanged numbers while on the plane, but each time he attempted to place the call, he didn't know what to say. Shaking his head at the absurdity of it all, he settled into the seat. Since when did he not know what to say to a woman? He almost laughed out loud.

"You okay man?" Sergio asked.

"Yes, why do you ask?"

"You seem a little uneasy...nervous."

"No, no, I'm good," Jarrett replied as he wiped his sweaty palms on his pants.

The lights dimmed and he couldn't have been more grateful. For at least the third time in the last hour, he wondered if he should have come. He was glad he asked Sergio to come with him at the last moment. Sergio, with his crazy sense of humor would set things at ease if needed.

"I'm glad you came man."

"Shh," the woman next to him said as the music began.

"Sorry," he said then turned his attention to the stage.

The music was playing to a dark stage. Dancers entered from both sides dressed in black as they jumped across the stage in unison. As the dancers left an opening in the center, a spot light grew on a curtain at the back of the stage. Before the dancer moved he knew the silhouette behind the curtain was Paige. A smile touched his lips as he sat forward with his elbows resting on his knees and chin resting on his folded hands.

Her body moved to the slow rhythm of the music as she eased from a sitting position, stretching upward until her full height was reached. She paused, the music stopped and a hush came over the audience. Suddenly she burst through the curtain with a series of twirls and jumps that had the audience reacting in awe. Her movements were nonstop from beginning to end. When she leaped in the air, Jarrett's heart stopped. Her partner caught her midair, then flipped her twirling body to another. She slid down his body onto the floor in a split displaying her long slender legs. Jarrett's gut crunched as if someone had punched him.

The music stopped again as her body lay flat on the stage, arms stretched out in front of her. It seemed like no one in the audience breathed. Slowly, she turned onto her back as the music followed, her legs came up into a fetal position, she eased onto her feet and began spinning slowly. As the rhythm of the music increased, the speed of her spin increased, and increased and increased until she looked like a spinning top twirling on one leg. Then just as suddenly, the music stopped, the stage went black and she disappeared off stage.

His hands were sweating, his heart was beating fast and he didn't know why but Jarrett had to stand to relieve some of the pent up energy from holding his breath. That was only the first scene. He sat back down. He was in trouble.

"Damn."

For a moment Jarrett thought he had spoken out loud. Then he turned to Sergio and saw the look of astonishment on his face. He felt validated. Jarrett held out his hand. "It got you too...right."

Sergio slapped Jarrett's hand once up, once down then a fist pound. The two men sat back and exhaled.

Jarrett sighed. "I feel like I just hit a home run."

By the time the performance was over, Jarrett was a goner and he knew it. Paige was going to be his undoing. For over two weeks, he had done all he could to keep her from creeping into his mind, but it was fruitless, she had anyway. The first week it happened, it didn't faze him, he just chalked it up to meeting a beautiful woman. But the last week, well he put the effort in to make it stop and he lost. Now, it was time to face the music... or the woman in this case.

CHAPTER SEVEN

After the performance ended, Jarrett approached one of the attendants asking permission to go backstage to meet the performers. It wasn't often he used his celebrity status, but this time he would have insisted if necessary. It wasn't. Smiling, and signing autographs for the small crowd that waited to meet the dancers and congratulate the director and producers, he welcomed the distraction. It helped his nerves to settle a little...then he saw her.

Dressed in a simple black sleeveless dress that hugged her body, black heels, her hair changed from the bun for the performance, to waves that fell right at the nape of her slender neck and a beautiful smile, his heart slammed into his chest. This wasn't the chatty young girl he'd met on the plane. This was a confident sensuous woman who knew how to handle an audience. She was grace in motion.

"Jarrett Bryson, what an honor to have you backstage."

Jarrett did not register the woman speaking to him until Sergio gave him an elbow. He turned to the woman as he finished signing the autograph for the person standing in front of him. He then shook the woman's extended hand.

"Hello." He nodded.

"Jolene Cadet." She held his hand as she smiled. "Did you enjoy the performance?"

"Immensely," he replied as he looked over her shoulder trying to find Paige again.

"I'm pleased to hear that. We have a vigorous rehearsal schedule, which pays off. I'm sure you understand the dedication it takes to stay in shape." She rubbed his bicep.

Finally taking a look at the woman, he found her to be attractive and she had a banging body, but...she wasn't Paige.

On the other side of the room, Victoria approached Paige while she was signing a program for a couple.

"Good evening," she said to the couple then turned to Paige. "May I have a moment of your time?"

That was the line Victoria would use to rescue her from a too eager admirer. However, this was a couple and Paige wasn't sure why Vic would think she needed to be rescued.

"Thank you for coming. Would you excuse me?" Paige stepped away from the couple and turned to Victoria. "I don't think the gentleman would hit on me with his wife standing right there."

Victoria took her hand and led her through the small crowd. "I want to show you something."

"Okay."

Taking a few steps to the side, Victoria stood in front of Paige.

"Look over my shoulder near the door."

Paige stepped to the side and peered over Victoria's shoulder. The expression on her face was priceless. A slow smile appeared and her always dancing eyes seemed to beam brighter.

"He came."

Victoria took Paige's hand to keep her from moving.

"Do you see who he is talking to?"

Paige looked over Victoria's shoulder again, then nodded.

"You and I know she will stop at nothing to get what she wants," Victoria warned. "Don't let her upstage you."

Paige took another look over her shoulder. At the same moment, Jarrett looked up. Their eyes met and held. His smile emulated hers and in that moment she knew he had come to see her.

Paige squeezed Victoria's hand as a show of appreciation for her concern. She looked into her friend's eyes.

"What's for me is for me. No one can take it, especially not Jolene Cadet." Paige stepped around Victoria.

"Well...all right now." Victoria smiled and followed her friend.

Paige never took her eyes from his. A few people congratulated her on the performance as she walked by. She smiled, thanked them and continued to stride purposely towards the man who was making her hands sweat, her body tingle, and her heart skip a beat. She watched as he took a step away from Jolene and reached out his hands to her.

"Hello, Jarrett. You came." She smiled brightly.

"Paige." He grinned taking her hands. "I told you I would."

"Why did you make me wait so long?"

"I have no idea, but I promise, it will not happen again."

The heat building between the two could be felt by all standing around them. Several people in the crowd turned and just watched the couple standing there holding hands.

"Hello, Jarrett." Victoria extended her hand before the two drew more stares.

Paige looked over her shoulder at Victoria. She released one of Jarrett's hands and pulled Victoria closer.

"Jarrett this is my roommate Victoria Gaye. Vic, this is Jarrett Bryson."

Taking Paige's arm and pulling her closer to him, unintentionally pushed Jolene further away.

"It's nice to meet you Victoria." Jarrett turned to his left. "Sergio, this is Paige Cartwright and Victoria Gaye."

"Good evening," Sergio said to Paige as he shook her hand. He then turned to Victoria. He took her hand, brought it to his lips and kissed it. "You are as beautiful as you are graceful."

Victoria raised an eyebrow as she smiled at the man. "Thank you and I love the accent."

Sergio then spilled a series of words, dropped her hand and smiled.

"I have no idea what in the hell you just said, but the answer is yes." Victoria raised an eyebrow and smiled.

Jarrett and Paige laughed until they heard Jolene clear her throat.

"Oh, I'm sorry, Jolene." Paige frowned. "I forgot you were standing there. Please forgive my bad manners." She then smiled. "Have you been introduced to Jarrett and Sergio?"

"Yes, we were having a conversation before you interrupted."

"It wasn't important," Jarrett said to Paige. "Are you free for dinner?"

Victoria snickered. Paige gave her a warning look, then turn to Jolene.

"He was in no way insinuating that you were not important." She looked at Jarrett. "Isn't that right, Jarrett?"

That was exactly what he was saying. The woman was coming on to him shamelessly. However, he could see Paige expected him to be nice.

"No not at all." Jarrett apologized.

Paige squeezed his hand and looked at him in anticipation.

No. He tried to respond with his eyes. She apparently chose to ignore his answer and squeezed his hand again. He turned to Jolene.

"Would you like to join us for dinner, Ms. Cadet?" Jarrett asked through clenched teeth.

"Actually," Victoria interrupted, "Jolene, the producer is looking for you. Something about changing the lineup."

Jolene's eyes grew large at the announcement. "Really? Why didn't you tell me that?"

"I just did," Victoria replied to Jolene's back as she briskly walked away.

"Victoria." Sergio took her hand. "Will you be joining us for dinner?"

The sweetest smile appeared on her face as she turned to Sergio. "Why, I thought you'd never ask. Yes, I would love to join you." She stepped closer to the group. "May I suggest we find our coats and use the back door to escape? It would be great if we leave before Jolene finds out I lied. Could you have your driver meet us in the back?"

Jarrett and Sergio laughed while Paige looked stunned, as Victoria pulled her towards.

"You lied to Jolene?"

"Yes, Paige. Keep walking." Paige looked in the direction of Jolene then hurriedly followed Victoria.

"Paige, I swear, you are the only person who would invite a barracuda to your party."

Jarrett coughed to cover his laugh. Paige turned to him.

"Please don't encourage her."

"I'm sorry, but she's right," he said as he pushed open the stage entrance door. "Where would you like to eat?"

None of them picked up on the look of rage Jolene sent their way after being embarrassed by the producer in front of the other performers.

*****

"Of all the places we could have gone to eat, you wanted to come to Coney Island, in the cold, for a hot dog and cotton candy?" Jarrett marveled at the woman who was walking backwards, a little ahead of him, while eating cotton candy and smiling as if she didn't have a care in the world.

Less than an hour ago she was on stage, transformed into a temptress. Here she was childlike, marveling at the things most New Yorkers don't even notice. This woman was a chameleon and he liked that.

"I love amusement parks, ballparks, the beach, the Ferris wheel and snow." Paige twirled around with her arms in the air. "I love it all. It's like having a little piece of heaven right here on earth. Doesn't being here give you a burst of energy?"

"Seeing you smile again is like a little piece of heaven to me."

The sincerity in his eyes touched her heart. She stopped walking and watched as Jarrett stepped closer to her.

He was so handsome, confident and powerful as he walked towards her. She could feel the power radiating from him. It gave her a sense of being safe, protected. The same feelings she got from her father. Well, not quite the same.

The cashmere coat he wore was unbuttoned. Jarrett had removed his tie, and stood with his hands in his pockets as he stared down at her. In heels, she still had to look up to meet his eyes. All Paige could do was marvel at how magnificent he was. She pulled a piece of the cotton candy off the stick and held it out on two fingers.

This woman was perfection in his eyes. The trim white coat fit her body like a glove, showing every curve, enticing him. Her smile embraced him, but it was her eyes that called out to him. He wondered if she had any idea how much of a temptress she was.

Jarrett smiled as he parted his lips, took the candy and the fingers that were offered. As the candy melted on his tongue, he continued to hold her fingers between his lips. He wasn't sure which was sweeter, the candy or the look in her eyes from his touch.

The cold air did not stop the warm sensation from seeping into her veins like a surge of electricity running through a wire. Her reaction to his touch was evident before she could sensor it. Her lips slowly parted to release a little air from the pressure building in her stomach.

His hands were in his pockets, no other parts of their bodies were touching. Why did it feel like she was wrapped deep in his warmth? If he didn't break this contact soon, he was going to lose the little composure he'd managed to keep since seeing her on the stage.

Reaching up, Jarrett took her hand and slowly pulled her fingers from his mouth.

"I've thought about that light in your eyes for two weeks."

"I know," she said softly. "So have I." She shook her head. "Not about the light in my eyes, I mean." Paige blushed, never taking her eyes from his. "I thought about you and the way I felt talking to you."

"You're very easy to talk to."

"You should call when you need to talk to someone."

He kissed her fingers, then began walking with her hand in his. "Your hands are cold."

"Really? I feel warm all over."

Jarrett smiled as he thought about her offer. "I don't open up to people easily."

"I know. If you did the media wouldn't say some of the things they do about you. They would have a better understanding of the man you are."

"Do you think I should change that?"

She thought for a moment before responding. "I think you should adjust it. You should allow them to see some of what I see."

He stopped as she continued to walk. The sudden change caused Paige to be pulled back into his embrace.

"What do you see?" he asked standing there, with her hand in his, the other hand in his pocket.

The intensity in his eyes caused her to proceed with caution. Her response was important to him. She could tell by the vein in his neck that was pumping fiercely. The impulse to kiss it crossed her mind, but that would have been too forward.

He saw the look in her eyes as she began to formulate her response.

"No. I don't want it sugar coated. I need to know what you," still holding her hand in his, he pointed to her chest, "see when you look at me."

"I see a proud man filled with respect and integrity in all that he does. I also see a man filled with doubt about who he is and what awaits him in life. You're longing for something, and it's standing right in front of you. All you have to do is get out of the way and let it happen. All your life your dedication has been to the game. You haven't allowed anything to come between you and success. Now, you're wondering what comes after you stop playing. As my Grand'Mere would say, throw the balls in the air and let them land where they may." She tilted her head as she spoke to him. "You can't control the future, Jarrett any more than you can control the feelings you have for me."

"You think I have feelings for you?"

"No. I know you do. I felt it from the moment you shook my hand on the plane. So did you. Just as both of us feel it right at this moment. What is puzzling me is why you took so long to come and get me?"

"That's a difficult question to answer."

"Please try. Your answer is going to determine if you get to kiss me or not, and I so want to kiss you."

He loved the way she just spoke her mind. Taking her other hand in his, he took a step closer.

"Then I better get this right, because I also want that kiss." He placed his arm around her waist. Standing toe-to-toe, nose-to-nose, lips a breath apart, he spoke. "My life is so complicated."

"Un-complicate it," she said as her eyes held his captive.

Against her lips he whispered, "It's not that simple."

"Yes, it is."

Her lips moving against his caused a tidal wave of emotions to surge through him. Her lips were soft, inviting. The rainbow cotton candy, mixed with her vanilla scented body, was like a sensual aphrodisiac to his senses. The temptation to taste more was too strong to resist. His tongue rolled across her bottom lip, then eased her lips apart. His heart skipped two beats when their tongues met. He moaned, and he knew it was him because it vibrated throughout his body. Pulling her body closer, he loved the way it fit to his. *This must be heaven,* was the last sensible thought he had.

Paige heard her purse and cotton candy hit the ground the moment his tongue touched hers. The heat on her back from where he held her penetrated through the material of the coat and dress, to spread throughout her body. Her arms, as if of their own will, circled his neck, fusing their bodies together. *This must be heaven, because nothing on earth could ever feel this good,* was her last sensible thought.

Jarrett's body was telling him it was time to stop. Damn if he wanted to. He danced with her sweet tongue one last time then ended the kiss. He looked down into her eyes. The look in them screamed at him to kiss her again. He shook his head as he took her hand, picked up her purse and placed the cotton candy in a trashcan.

"I am in trouble," he said as they continued to walk.

"I'm right there with you."

"I don't think I want this night to end."

"If tonight doesn't end, there will be no tomorrows." Paige stepped around in front of him. "I want my tomorrows to be with you."

He kissed her temple. "I'm so gone," he laughed.

Victoria and Sergio sat on a bench watching. Sergio shook his head. "I can't believe Jarrett is kissing a woman in public and now he's laughing about it."

"Well...I'll be damned. It's snowing and they are acting like it's springtime out here," Victoria said in disbelief, then smiled, happy for her friend. "He is as gone as she is."

*****

Jolene sat in the mid-town apartment that she shared with another chorus line dancer, Carin Tomey. She was fuming.

"So are you going to let her get away with the principal and Bryson?"

Carin sat Indian style on the floor eating from a container of ice cream as she asked the question.

"No." Jolene gracefully stood as she walked to the window watching the light snow falling. "The only reason I am her back up is because of her heritage and money." The snarl was clear, crisp and deadly.

"You can always put broken glass in the toe of her slippers like you did with Melanie."

Jolene turned quickly on her roommate. "I told you to never mention that."

"It's just you and I here," Carin yelled back. "I know you from way back, Jo. You don't scare me." She put another spoonful of ice cream into her mouth. "So...what are you going to do? Break her legs?" she laughed.

"That's been done." Jolene sat on the sofa then leaned forward. "Remember the trick we pulled on Marcia Greene?"

Carin stopped eating and dropped the spoon into the container. "Need I remind you that Marcia died, Jo?"

"Marcia died from exposure to cold weather."
"Duh...It's cold, here in New York."
"Your point?"

CHAPTER EIGHT

The phone vibrated on the nightstand. Paige scooted further down beneath her comforter. She was having a wonderful dream and did not want to wake from it at that moment. Just another minute and she was sure he would kiss her again. The phone vibrated again. With the sheet still over her head, she reached out and pressed the button on the phone.

"Hello."

"Good morning."

Paige pushed the sheet off and sat straight up in bed. She looked at the phone. There was Jarrett's smiling face staring at her. She pushed her hair back and smiled. "Good morning."

"Are you always this beautiful in the mornings?"

The blush was so bright she covered her face with her hand.

"Thank you and no, I'm a mess early in the morning until I wash my face, brush my teeth and comb my hair. But you look wonderful. Since you're calling, I take it last night was not a dream."

"No, I'm afraid you stole something from me last night."

She frowned. "I did?" She was thinking. "I'm sorry. What was it? I will return it today."

He laughed. "I wouldn't take it if you tried. I think I like you having control of my mind right now."

Smiling, Paige lay back on the pillows.

"You shouldn't make me blush so early in the morning. I'll never get my workout or rehearsal on point after this. I'll spend the day thinking about you."

Seeing her lying against the pillow with her hair loose was causing his body to react. The vision was seductive without her meaning it to be. It was six in the morning and he still had to work out before catching the flight to Texas.

"You know I didn't get any sleep last night, after we dropped you off."

"I think that's only fair, since I didn't get any rest and Victoria threatened to put me out in the snow if I didn't stop talking about you. She hurt my feelings when she hit me with a pillow and locked me out of her room around four this morning."

Jarrett laughed at the pout on her face. "God, you are so adorable. I think I like seeing you like this early in the morning."

"It is a nice way to start the day." She smiled. "Now, I'm hungry."

"Have you ever eaten at Jake's, the little bistro around the corner from your place?"

"Yes!" She sat up in bed. "I love his bagels."

"You're a dancer and you eat hot dogs and bagels?"

"Yes, and I have to work overtime to keep them off my hips. Jolene says I have thunder thighs, that's why I shouldn't be the principal in any production."

"Don't listen to that. You were on point. You're movements were flawless."

"Thank you." She blushed again.

"You don't take compliments too well, you know that?"

"I know. Victoria says I have to toughen up. My Grand'Mere says all you have to know is that if you are good on the inside then only good will shine through."

"It shines through you." Seeing her smiling face on the phone caused him to lose his train of thought for a moment. "I don't live far from Jake's. Would you like to meet me there for breakfast?"

"I'd love to." She jumped out of bed and stepped into her slippers. "Give me ten minutes to shower and dress and I'll be there." She disconnected the call.

Jarrett looked at the phone and wondered, what in the hell was wrong with him. He had just dropped her off at her condo around two in the morning, after they had walked the boardwalk and talked just about all night. Then he came home, sat on the balcony of his condo watching the snowfall and wondering which window in the building across the street was hers. It didn't matter, he knew she was in that building. Once in bed he went to sleep thinking of her. Now, he did the unthinkable and let her know he lived close by. Shaking his head, he walked into his shower, excited that in ten minutes he would see her again.

It took him less than five minutes to walk to Jake's. The only reason it took that long was because someone stopped him for an autograph. Unlike some athletes, he knew and appreciated the value of his fan base. Any opportunity he had to thank them or show them how appreciative he was, he took it. He rarely turned anyone down for an autograph.

The snow had stopped, leaving an angelic like coating on the sidewalks. Jarrett wiped his feet before entering the bistro.

Jake's crowd was light at six thirty on a Sunday morning. During the weekdays, it was packed from six until after ten in the mornings, then the lunch rush hour would take over. The evenings would vary depending on what was happening in the city. This was one of his favorite places to come and just chill, when he needed some down time from the celebrity status and good conversation.

"Jarrett," Jake Weingart called from behind the counter. His salt and pepper hair showed the wisdom. The wrinkles on his olive tone skin were traces of the welcoming smile he always gave his customers when they entered the door. Jarrett swore he knew every person's name that walked in.

"Good morning, Jake." Jarrett shook the hand that was extended across the counter.

"Morning, Jarrett," his wife Celia called out with a pan of fresh bread in her hand. "The raisin bread is piping hot, just like you like it."

"What are you doing here, aren't you flying out today?"

"Yes, sir, the team is flying out around nine," Jarrett replied as he placed his jacket on the back of the stool. "We play tonight at seven. You're going to watch the game?"

"Are you serious? Haven't missed a game since sixty-three." Jake looked out the window. "Oh, do you remember when I told you about our new friend that has the eyes of an angel? There she is coming across the street. Isn't she beautiful?"

Jarrett looked out the window. There was Paige skipping across the street. The long white coat swirling around her boot covered legs, her hair bouncing as she moved. His heart pounded with anticipation with every step she took.

Celia turned around just as the door opened. "Look who's here! Hello, Paige. You beautiful girl you. How did the performance go?"

"Good morning, Mrs. Weingart." Paige beamed as she wiped her feet, closing the door behind her. "It was wonderful. The audiences were very kind. Good morning, Mr. Weingart."

He waved his hand in the air. "Jake, no Mr. around here."

Paige smiled. "I'm sorry. Good morning, Jake."

She turned her attention to Jarrett and he thought he would fall off his seat. Her face was clear of the theatrical makeup from last night and he swore she was even more beautiful this morning.

"Hello, Jarrett." She stopped at the stool next to him.

"Do you brighten up everyone's day or is it just me?"

She leaned in and kissed him. "I think I like you very much."

Jarrett wrapped his arm around her waist and pulled her closer. "I'm happy to hear that." He kissed her again, as if he was marking his territory. "The next time you kiss me, that's how I want it."

"I will do my best to comply with that request," she replied as he assisted her with her coat. "I'm starving."

"Let me take that for you." Jake reached for the coat. "I knew you had good taste," he teased Jarrett. "Now, this young lady is quality," he said after placing the coat on the rack. "Not to say anything about those other women you date. But this one...like I told Jake Jr. when he brought Valarie home." He put his fingers to his lips and kissed, "Quality, my boy, quality," then he walked to the back.

"You better treat her good, or you'll be dealing with me." Celia pointed a spatula his way.

He looked at Paige. "I've been coming into this place for at least five years and this is the first time I've ever been threatened."

"I won't let them hurt you. I'll protect you."

Jake walked back out with a tray in his hand.

"In honor of two of my favorite customers finding each other, you get my special." He walked from behind the counter. "Join me at my special table."

Jarrett took Paige's hand and led her over to the table by the window. He pulled her chair out, then took the one directly in front of her. Jake uncovered the plate, which he had filled with bagels, fruit and a variety of spreads. Celia joined them with a cup of coffee for Jarrett and hot tea for Paige.

"This is on the house, enjoy, enjoy." Jake and Celia walked away before either of them could say thank you.

"They are the sweetest people I've ever met." Paige smiled.

"I've never gotten free breakfast from them before. I'm going to bring you here more often."

"Is that a promise?"

He held her gaze. "Yes, that's a promise."

She sighed, then looked out the window where the street was still pretty empty. "There is something magical about the first snowfall of the year. It lifts your spirits and cleanses the air." She sighed. "Jarrett, Jake mentioned other women you date. Are you dating them now?"

"No." Jarrett wanted to reassure her, but wasn't sure how. He'd never been in a position where he felt compelled to explain his dating behavior. He reached across the table taking her hand in his. "I don't double dip, Paige, I never have. I can't explain all that I'm feeling for you, because I don't understand it all myself." He shrugged his shoulders. "I'm not interested in anyone but you."

She squeezed his hand. "I'm not as sophisticated or as 'in the know' as some of the women you've dated." She looked up. "You should also know I'm twenty-four years old and I've never reacted to a man the way I did with you last night. I've been kissed, made out a few times, but I've never made love. I don't think that will scare you off, but I thought you should know."

Jarrett sat his coffee cup down on the table. "I've dated many women. None of them made me feel the way you did the first time I met you or the way you made me feel when you kissed me last night. I don't know where this is going. I do know nothing that you said or could say would make me walk away from the thought of you being a part of my life." He kissed her fingers. "We can take things as slow as you like. When you are ready we'll move forward." He looked out the window as he gently rubbed her fingers. "There are so many things in my life that are a pretense." He looked back at her. "You're not. There isn't a pretentious bone in your body. It's like you fell from the sky into my life just when I needed you. I want to know everything about you. What do you like to eat, other than hot dogs and cotton candy." Paige smiled. "I want to know what makes you laugh, what makes you cry. Everything. Will you give me a chance?"

Tears were on the verge of falling from her eyes. She knew some hurt was going to be a part of their lives, but she didn't care. She wanted what he was offering and more. "I can do that."

He held her fingers to his lips and kissed them.

"Hey," Jake yelled from across the room. "You don't like my bagels anymore?"

Celia hit him with the spatula. "He's found something that tastes better than those bagels."

Jarrett and Paige laughed at the couple, then began eating.

"I don't know if I told you, but we are flying out today for a five day road trip. What's your schedule like this week?"

"I have three more performances this week, including a Saturday matinee. Then I'm off for three days. Where are you going to be?" She picked up a strawberry and bit into it.

Jarrett hesitated as he watched her. "Two games in Detroit, three in Texas, then we're back home on Sunday. Will you go to dinner with me Saturday night?"

"I'd love to."

The two talked, enjoyed the bagels and the peace of having the place to themselves. As other customers began to enter, they gathered their things, waved good bye to the Weingarts then walked out hand in hand in the snow.

"Love is in the air." Celia smiled to her husband as she watched the couple through the window.

*****

Waking up and falling to sleep at night for the last week did not satisfy Jarrett's need. It increased his desire to be with Paige every hour of the day. The benefits were his stats were off the chart. His batting average was 376, his runs batted in numbers had doubled and his home runs for the year were twice what he had this time the year before. To top things off, he was thoroughly enjoying the game again. They had clinched a spot in the playoffs with twenty games left to play in the regular season. All he had to do was stay healthy and get through the negotiations.

He had spoken with Nick about the topic, however, it just was not at the top of his priority list these days. Paige held that position. He was the top short stop in the league, as it was, but being with Paige brought a new element to the game. Talking to her before each game, she lifted his spirits and encouraged him at the end of every call with the same words. *'Enjoy the game, I'll be watching.'* That's exactly what he did, each time he hit the field. It was no longer about a paycheck. It was now about his love for the game.

The change was all her doing. It was also Paige who had him longing to hold her in his arms again. Last night, around two in the morning, she fell asleep while they were still on the phone. She had her phone on the nightstand while she was lying on the pillow. For the longest, he just held the phone watching her sleep and wishing he were there beside her.

Jarrett had finally finished the last interview after the game on Saturday. He jumped in the shower and was at his locker, dressed and ready to leave. The excitement of seeing Paige was consuming him.

"We're going to Jake's." Ron hit Jarrett on the shoulder just as he grabbed his coat.

"Can't do it tonight, man." Jarrett shook his head.

"What's up, man? You brushed us off the whole road trip and again tonight? What's up with that?"

Jarrett closed the locker door. "I have a date." He grinned.

"With who?"

"Paige." Jarrett smiled. "I'll catch you guys later."

"Hold up, man. Suzette is waiting outside and she's not alone. Lacy is with her. We thought it would be great if we hit Jake's, get a little dancing in then headed back to the house like we used to do."

"Sorry, man, I can't tonight. I have plans."

"Who is this Paige woman?" Ron asked, a little agitation clear in his tone.

"Leave it alone, Ron," Sergio said as he walked up.

"Since when did we start keeping things from each other, Jarrett?" Ron questioned.

Jarrett exhaled, "Look." He walked back to Ron. "I'm not keeping things from you. It's just..." Jarrett hesitated. He placed his bag on the floor. "It's new...different...you know. I just want to have her to myself before the craziness starts."

"But, you can share her with Serg?"

"I don't have a wife that's trying to push Lacy on him." Sergio hit Jarrett on the shoulder. "I'll check you later man."

"Is that what all the secrecy is about? Lacy?"

"Suzette is outside waiting, who's with her?" Jarrett picked up his bag. "We're still cool, man, and I love Suzette. The thing with Lacy is over. She is not the one for me."

"And this Paige woman is?"

Jarrett smirked. "I think she is."

"Yeah?"

Jarrett's face displayed a full-blown smile. "Yeah."

Ron pulled out his cell phone and took a quick picture of Jarrett smiling, then turned the phone to him. "This is how ridiculous you look."

Jarrett looked at the picture and began to laugh. Ron joined in. "Yeah, well, that's where I'm at, right now."

Ron put the phone away. "I'll walk out with you and play interference with Suzette. Tell me about this miracle woman who has you acting like a teenage boy who's about to get his first piece."

Jarrett laughed. "I can't deny it. She got me - heart, body and soul. There is not a part of me she hasn't touched. I can talk to her about anything. When the front office pissed me off the other day, I talked to her about it and we were laughing before we hung up the phone. That's another thing. She makes me laugh, even when we aren't doing anything but eating a damn bagel, I find myself smiling all the time. It's as if she has put a spell on me to be happy. You know, it's the craziest damn thing."

Ron stared, amazed by the emotions rolling out of his friend. "I don't think I've ever heard you talk about a woman this much."

"Hell, I don't think I've ever heard him talk this much, period," Jake laughed.

Jarrett shook his head as he looked around at his teammates, laughing. "Well, there you go."

Ron stopped and stared at Jarrett's back. "What in the hell does that mean?"

CHAPTER NINE

"**M**s. Cartwright, this is Alex from the front desk. You have a visitor." He sounded excited.

"Thank you Alex. Would you send him up please?"

"Visitors have to be signed in, Ms. Cartwright," he replied hesitantly. "But, I think we can overlook this visitor. You can come down to sign him in at your convenience."

"Thank you, Alex." Paige hung up the telephone and exhaled. She was nervous, excited, and happy. The feelings inside of her were hard to put into words. It had been a long week with Jarrett away. Now he was back and she was going to get those kisses he had promised all week.

She was wearing a halter-top black dress that fell just above her knees, 3-inch, strappy black sandals, her hair held up with a diamond comb, dangling, tear drop, marquis diamond earrings, and a matching tennis bracelet. She stopped in front of the mirror in the foyer. Her appearance wasn't something she ever worried about. She was taught how to dress to impress by her mother and Grand'Mere. There weren't any women more elegant than them. However, tonight it wasn't about elegance or impressions. She was stepping out as the woman in Jarrett's life. When she opened the door to him, she wanted him to see the woman he can't live without. She closed her eyes, said a short prayer, then walked through the foyer and opened the door. There were four apartments on her floor. The elevator was in the middle of the hallway. Why was it taking so long for it to reach the twenty-first floor? She did not know and the wait was killing her. The elevator's ding indicated it had stopped. Her heart began to pound harder, faster, then he stepped off the elevator and her heart stopped.

This was his first time at her condo. Jarrett wasn't sure which way to turn. He looked to his left, then to his right and there she was. Standing in the doorway, waiting for him. The sight of her stole his breath away. Then she smiled. He knew this was his blessing...a woman with a smile that he wanted to see each day for the rest of his life. A glow surrounded her. He wasn't sure who took the first steps, as he cradled her face in his hands midway between the door to her apartment and where he'd stepped off the elevator.

"I missed you," he said as he stared down into smiling eyes. Jarrett gently kissed her lips, as she wrapped her arms around his neck. "I missed you so much." He kissed one side of her mouth, then the other. He wrapped one hand around her waist picking her up, the other held her head as his tongue parted her lips for the sweet taste he had been longing for. The intoxicating smell of her jasmine scented skin, the tantalizing feel of her body clinging lovingly to his, sent surges of desire through him like a bolt of lightning. He had kissed many women, but none made him feel like he was in heaven. It was a feeling he didn't want to let go.

This was it. The look she'd seen between her parents when they kissed. The feeling that no one else in the world existed except the two of them. The sensational feeling of heat that was building with each taste of his tongue. The protective, caressing hold of his arms, the throbbing generating from his thighs. The profound feeling that was indescribable, pulsing through her at the thought of this man wanting her.

Walking her backwards, into the open doorway, Jarrett kicked the door closed. He sat her on her feet, leaned her against the door, then moved the kiss from her lips to her beautiful sleek neck, across her shoulders, over the rise of her breasts. His hands followed his trail down the side of her breasts, the curve of her waist, until he dropped to his knees, kissing her navel through the material of the dress. He wanted to kiss every inch of her body. He cupped her behind and pulled the essence of her intimately against his lips. Hearing her whimper, Jarrett knew he was going too fast...too fast. The need to have her was overwhelming him. He could just imagine the effect this was having on her. Her innocence was evident in her touch, which was maddening to his senses. Pressing his forehead against her stomach, he exhaled to bring some kind of control to the moment. "Paige."

'When it comes to making love, you simply go with what you feel. It will never steer you wrong.' That's what her mother had told her when they had the talk when she was sixteen. His hands, his lips, the heat, were profound. Nothing, nothing had ever made her feel as sensuous as his touch, so precious as his kiss, so wanted as his voice. She didn't want any of it

to end and all she had to work with was what she was feeling.

Dropping to her knees, she cupped his face in her hands and looked into his eyes.

"Love me, Jarrett."

She kissed him so deeply her insides quaked. The moisture, that began building from the touch of the bulge in his pants in the hallway, was flowing like a stream. The wanting increased and the need was pushing her over the edge.

Taking over, Jarrett's tongue danced with hers, touching every corner of her mouth, drinking up every drop of sweetness she released. His hands traveled up her thighs. Sensations from the touch of her, seared him, but he couldn't stop as he fell backwards onto the floor in the foyer bringing her with him, pulling her closer to his growing desire for her. The smooth silky feel of the globes of her behind, sent him into overdrive again. When his hands felt the wetness of her essence, it sent his senses overboard. Rolling her over onto her back, he pushed her dress up, pulled her panties down and threw them in the corner then buried his head between her legs. Her scent was intoxicating. Her taste was like honey. He was lost in the essence of her. The newness of tasting a woman here, didn't deter him from working his tongue lovingly around her, into her, over every inch of her until her fingernails dug deep into his shoulders, her breath hitched, and her insides pulsated. Then and only then did he feel compelled to see the look on her face.

Lifting his head, he wiped his face and looked at her. That was the wrong thing to do. The passion on her face, that perfect face, only increased his need.

"Paige?" She looked at him and that was his undoing. "Where's your bedroom?" he asked more harshly than he intended.

She heard him, wanted to answer him, but the glorious shivers going through her body controlled her.

He couldn't help but smile at her trying to answer him. He loved her reaction to his touch. "Bedroom Paige," he choked out in a laugh as he gathered her in his arms.

"Don't you dare laugh at me," she said as he carried her through the foyer.

He kissed her. "I am laughing at both of us." He loved that spark of passion that was beaming in her eyes. "Tell me where your bedroom is before I make love to you in this hallway."

"At the end of the hallway." She kissed his neck.

He closed his eyes for a second to the sensations building. Reaching the bedroom, he laid her on the sleigh bed, then just marveled at her. "Would you be terribly disappointed if we skipped going out tonight?"

"No."

She had transposed from the bashful girl of a minute ago, into the tempting tigress he saw on stage. Every woman he would ever need was wrapped into this one. Holding her eyes as she watched him from almost closed lids, he began to undress. Her eyes didn't move until he was completely naked. When he placed the condoms on the nightstand, her eyes traveled up his body and stopped at his manhood. "You have a powerful body."

He held out his hand to her. She placed her hand in his and the calm feeling he felt that first time on the plane touched him. Pulling her up he turned her around and unzipped her dress. Slowly he pushed the straps over her shoulders, hearing the swish when the dress hit the floor. She turned to him. Incredible. She was exquisite. They say that beauty is in the eye of the beholder. Well...her beauty was dazzling. He pulled the diamond comb from her hair. The strands unfolded, stopping at the nape of her neck. He dropped the comb to the floor, then bent down to remove her sandals. What amazed him was her comfort level with her body and his. Not once did she shy away as she stepped out of the sandals and he ran his hands up her calves, her thighs, over her behind, around her waist, to cup her breasts. Kissing one nipple he heard the hitch in her breath and he jerked in response. As he opened his mouth and closed it over her breast, he wondered if he was going to survive the night. Switching to give the other breast a little attention, he felt her legs buckle. Wrapping his arm around her waist, he guided her body back onto the bed as he continued his assault from one breast to the other. Her body moving seductively under his as he suckled and caressed her.

"Jarrett," he heard her call out as her hands trailed over his shoulders. Her voice alluringly angelic, it almost cracked his concentration. Shaking the effect away, he continued as his lips stayed on her breast and his hands traveled down her body until his finger entered her. Her body bucked at the intrusion. But he couldn't ease up. The outcome of this night was too important to allow any interruptions to the plan in his mind to brand her so deeply that she would never want another man to touch her--never. If that meant delaying his pleasure, so be it. He wanted this woman forever. With that set firmly in his mind, he continued to arouse her until he felt her explode again in his hands. Watching her explode a second time was his undoing. He reached over to the nightstand and covered himself with protection. He positioned himself between her thighs and lay on top of her. He kissed her swollen lips while brushing her hair from her face.

"Paige, I need you to look at me." Her eyes were so filled with passion he had to smile. She smiled back. "I'm going to make love to you now."

"Isn't that what you have been doing for the last hour? It feels like it."

"Yes," he laughed. "That's exactly what I've been preparing you for."

She held his gaze. "You're not going to hurt me Jarrett." She kissed his lips. "The anticipation is what's killing me. Ease my pain."

Damn if she didn't steal his heart--again. Kissing the side of her mouth, he slowly positioned himself at her opening. He kissed the other side of her mouth as he eased into her. She surrounded him like a warm wet blanket as he submerged deeper into her. A moan of pleasure escaped as he went deeper. When he reached her blockage, he rested his forehead on hers. Perspiration was popping from him straining to hold back because he did not want to hurt her.

"Love me, Jarrett," she breathed into his ear "Please love me."

The strain was killing him and she wasn't helping. Holding her face in his hands, he kissed her deep, and plunged through the barrier. He continued deeply kissing her until the cry he heard in her throat turned into a moan of passion. The kiss changed, from protecting, to sensuously charged, then to passion filled, as her body began moving in rhythm with his. The dance that was as old as time, escalated to a magical erotic movement of two lovers digging deep to satisfy an urge that could not be tamed. It would take a lifetime. All they could do was pacify the desire. Her movements were graceful yet demanding. She moved upward to meet each of his magnificent strokes, after stroke, her nails digging into his back with her efforts to pull him deeper. Jarrett arched up, placed both hands on the bed beside her, then began pumping feverishly into her, until they both screamed at the powerful bolt of passion that took them into another hemisphere. Even after the bolt, Jarrett continued to move within her, slowing the strokes, easing the intensity, loving the glorious feel of her.

Still on his hands, he stared down at the woman that had become a tigress. Her hands holding on to his lower back as if she was afraid he would pull away. Her face was glowing from satisfaction. He knew in that moment, he would never let her go. Never.

"Paige."

He sounded afraid to her. But that couldn't be. They had just crossed the threshold of togetherness. Nothing could separate them now, for she had tasted him and he her. No one else would ever be able to quench his or her thirst. She opened her eyes and looked at him. Worry was staring back at her. "Yes."

"Are you okay? Did I hurt you?"

"You are such a caring man." She touched his cheek. "I have to call Grand'Mere and tell her she was right." Paige smiled.

"I just made love to you. Still inside of you and you want to call your Grand'Mere?"

She sat up, kissed his lips then lay back down. "She said you would be like a one hundred mile per hour fast ball, and the explosion would knock us out of the ball park. She was right."

The twinkle in her eyes at the outrageous statement made him laugh. He kissed her, then gathered her in his arms as he rolled onto his back, pulling her on top of him, staying deep inside of her, still laughing. "I have to keep you."

She folded her arms under her chin and laid on his chest. "I'm falling in love with you, Jarrett. Does that frighten you?"

Jarrett was rubbing her back, the motion stopped. He latched both hands behind his head as he looked into the wonderful innocent brown eyes and pondered her question. Women had said that to him before and he immediately put an end to the relationship. He wasn't there with them and he thought it would be cruel to allow them to hope that would change sometime in the future when he knew it wouldn't. With this woman he was afraid he would be on the other side of the table.

"No, it doesn't. I'd be scared as hell if you weren't. But you already know that, don't you? Just like you knew I was going to come looking for you before. Why do you have so much faith in me?"

Paige inhaled, then kissed his neck.

"When I boarded that plane, my stomach became nervous, like right before I go on stage. I knew something was going to happen. My family is intuitive like that. When I touched your hand, I knew then you were the man I would spend the rest of my life with. I'm coming to terms with that. Now, I have to be patient and allow you to find your way." She exhaled. "Then I have to prepare." She laid her head down and listened to his heart beat.

The woman fascinated him with her old school wisdom or intuition as she put it. "What do you have to prepare for?"

"The hurt."

"I'd never hurt you, Paige."

She put her chin back on her hands and held his eyes. "You won't mean to, but it will happen. Our love is like a traditional romance. We've found each other, then something is going to happen that's going to hurt one of us. We'll lose each other."

"No, we will not," Jarrett demanded. "I will not lose you."

Feeling the tension building up in his body, she kissed his chest. "We'll find each other again." She squeezed her inner muscles, as she pushed up on his chest. He put his legs up to support her back as she sat straddling him, his hands at her waist, hers playing with the hair on his chest. "Our love is not one that can be destroyed. People will try, because of who you are."

"Paige, I want you to listen carefully to me. I've been around. You know that. This is the first time the word love did not send me packing. The first time in my life that I did not wake up with baseball on my mind. I don't know what your intuition is telling you, but I know what I'm feeling and I don't want that feeling to ever stop."

This was a path they should not have gone down, Paige thought. He didn't understand that sometimes you have to lose what you have to appreciate it more. Her Grand'Mere had told her that. She knew, once the world knew about them, there was going to be trouble in paradise. However, that time was not here now. Right now, she wanted to feel the euphoria of his lovemaking. She squeezed her inner muscles around him. He closed his eyes and moaned. "Is that the feeling you don't want to stop?"

He opened his eyes to the mischief in hers. "No, and you know it's not."

She squeezed again. "No? You don't want to feel that?"

He moaned again. "Paige."

"Yes?" She moved in a circular motion. "You know I could do my whole floor routine right from this position." She wiggled around until his hands tightened around her waist. She rubbed his arms. "Dance with me again, Jarrett." She closed her eyes and relished the feel of him growing inside of her. "Dance with me," she breathlessly asked.

How in the hell could he resist her? The dance began again.

*****

The scent was exquisite, the feel, silky and warm. His arousal, erect. A smile spread across his face as his eyes opened. It was Paige's hair that was on his chest that he smelled, and her body that he was feeling. Her leg over his thigh was causing the arousal. This must be heaven, he thought again. He kissed the top of her head, then eased from the bed so he would not awaken her. They did not fall asleep until the wee hours of the morning. She needed to rest. Looking around, he marveled at the room that was tastefully decorated in peach and cream. Smiling, he thought it fit the personality of its occupant. The sight of her sleeping soundly tugged at his heart. She was beautiful and he was in love with her. How in the hell did it happen so fast? The other question that hit him was why did he feel so damn happy about this? He picked up his pants then walked over to the bathroom to take a shower. Afterwards, dressed only in the pants he'd worn the night before, he stepped out onto her balcony, to watch the sun rise. It was a clear morning. Cool, but not cold. He was right, he could see his condo from her balcony. *How sweet is that?* He pulled his cell from his pants pocket and pushed a button.

"Hey, Pop."

"Jarrett?" his groggy father replied. "Is everything all right, son?"

"Yes, I'm fine Pop. I want you and Mom to fly up for the game today. I'll have Nick send the jet."

"What's the occasion?"

"I want you to meet someone."

"A woman?" his father asked.

"Pop, she is amazing. I wake up thinking about her. I close my eyes at night and her smile is there."

His father began laughing. "See, there you go."

Jarrett looked around to see if Paige had said that or his father. He still had no idea what it meant, but he had to laugh.

"Connie, Connie, wake up. Jarrett has met a woman."

Jarrett could hear his mother stirring in the background. "Tell me about her. What's her name?"

Jarrett sat in one of the lounge chairs on the balcony. "Her name is Paige Cartwright."

"Is she pretty, son?"

Jarrett looked through the sliding glass door and saw Paige sit up in bed wiping the sleep from her eyes. She looked around and when she saw him, her eyes lit up, then she smiled. It was like the sun had just begun to shine. "Yes, Pop, she is beautiful; inside and out." He saw her grimace as she moved to wrap the sheet around her body. "Pop, I have to go. See you soon."

He walked back into the room closing the balcony door.

"Good morning." He leaned against the doorway, with his hands in his pockets. The temptation to go back to bed and make love to her was so strong he decided not to go any closer. "Are you sore?"

"Good morning. Why are you so far away?"

"If I come any closer to you, I'm going to make love to you again."

"Is that a problem?" She raised an eyebrow, as she brushed her hair out of her face.

"A little." He nodded. "That's why I'm keeping my distance for now."

"Does that mean I don't get a good morning kiss?"

He growled, as he walked over to the bed. "No hands." He placed his hands on the bed to the side of her. She laughed as he kissed her good morning.

Her cell phone buzzed. Without looking at the phone she sighed happily. "That's Grand'Mere. She knows."

He looked at the picture and name that appeared on the face of the phone, then frowned at her. "How did you know that?"

"The women in our family are very in tune with each other. Well, with the exception of my cousin, Grace, but that's a whole other story." She reached for the phone, while he continued to stare down at her. "Good morning, Grand'Mere."

"Is he still there?"

"Yes."

"Let me speak to him."

She held the phone out to Jarrett and smiled. "Grand'Mere would like to speak to you."

Jarrett's face frowned with confusion as he took the phone. "Good morning, Grand'Mere."

"Good morning, Jarrett. You're a good man, son. Paige is a wonderful woman. Treat her as the precious gift she is or you will have to deal with me. Are we clear?"

"Yes, ma'am."

"Good. Now here's what I want you to do to help with the soreness."

Jarrett laughed, "Excuse me?"

"Listen, son, this is important. Go into her bathroom and tell me what she has on hand."

Jarrett walked into the bathroom and gave a rundown of the contents of her cabinet. "Now what do you want me to do with this?" He listened intently and followed the directions given.

"Draw a nice warm bath, add the tea tree oil and her jasmine bath oil. This is the most important step, Jarrett."

He stood up from the tub as if at attention. "What's that?"

"You slide into the tub behind her and hold her while she bathes. Then love my Paige. Not make love to her, just love her."

Jarrett turned to Paige standing in the doorway with the sheet wrapped around her. He smiled. "I can do that."

"Goodbye, son."

"Goodbye, Grand'Mere." Jarrett hung up the telephone and held his hand out to Paige. "Let me love you."

On the other side of the balcony, Victoria was sitting outside her bedroom, worried. When she walked in last night, she'd found Paige's underwear in the foyer and knew that meant Jarrett was there. All night she worried if this was just a conquest for him that would leave her friend hurt. Jarrett Bryson was a media disaster waiting to happen for any woman that walked into his life. The publicity of their relationship was going to kill Paige. That aside, at least she had some idea where Jarrett's head was at, after listening to his call with his father. Now she could get some sleep. That is until all hell breaks loose. She sighed at the thought of Paige going through what was coming her way. She prayed she was wrong. Maybe, just maybe things would be okay.

CHAPTER TEN

The crap began sooner than expected. Jarrett and Paige arrived at the stadium hours before the scheduled two o'clock game.

"Are you sure you are feeling okay?" Jarrett asked for the third time as he opened the passenger door for her to get out.

She cupped his face, pulled it down to hers and kissed his lips with a smack. "Yes, I am fine. Are you sure my being here unplanned is not a problem for you?"

He kissed her. "Now who's the worry wart? I'm positive," he replied as he pulled his bag from the back seat. "You will be sitting with some of the other players' wives." He wrapped his arms around her waist, then turned towards the players' tunnel that led to the locker room. "Introduce yourself to them and they will welcome you with open arms."

"Jarrett."

He turned to see Jake, and his wife Valarie.

"Perfect. Hey, Jake, Val." Jarrett was smiling from ear to ear. "Paige, this is Mr. and Mrs. Weingart's son, Jake and his wife Valarie. This is Paige Cartwright."

"My parents speak very highly of you. You're the dancer, right?" Jake extended his hand.

Paige extended her hand and shook both of theirs. "Yes, I am." She smiled as she felt Valarie appraising her.

"It's nice to meet you." Valarie smiled.

"Thank you," was all Paige said.

"Would you do me a huge favor, Val?"

"Sure, anything, Jarrett."

"Introduce Paige to the ladies and make sure she has a good time. I want to make sure she comes back."

"I can do that." Valarie replied.

Paige noticed a bit of apprehension on Val's part. "You know, I can sit in the outfield and watch the game from there."

"Nonsense," Val said. "You're a guest of Jarrett's. You are welcome to sit with us. You guys go on. We'll see you on the field," Val added.

Jarrett pulled Paige into his arms and kissed her. "I'll see you after the game. I want you to meet some people."

"Enjoy the game." Paige smiled and watched as the two men walked away.

"You know you just put her in the lions' den," Jake said as he walked beside Jarrett.

Jarrett turned and looked back, to find Paige looking back at him. "Paige can handle it."

Paige ended up watching the game from her family's Skybox. As the wives began arriving to the game, it became more and more evident that she was not welcomed. Each person that arrived in the wives' box looked at her as a misfit. First she was dressed in white slacks, a cardigan top, with a gold belt at her waist, and flat boots and a leather jacket. The others were dressed as if they were going to a club. As Val introduced her around, a few of them made her feel uncomfortable. That was expected, after all she was the new girl and they didn't know her. Once they had a chance to spend some time with her, they would like her, she was sure of that. Most of them were cordial but kept their distance.

"You know, it's not you, they are shunning," Val said as she sat next to Paige with a plate of food from the spread in the room. She pushed the plate towards Paige. "Some are concerned with your looks."

Paige looked down at what she was wearing then back up at Val. "What's wrong with the way I look?"

"Nothing, that's the problem. The women who are married to, or dating ball players have to deal with groupies and others that want what they have. You are a concern because they do not know your status. And, well to be honest, Jarrett doesn't keep a woman around long. Which means, you may be a free agent and may catch their man's eyes."

"No one can take what is theirs, if it's truly theirs. That's what my Grand'Mere always says."

Val smiled at the young woman. "I believe that is true." She picked up a shrimp and put it in her mouth. "However, some of them schemed to get their man and they are afraid another woman will do the same."

"Karma does have a way of coming back and biting you in the behind." Paige picked up a grape and popped it into her mouth.

"That's true," Val laughed. "The others know that Suzette will not be happy because Jarrett's ex is her friend and they don't want to get caught in the crossfire."

Paige picked up another grape and popped it into her mouth. "What's your take?"

"Well, I called Momma Celia and she vouches for you." She ate a shrimp. "Other than that, I've known Jarrett a long time. I've never seen him be openly affectionate with any woman he has dated. He can't seem to keep his hands off you. That will not win any points for you with Suzette." She heard the woman laughing in the distance. "Be forewarned."

"Who is Suzette?" Paige ate another grape. "Why aren't you afraid of her wrath?"

"I'm a wife who is loved dearly by my husband. She goes too far with me and she has to deal with him." She ate another shrimp. "She doesn't want to go up against Jake. As to who she is, well she is the self-appointed leader of the wives or significant others. We are called the Queens. We do charity work and we also support each other. We're not a bad group. Some of us just have a misconception about priorities in life."

"So, Val, who do we have here?" A strikingly beautiful woman dressed in a black designer dress and heels, with diamonds flashing from head to toe, sneered at Paige.

Paige extended her hand. "Paige Cartwright."

The woman looked her up and down. "You are supposed to be Lacy's replacement?" she laughed. "Jarrett must have lost his mind."

Paige looked at Val, who only raised an eyebrow then looked away. "I'm sorry, I didn't get your name." Paige dropped her hand and waited.

"That's because I did not give it. I'm Suzette Mackenzie. Ron Mackenzie's wife." The emphasis was on the word wife.

"It's nice to meet you, Suzette. I've watched your husband play a few times. He's very good. You must be proud of him."

Suzette frowned, turned and looked at the other wives sitting around the room, then she turned back to Paige. "It's Mrs. Mackenzie to you. We have a certain dress code around here. We represent our husbands and in doing so we must be prepared to be in front of cameras 24/7. While you are with Jarrett, you are to conduct yourself with the utmost dignity and stay camera ready. As I said before, you represent Jarrett." She looked Paige up and down. "Your hair is too short. If you can't grow more, buy some. The next time you step into this area, I expect you to be presentable. For today, there are a few seats at the lower end of the box. You can sit there."

At first Paige was a bit offended by the woman's words and was about to tell the woman that the blouse she was wearing cost more than her entire outfit, but that would be rude. Her Grand'Mere once told her, *you can catch more bees with honey than you can with venom.*

"Mrs. Mackenzie, you are a very pretty woman. I'm sure your husband is very proud of the way you represent him." Paige picked up her purse. "Thank you for the advice." She looked at the other women. "It was nice meeting you all." Then she turned to walk out of the area.

"Paige, wait." Val followed her. "Where are you going?"

"My family has a VIP box here. I'll watch the game from there."

"Do you know where to meet Jarrett after the game?"

"No, but I'll figure it out. It was nice meeting you Val." Paige smiled then walked off.

"Where is she going?" Suzette asked as she filled her plate.

"To her parents' VIP box."

Suzette paused. "Her parents have a VIP box here? Who is she again?"

Val wanted to laugh at the look Suzette was attempting to hide when she mentioned the VIP box. The cost of that area ranged from a mere one hundred thousand and up a year.

"Jarrett's friend who you just put out. Her name is Paige Cartwright. According to my mother-in-law her father is a big time Judge and her mother is an attorney in the DC area. I would say you have a few hours to put together a good lie that will not piss Jarrett off. After all, it looks like this one is going to be around for a while. Which means." She popped a grape in her mouth to hide the smile. "Your status as Queen of the Queens may be in jeopardy." Val cleared her throat, turned and walked off.

Suzette stared at the woman's back as she walked away. There was no way she was relinquishing her role to some woman Jarrett just met.

Following the game, Jarrett bypassed the locker room and reporters, and went directly to the seating area for the wives and families. They had a good victory over the visiting team. It felt good knowing Paige was in the stands watching. Where exactly, he wasn't sure. The few times he looked up at the area for the wives, he didn't see her. It didn't matter, he knew she was there.

Walking into the area, he looked around, but did not see Paige. "Suzette," he called out as he spotted her standing with a few wives. "Good afternoon, ladies. He nodded as they were leaving the area. "Did you meet Paige?"

"Hey Jarrett," Suzette replied. "Yes, I met her."

"Where is she?"

"She left earlier."

"What do you mean she left?"

"She said something to Val about watching the game from her parents' VIP box. I guess sitting out here with us was beneath her."

Jarrett knew better than that. "Did she say which box?"

"She didn't really talk to me or any of the other wives, Jarrett. I couldn't say. I'll walk down to the tunnel with you. I am going to meet Ron."

"I need to find Paige." Jarrett turned to walk away.

"What are you going to do, walk around the stadium until you find her? I've never known you to run after anybody. You never had to search for Lacy."

"Let it go, Suzette." He kissed her cheek. "I'll talk to you later." He walked back down to the locker room and pulled out his cell phone. "Give me a minute," he said to the reporters, then pushed a button on his cell phone. "Hey beautiful. Where are you?"

"Standing outside the locker room with a bunch of your fans. They are wonderful and they love you. You should hear them raving about your game today."

Jarrett couldn't help but smile at the laughter in her voice. "What are you doing out there?"

"It is so much fun. You should come out here and say hello to them."

He laughed. "Tell me where you are."

She looked around. "Near the tunnel entrance where we parked."

"Is there a tall guy with a goatee directing the people?"

"Yes."

"Go to him and give him your phone." She did as he asked. "Julio, this is Jarrett. Would you bring Ms. Cartwright to me?"

"This little lady with the phone?"

"Yes, Julio."

"I can try, but along the way I'm going to try to take her from you, she's a beauty."

Jarrett laughed. "Thanks, Julio." He disconnected his cell and dropped it back in the locker as the reporters emerged.

Thirty minutes later, after the interviews, he showered and was dressing when Ron approached him.

"Suzette said your new girl was rude and walked out on her." Jarrett looked at Ron and just smirked. Ron laughed at the look. "I know, she's exaggerating. You want me to talk to her?"

"Val said Suzette put the girl out." Jake joined them.

"Suzette put Paige out of the area, why?" Sergio asked as he walked up.

"Suzette wouldn't put her out. She would just make her uncomfortable enough to want to leave," Ron stated. "If your girl allows it, Suzette will bully her. Do you want me to talk to her?"

Jarrett looked around at his friends and teammates. He knew them and their wives well and understood their relationships at home were important to their happiness, just as his relationship with Paige was to him.

"I appreciate everyone's concern. Paige is going to be fine." He looked at Ron. "I don't want you to tell Suzette anything that will get you in trouble." The guys laughed as Ron nodded. "Just let your ladies know. Paige is here to stay. Where I go, Paige goes. If Paige is not welcome, neither am I." Jarrett picked up his bag. "Now, if you gentlemen will excuse me. I'm going to introduce Paige to my parents."

"She's meeting the parents?" Ron asked, surprised at the implications.

"Momma Connie is here?" Sergio asked. "Is she cooking?"

Jarrett laughed. "Yes, Ron, she's meeting the family. Sergio, would you like to join us for dinner?"

Sergio did not reply, he walked over and opened the locker room door. "I'll follow you home."

*****

The usual crowd of fans was outside the door as Jarrett and Sergio emerged. The media was out in full force as they approached the area where the wives held court with the fans. The cameras and microphones were directed at Suzette and her band of friends, catching husbands and boyfriends as they met up with their women to take the after game media circus photos and occasional interviews with the paparazzi. This was the round where the players who weren't sought out by the top level media core, hung out to get their shine. As soon as the media spotted Jarrett they turned in his direction.

"I don't see Paige."

"You look for her. I'll run interference for you," Sergio offered.

"Bryson, get over here," Suzette called out using her sexy Jersey accent as she motioned for him to come towards her and the camera. "We are talking about Queen of the Knights."

"Do you have a queen to add to the reality show?" the reporter called out to Jarrett.

"Of course he does," Suzette replied for him as she reached out to grab his arm. "Lacy is considering becoming a part of the cast along with the other wives."

"Jarrett, are you and Lacy on again?" the reporter asked as Suzette squeezed Jarrett's arm.

He knew what she wanted him to say, however, it was time for Suzette to learn she cannot manipulate every man.

Jarrett held up his hand, smiling and shaking his head. "No." He patted Suzette's hand then removed it from his arm and placed it on Sergio's arm. Sergio clamped down on it and held it so she could not pull at Jarrett again. It was a smooth, practiced motion that would save face for Suzette with the media.

"You know Jarrett has always been camera shy." She smiled at the cameras.

"Sergio, will you make an appearance on the show?" another reporter asked.

"Why not. I may have a queen by then." The reporters laughed.

"Do you think Queen of the Knights will be a contender against the other housewives shows without the captain's queen?"

"I am certain Suzette is going to give you plenty of drama."

"That I am."

Jarrett heard Suzette's strained laughter as he continued in the direction he was previously walking. *Ron is going to catch hell when he emerges from the locker room* was his thought until the sight of Paige came into view. Approaching the end of the roped off area, leaving behind the paparazzi and fans, he could see Paige in the distance, helping the cleanup crew with the trash from the concessions. Her back was to him as Julio looked up with a bright smile and waved. The women and men around her were laughing and listening to music as they worked. A song came on and the group threw their hands in the air and began singing and dancing to the song. Paige joined right in. Jarrett was mesmerized by the essence of her. He was standing there watching her as Sergio walked up next to him.

"You are so gone."

Jarrett turned to him laughing, then back to Paige and the workers dancing. "Tell me that doesn't make you smile."

Ron and Suzette and some of the other couples approached them. "It's disrespectful, if you ask me."

"Disrespectful?" Sergio frowned. "How?"

"She chose to be with the cleaning crew rather than with us." Some of the women behind Suzette nodded in agreement.

"Oh, I don't know, Suzette," Valarie replied. "After the way you all shunned her this afternoon, I'd rather be with them too."

Suzette took a step towards Val. "No one shunned her. We simply schooled her on what is acceptable. We have a reputation to uphold. If she expects to be accepted, she needs to know that and get in line."

"In line for what and behind who?" Jarrett turned to Suzette. He held her gaze.

"Come on, Jarrett," Ron interceded. "You know how Suzette is with our Queens. She takes the organization seriously."

Jarrett's eyes never left Suzette's as he spoke. "Does she? I suggest she check herself if she wishes to remain their leader." He turned back to Paige and walked away.

"Did he just threaten me?"

"I strongly suggest you tread lightly on this one, Suzette," Valarie said as Jake took her hand and followed Jarrett.

Sergio grimaced then slowly walked backwards. "I'm going to have dinner with the family." He grinned then turned towards Jarrett.

Suzette turned to her husband. "The family?" She frowned.

"Yes," Ron sighed as he took his wife's hand and walked towards their car. "He is introducing her to his parents."

"What about Lacy?"

"I think Jarrett has moved on."

Suzette stared at the group of people as they laughed aloud.

Paige noticed the flutter in her chest and knew Jarrett was near. She turned to see him and some of his friends walking towards them. She couldn't help it. A smile as wide as a canyon appeared on her face as she watched the natural swagger of his stride approaching her. The look in his eyes intensified the closer he got, causing her mouth to water, anticipating the taste of him. The people around them faded into the background as the heat between them increased with each step. Her feet began to move towards him, one small step at first, which turned into a speed walk as his arms opened. She jumped into them as his bag hit the ground. Jarrett swung her around as laughter filled the air. The kiss that followed was deep, loving, and all-consuming. Everyone - Ron and Suzette, Jake and Valarie and the other couples stopped. Sergio was the only one who did not seem phased by what was occurring. He picked up the discarded bag as the cleaning crew and Julio cheered for the loving couple.

"Now, that's how you kiss a woman." Julio whistled.

Jarrett had no idea what came over him. The closer he got to her, the more the urgency to taste the sweetness of her lips increased. As he reached her, he realized this was what it felt like to be in love. In that moment he knew he would do anything to have this woman's love. The moment her arms wrapped around his neck he was lost, gone into her beautiful world and he was okay with it. Her kiss held back nothing as she surrendered her all to him. And he was okay with that too, for he did the same.

The giggle in her throat caused him to do the same. Jarrett broke the kiss and held on tight to her.

"Don't you ever let me go, Jarrett Bryson."

He looked down into her dancing eyes, with a grin as wide as hers. "Have no doubt, if I ever do, I will come back for you."

"Okay, you two," Sergio laughed. "I think you've put on enough of a show. Can we go eat now?" He held the bag out for Jarrett.

Jarrett took the bag, holding Paige at his side as he walked towards the SUV. "Julio, thank you for bringing her to me."

"You better hold on tight to that one, or I will teach her some Spanish love and make her forget all about you."

"Las manos fuera."

Julio threw his hands in the air. "Hands off."

Sergio nodded. "Good," Sergio said from his truck. "Now can we go eat?"

Jarrett helped Paige into the vehicle as everyone got into their vehicles.

"Since when does Jarrett act like a horny high school boy?"

Ron shook his head as he held the door for his wife. "Looks like a man in love."

"Oh don't be ridiculous, Ron," Suzette hissed as she got into the vehicle. "This is Jarrett we are talking about. What is she, girlfriend number 52?"

"Looks like she may become wife number 1." He smiled and closed the door on his wife's incredulous look.

"We'll see about that," Suzette said to herself then snapped a picture with her cell phone before Ron got into the car.

CHAPTER ELEVEN

The moment the elevator door opened into the foyer of the penthouse the aroma from the homemade lasagna hit them. Sergio pushed past Jarrett and Paige with arms opened wide.

"Momma Connie, I could smell your lasagna a mile away from here." He hugged Connie, picking her up as he kissed her cheek.

"I'm standing in the room while you are mauling my wife," Frank growled.

Sergio put Connie down as she laughed at the rambunctious young man. "Oh, no worries, Frankie, he doesn't hold me like you do."

"Let's keep it that way." Frank held his hand out as Sergio grabbed him in a bear hug.

"How you doing, Mr. Bryson?" Sergio made quick work of shaking his hand then moved past Frank into the kitchen.

Connie watched as Jarrett walked into the room. There was an ease, a calmness about him that she couldn't quite explain. Frank stood next to his wife, holding the small of her back as their son approached.

"Hi, Mom, Dad." He kissed his mother, then hugged his father. Stepping back he put his arm around Paige's waist and pulled her forward. Proudly, he said, "This is Paige, Paige Cartwright. Paige, my parents, Frank and Connie Bryson."

Paige could feel the fear in Jarrett's mother. She wasn't certain how to ease the woman's fears.

"It is an honor to meet you both." She then stepped forward, putting her arm around Connie's and then walked into the living room with her. "You know, my Grand'Mere says, let all the butterflies out of the jar so there will be no questions about who you are. I am an open book into my world." They sat on the sofa facing the window with the park as a backdrop. Paige crossed her legs and began. "I am the only child to Horace and Eleanor Cartwright. They had me late in life and spoiled me relentlessly. My Grand'Mere says I was born an old soul, raised by old souls and live by old souls' standards. For me, respect thy mother and father in all things, is in my top ten do's and don'ts. So ask away. Whatever you want to know I'm sure I can answer or feel free to call my parents, Grand'Mere or Leona; they will tell you all you need to know about this woman who has invaded your son's life."

Connie sat there stunned for a moment, then she realized the beautiful creature sitting next to her was an angel. There was no other way to explain the calmness that suddenly surrounded her. It was a moment later that she realized the woman had stopped talking. Jarrett and Frank stood in the center of the room while Sergio had stopped eating the garlic bread and was listening too.

"Leona?" Connie asked.

"She's the one I call my number 3 mother. See there's my mother, Eleanor who is like a twin sister to me. My father constantly mistakes me for Mother and Mother for me. Of course that's his way of charming her, but we play along. Then there's my Grand'Mere who was there to catch me when I popped right into this world. Why if she hadn't been there I would have hit the floor. At least that's what my father says. More to the point there is Leona, who the lord only knows how our family would have survived without her being there to keep us organized and to let us know when we have stepped out of line. I promise you, when you meet her you will think she is the head of the family instead of our housekeeper. But then to tell you the truth, she is more than just a housekeeper. I consider her children my brothers and sisters."

Connie began smiling somewhere in the middle of this round of the life of Paige. Jarrett had taken a seat across from them watching the expression crossing his mother's face. He began laughing at the same time she did.

Paige turned to Jarrett. "Are you laughing at me again?"

"Yes." He bent over and kissed her. "You are a ray of sunshine to my life."

Frank and Connie glanced at each other and smiled.

Taking Paige's hand and walking between her and Jarrett, Connie was satisfied. "Let's go to the kitchen and put more bread in the oven." She hit Sergio with the dishtowel. "I'm certain Sergio has eaten what I made before."

Frank sat across from Jarrett watching his son watch Paige's every move. "She's beautiful Jarrett."

Jarrett turned to his father. "I'm in love with her."

Of all the women Jarrett had dated, and there had been many, this was the first time he had said those words to him. Frank nodded. "She's a burst of energy, that I can see." He sighed. "Is she going to be strong enough to deal with what comes along with being in your life, son?"

Jarrett glanced into the kitchen, then sighed. "We had a round with the queens today during the game."

"How did she handle it?"

"She walked away."

"A big part of being the captain of the team is keeping harmony amongst your teammates. Their wives are the key to their stability. A permanent woman in your life is going to impact the present hierarchy of the Queens. Suzette is going to fight you tooth and nail."

Jarrett nodded. "It's already begun."

"Do you want your mother to step in?"

"No." Jarrett sat back. "Paige will have to establish her place with the women in her own way."

Frank smiled. "She does have a way." They watched the women and Sergio in the kitchen laughing, while they set the table. "What about the media? Has Brooks put anything in place?"

"No." Jarrett shook his head. "I thought I would keep her to myself for a while."

"Ha," Frank laughed out loud, causing the people in the kitchen to look their way. "You have not been able to keep any portion of your life a secret since high school. The media gets wind of how serious you are about Paige and you can forget stepping out the door without questions being thrown at you and so can she. Is she going to be able to handle the press?"

"She handles the press now. Paige is a principal in a ballet. She deals with the press regularly."

"Are the press at her front door when she goes to work, to the store, to a restaurant, to buy her tampons?" Frank sat up. "They will hound her the same way they hound you."

"Dinner's ready," Connie called out while laughing at Paige.

Frank stood patting Jarrett on the back. "Prepare her for what's to come before it hits her in the face, son."

*****

"Your parents are wonderful," Paige said the moment they stepped into the elevator.

Frank and Connie had talked for hours about Jarrett and his sisters and the antics they pulled. Sergio added his stories about Jarrett in the locker room as they laughed for hours at Jarrett's expense.

"You are a blessed man, Jarrett." Paige smiled as she took his hand. "My Grand'Mere would say, a man who is loved by many carries a loving heart. For only a man who knows how to give love receives love in return."

Jarrett laughed. "I will have to meet your Grand'Mere one day soon."

"Oh, she is going to love you. She already does." Paige smiled up at him.

The gleam in her eyes caused his heart to skip a beat. He could not explain why, or how he knew that the sparkle reflecting back at him was for Jarrett the man, not the ball player or the celebrity. That sparkle was all for him. What on earth had he done to deserve her looking at him in this way, he would never know. He cupped her face between his hands, then gently kissed her lips. "You are a spark of magic."

"What a beautiful thing to say. Thank you." He took her hand just as the elevator door opened into the garage. "Oh, Jarrett, it's a beautiful night. Can we walk?"

He hesitated as he pulled the collar to her jacket up. "I'm not sure that's a good idea. It's a little cold out."

"We have warm hearts. Besides, I had no idea you lived this close to me." She held his hand as she smiled up at him. "Let's walk."

Finding it difficult to say no, Jarrett looked around the garage towards the back entrance. "Okay. Let's take the back door."

Jarrett looked in both directions before he allowed her to step out. The street looked clear of the paparazzi.

"Why are you tense?"

He looked down at her worried face, then smiled. "People stake out the place sometimes. I don't want you to be impacted by that. It can get a little wild."

They walked hand in hand. "Are these people you are hiding from a part of your life?"

"I'm afraid they are."

"My Grand'Mere says people are people. You can't change or control others. The only thing you can control is your reaction to their action."

He smiled down at her. "Is that so?"

"Yes, it is. Of course the wonder of you is new to me. In my eyes, you are invincible. Nothing can touch you."

"Be careful. You're putting me on a high pedestal."

She looked up at him so innocently. "Yes I am. It's where you belong in my eyes."

He placed his hand on the side of her face, staring down into her eyes with unbelievable joy in his heart. "What did I do to deserve you?"

Paige smiled, as she covered his hand with hers. "You were born, Jarrett. Whatever you have to deal with, be it people, the Queens, the craziness of being deemed a superstar, is now a part of my life too. Do I want it? No. However, if the choice was between learning to live with it, or not having you in my life . . . I choose you."

His lips met hers with a tenderness akin to the handling of a one of a kind Tiffany vase. Her lips parted giving him the sweetness of her taste. Causing the world around them to disappear. Her embrace eased his soul, calmed his spirit and aroused his body.

Victoria was sitting on the balcony of her room as she did most nights. She could see the paparazzi in front of Jarrett's building. They had been there before, but she wondered why so many were out there tonight. She pulled out her tablet, then searched his name to see if anything of significance was posted. There was.

"Holy shit."

There was a picture of Jarrett and Paige kissing in what looked like a parking lot with Serg and a few people she did not know watching. She pulled out her cell phone and called Paige.

Paige's head fell onto his shoulder as the ringing of her phone interrupted the romantic moment. She exhaled. "I'm sorry," she said while pulling the phone from her pocket.

"Hey," came the voice on the other end of the call. "Is Jarrett with you?"

"Yes, we are walking back to the condo."

"Where?"

Paige looked around. "We are right around the corner. Why?"

"Let me speak to Jarrett."

"Okay?" Paige looked confused as she gave him the phone. "Victoria wants to speak to you."

Jarrett took the phone. "Hello."

"Jarrett, I'm on the balcony looking towards your building. There is a shitload of reporters with cameras in front of your building."

"There are usually four or five out there. That's why we came out the back."

"No, Jarrett, they are lining the street."

Jarrett looked around, pulling Paige close to him. "On the front side?"

"Yes."

"Do you have any idea what's going on?"

"There is a picture of you and Paige kissing in a parking lot on the web."

"What?"

"I'll alert the doorman. See if you can get her to the side. . . Oh hell. I think one of them just spotted you."

Jarrett looked behind him to see a cameraman's lights come on. Suddenly there was a crush of reporters behind him.

"Jarrett Bryson, who's the woman?" one yelled out as they rushed towards them.

Jarrett pushed the panic button in his pocket. But he knew it would be ten minutes before his security team would reach them. He grabbed Paige's hand, then held up his other hand to stop traffic. They ran across the street as he yelled into the phone. "Bring a coat to cover her head. Meet us downstairs." He hung up the phone.

"What's happening?"

"Those people we were just talking about have found us. Stay behind me when we reach the corner. Victoria is going to meet you at the door."

"What about you?"

Before he could answer, a mob of reporters with microphones and cameras were upon them. Cameras were flashing. Reporters were circling them. Jarrett kept Paige behind him with her face turned towards the building.

"Hey," Jarrett called out. "Take it easy, people. Please, take it easy."

"Jarrett," Paige called out. She was losing her step because there were so many people pushing to get to her.

Jarrett turned, covering her face by wrapping his arms around her.

"I don't want my parents to find out about us like this, Jarrett."

He picked her up, her face buried in his chest, as he walked swiftly towards her doorway. His pathway was blocked.

Alex and Victoria appeared pushing through the crowd until they reached them.

Victoria wrapped the blanket over Paige's head, as Alex took her from Jarrett's arms. They rushed back into the lobby of the building leaving Jarrett to deal with the reporters.

Once inside, Alex locked the front entrance and called more security to guard the door. "Is everyone okay?"

Victoria pulled the blanket away to see the stunned look on her friend's face. "You okay?"

Paige glanced at her. "I don't know what happened. We were walking from his place. We stopped and kissed then all of a sudden we were surrounded by a crush of people. Where is Jarrett?" The worry in her voice was clear as she stepped towards the door.

"Paige, no!" Victoria grabbed her arm and pulled her back. "Jarrett knows what to do. He deals with this every day. Now look at me."

Paige turned to her. "Are you okay? Are you hurt anywhere?"

"No, no. I'm fine, but Jarrett . . ."

"Let's go upstairs. Jarrett is a pro with the paparazzi. You on the other hand are not."

"Who's the lady, Jarrett?"

"Is she someone special?"

"How long have you two been dating?"

"Does this mean Lacy is out of the picture?"

Jarrett held his hand up as the lights glared in his face. He smiled but inside he was seething. He knew better. He knew the moment they had her name she would have to deal with every reporter in the continent trying to dig into her life. He did not want that for Paige. Not now. Not this early in their relationship. He should have protected her privacy better.

"Listen, guys and ladies." He nodded to some of the female reporters. "I'm only one person. I can't answer all of you if you are talking over each other." He took steps towards the corner, away from the entrance to Paige's condo. In his mind, he figured he had another five minutes before his team appeared.

"Jarrett, who is the lady?"

"I can't tell you that."

"Jarrett there's a picture on the web. Seems like a special lady." The reporter put the microphone back in Jarrett's face.

"She is very special."

"Does this mean Lacy is done?"

"Lacy is and always will be a friend."

"How does your new lady feel about that?"

"No comment. Look, this is new for me. I don't want you guys messing this up for me. Can you cut me a little slack here?"

"Give us a name, Jarrett, just a name."

A group of microphones hung just below his lips.

"Not until she is ready."

"She lives in this building?"

Jarrett gave the reporter an incredulous look. "We were taking a romantic walk until you all decided to join us. Kind of takes the intimate moment away. You know what I mean."

A few reporters laughed, nodding their head in understanding.

A black SUV pulled up. Two burly men dressed in black suits stepped out, pushing their way through the crowd.

"Looks like the interview is over. Until the next time."

"Jarrett is she the same lady from earlier today, or another?"

"No further comments," one of the guards clearing the path announced as he pushed Jarrett's head down, and into the back of the SUV.

Jarrett still had Paige's phone in his hand. It was now locked. He did not have her roommate's phone number to call and check on Paige. There was no way he could get into her building with all the reporters standing on the corner.

"Mr. Brooks is on the line." One of the guards gave him his phone.

"Yeah," Jarrett spoke a bit irately.

"Having a nice date?"

"Ha ha."

"I just sent you a text with a picture on the web," Nick stated. "You can't really make out her face. I have my people on it to see how long it will be before the media has her name, address and history."

"I need to get to her."

"Where does she live?"

Jarrett smirked. "Where you just had me picked up."

"Damn. Okay give me her info."

Jarrett hesitated. "Her parents don't know."

"Is she under eighteen," came the surprised voice of his agent.

"No. We just wanted to keep it to ourselves for a minute."

"Give me her info."

"Paige Cartwright. I have her cell phone in my hand so I can't reach her that way."

"Hold on," Nick said then put him on mute.

The guard turned to the driver. "Hold up here."

The driver pulled over.

Nick came back to the phone. "Hold on."

Jarrett heard a click.

"Jarrett?"

"Paige," he sighed with relief. "Are you okay?"

"Yes, I'm fine. How are you? Where are you?"

"Around the corner in a car."

"I'm so sorry, Jarrett. This is all my fault."

"No, babe, no, this isn't on you. I've been so carried away with you that I did not take the necessary precautions. This is on me, not you."

"Victoria showed me a picture of us today. Who took it? How did the media get it so fast?"

Jarrett sat back, closed his eyes then sighed. "I don't know, babe. I don't know. But I will find out."

"In the whole scheme of things, I guess it's not really important. It just that, I've never kept anything from my parents."

"What do you want to do?"

"I have to tell them. My father is going to freak out if he sees this on the internet or news before hearing it from me."

"Do you want to fly out to see them? I'll go with you."

He could hear the sigh of relief in her voice. "Yes, thank you."

"I'll make the arrangements. I have your phone."

"I know. Call Victoria's number. She will get the info to me."

Paige gave him the number, then she disconnected.

"Nick?"

"The jet is en route to you. I just got off the line with the doorman in the building. They have a way to get her to the airport. I suggest you use this time to prepare yourself to meet her parents."

"I want to know who took that picture and sold it."

CHAPTER TWELVE

The plane landed on a private airstrip near Alexandria, VA. A black sedan was waiting as the couple walked hand in hand off the jet. Paige pulled away from Jarrett to run into the open arms of an older gentleman dressed in a black suit.

"Hello, Grey." Paige hugged him. "I'm so sorry to get you up this time of the morning."

"She would not have it any other way." The man smiled as he held her at arms' length.

Jarrett walked up behind Paige. She reached for his hand. "Grey, this is Jarrett Bryson. Jarrett, this is Grey, my Grand'Mere's everything," she nervously laughed.

Jarrett extended his hand. "It's nice to meet you. I apologize for the hour."

"It's an honor, son." Grey merely tilted his head. He then opened the backdoor to the sedan. Paige climbed in followed by Jarrett.

"Hello, Grand'Mere." Paige sat back and sighed. "The biscuits have burst in the oven."

Jarrett had to smile at the simplicity of Paige's thoughts.

"No, dear, they are simply baking at the moment. The burst is about to happen." Her eyes went to Jarrett. "Hello, son."

Jarrett stared at the older woman. Even in the dark, the wisdom of her grey eyes shined through. He understood the reason for the name. She was elegance personified. "Hello, Grand'Mere." he took her hand and kissed it.

Ophelia smiled as she nodded her head. "The first time I met my husband, he kissed my hand. You're a charmer Jarrett Bryson."

"Yes ma'am, I am."

"You're also falling in love with my Paige."

Jarrett felt the vehicle moving as he inhaled. "Yes ma'am, I believe I am."

Paige reached over and took his hand, twining her fingers with his.

"I'm afraid you've had all the private time allowed. Cultivating your love for each other will become increasingly more difficult. I'd say you have approximately twenty-four hours before the media frenzy will begin. This first step is going to be easy compared to what's to come."

"On the flight, we discussed the best path to take." He glanced at Paige. "After speaking with Judge and Mrs. Cartwright, I will instruct my agent to setup a press conference."

"I think we are making way too much out of this. Yes, I do want my parents to hear about this from me. That's why we are here tonight. As for the media"- Paige glanced at Jarrett- "they will get tired of us eventually. Right?"

Ophelia laughed as she reached across and patted her granddaughter's knee. "In about thirty years, dear." She also turned to Jarrett. "What are your thoughts?"

Jarrett wanted to agree with Paige, but he knew once the public discovered he had someone special in his life, they would hound her and him on everything from marriage to babies and all points in between.

"I prefer to keep my private life...private. However, I have no intention of hiding my relationship with Paige. If reporters ask questions, I will respond within reason."

"If? You mean when," Ophelia stated. "It will be interesting to see how the public handles your new approach to the media." The vehicle pulled into a driveway. "You are about to experience your first taste of reality to the news. Beware."

"Grand'Mere, behave please." Paige asked, "Are you coming inside?"

"Of course. I want a ring side seat to Horace's reaction. I may ask Leona to record it."

"Leona?" Paige questioned as the back door to the sedan opened. "She should be home."

"Oh, I called her, and your parents to let them know you were coming home with a guest."

Paige turned to look at the house. The lights in the kitchen were on. She frowned at her Grand'Mere. "Did you upset Father?"

"Yes," Ophelia replied then walked elegantly towards the entrance.

Jarrett took Paige's hand. "Don't worry. Things will be fine."

"Oh, Jarrett, I'm not worried about you or how my parents will accept the news once things settle down."

"What things?"

Before she could answer, the back door swung open. There stood three very concerned people staring back at them.

"Are you going to move so we can enter the house?" Ophelia asked, pushing her way through them.

"Paige." Her mother reached out first. "Is everything okay?" She hugged her daughter, not paying any attention to the man walking in the door behind her.

Horace's eyes, on the other hand, were on him. "Jarrett Bryson?"

Jarrett held out his hand. "Yes, Your Honor. It's good to see you again."

"That remains to be seen," Horace said as he took the man's hand, looking from Paige to Jarrett.

"Harold, come and sit down. Let the man in the door, for goodness sake," Ophelia called out. "Leona, a cup of tea with a dash of brandy would be nice."

The tone in his mother in law's voice, added to the fact that she called him Harold, caused Horace to inhale.

"Dealing with her in the daylight is one thing. Having to do it in the middle of the night is another. This better be good." he said to Jarrett. "Come in Mr. Bryson."

"Thank you, Your Honor," Jarrett said as he closed the door and followed the others into the kitchen.

Leona squeezed Paige's hand as she walked by. "Would anyone else like some coffee or tea?"

"Yes, thank you, Leona," Eleanor replied. "Why don't we all take a seat in the family room?"

Ophelia was already sitting in Horace's chair as they entered the adjoining room. Leona remained in the kitchen quietly preparing the beverages so she could hear what was being said.

Horace stood behind the chair his wife sat in, while Paige and Jarrett sat on the sofa. Horace watched as Jarrett's arm circled Paige's shoulders. "Son, why are you with my daughter?"

"Daddy!" Paige reached up taking Jarrett's hand from around her shoulder and holding it at her side. "Well, at times we close our eyes to reality. Now it's time to open our eyes and see things as they really are." She looked around at the three faces staring back at her. "I guess you are wondering why we are here at this time of night or morning, whichever you want to call it." She smiled nervously at Jarrett. "Well, I wanted you all to meet Jarrett."

There was silence.

"Hello," Eleanor smiled.

"Hello," Leona replied, still looking confused as she placed a tray on the coffee table.

Horace simply stared at them, more at Jarrett than at Paige.

The room grew silent, again.

"Oh, Harold, they are seeing each other. Have been for a few weeks, now. You should know the feeling, when you just can't help yourself. Well, your daughter, your only child has been running around with a man you know nothing about. A reporter snapped a picture of them and it's out on the internet. What do you think of that?" All eyes landed on Ophelia as she smiled up at Horace.

"Mother!" Eleanor cried out as she took her husband's hand.

"Grand'Mere!" Paige exclaimed. "Please, this is not the time for you to settle old scores with Daddy." She turned to her father. "Daddy," she spoke calmly. "Jarrett and I have been seeing each other...."

Jarrett held up one hand as he clutched Paige's with the other. "Judge Cartwright, Mrs. Cartwright. I met your daughter a little over a month ago. Since that time baseball is not the first thing on my mind in the mornings. It's Paige's smile. I am certain you are aware of the impact she has on people. Multiply that a hundred times over, you will find me. Last night a picture of us appeared on the internet. We did not want you to find out about us that way. That's why we are here tonight."

A look of concern came over Horace's face.

"I can imagine you have a number of questions for me." He looked directly at Horace. "That is the reason I made this trip with Paige. Would you like to speak in private Judge Cartwright?"

"No, we all want to hear what you have to say." Leona folded her arms across her chest as she spoke. "Didn't I just see you in the magazine with that actress...Macy somebody?"

"Lacy, Leona," Eleanor corrected.

"Okay than, that Lacy woman. Then the month before that it was some model named Gabriella. Now you trying to add our Paige to your list?"

"Leona," Eleanor cautioned, then looked at Paige. She could see the light in her daughter's eyes. "Why don't we all take a moment to breathe?" She tugged on her husband's hand then stood. "Sit here with me, darling."

Horace took the seat, then pulled his wife onto his lap.

"You need an anchor there, Harold?" Ophelia grunted.

"Horace, old woman Horace."

"It seems you should have your name changed to Karma. It's a bitch, isn't it?" She sipped her tea.

"Mother," Eleanor cautioned, then sighed. "Leona, bring Horace a hot brandy."

"Yes, please." Paige frowned at her Grand'Mere.

Ophelia glanced at her granddaughter, gave her a knowing smile, then winked.

Paige ducked her head trying not to laugh out loud.

"Don't encourage her, Paige," Horace scolded as he took the drink from Leona. "Thank you." He took a swallow, then looked at Jarrett. "Would you like a drink?"

"No, I have a game tomorrow."

Horace nodded his understanding then sat back a bit more relaxed. "Tell me about this picture on the internet. Do you know how it ended up there?"

"No," Jarrett replied. "My agent is tracking it now."

"What's in the picture?"

Leona put her tablet in the center of the table. "I searched the internet and found it."

Eleanor stared at the woman. "Thank you, Leona."

"Well, it was right there for everybody to see. It's had over a million views."

"Really?" Paige sat up to see the picture.

The picture showed Jarrett's face, with Paige's back to the camera.

Eleanor looked at the picture and smiled. All the questions she had were answered. She looked up to find Paige smiling at her. She nodded, satisfied.

"Where is this?" Horace asked.

"It was in the garage at the stadium."

Horace glanced at the picture. Relief was clear on his face. "You have your clothes on." He did not intend to say that out loud.

"Of course I do, Daddy."

"It would have been nice if my daughter had kept her clothes on."

"Mother," Eleanor sighed.

"Well, Grand'Mere, if she had, I would not be here."

He turned to Jarrett and exhaled. "My concern is not you. I know your reputation. I'm not talking about what's in the news, or in the media reports. I know your reputation as a man. However, the press can be damaging no matter your good intentions towards my daughter. How do you plan to protect her from them?"

Jarrett reached for Paige's hand. "I've been dealing with the media for a number of years. I don't wish them on anyone. However, I can't allow them to rule my life. I'm a public figure, Judge Cartwright. I can't change that. There is a circus around every aspect of my life. I don't invite it, but it's there. When we first met, I ignored the feelings. I did not want to deal with the media circus. Each day I kept my distance from Paige for that reason. The urge to find her continued to build until I came to the realization that finding her outweighed the displeasure of dealing with the media."

Leona put the cup on the table in front of him with a thump. "Those are pretty words. I still want to know about all these women." She glowered.

"Ms. Leona," Jarrett began. "In a perfect world I would have found Paige long before any of those other women existed. But I did not. I just found her. I thank God for placing her in my life when he did. Any time earlier, I may not have recognized the gift he bestowed on me." He turned to those at the table. "I can't say the craziness will not reach her. I'm certain it will. But, I give you my word I'll protect her with all the resources I have at my disposal."

"As will I," Horace replied with a poignant glare at Jarrett.

"Daddy." Paige stood then motioned to her mother. Eleanor moved from her husband's lap to take Paige's seat next to Jarrett.

"Oh Lawd, here we go."

Paige sat on her father's lap. "Do you remember the story you told me about the princess and the hound?" She put her forehead on his. "You said the hound was searching and searching for something in his life, but he could never figure out what. He tried bone after bone and found himself tasting, then spitting it out. Then one day he ventured into an unknown land called the Ponderosa. That's when he found the beautiful princess. He was afraid to touch her for he thought she might vanish. So for days and nights, he watched the princess from afar. One day he awakened to find the princess standing over him. The moment their eyes met, he knew that was his princess. Then she smiled. It was a radiant smile, so much so that it rendered him speechless. Then the princess bent over and kissed him. One taste of that princess and the hound was lost forever. Then the dogcatcher walked in, snarled at the hound. That hound growled and bared his teeth ready to defend his princess to the end. The mean old dog catcher pulled a gun on the hound, but that hound didn't care. No one was going to take his princess. The hound stood to his full height on his back legs and let out a vicious growl. But he didn't attack the dog catcher because he could tell his princess cared about the dogcatcher. But his stance let that dog catcher know, he wasn't going anywhere and neither was his princess. Once the dog catcher accepted the hound was in love with the princess, they all began a life together as a family. As it turned out the hound, the princess and the dog catcher lived happily ever after. The moral of the story is, at some point in their life, a person is going to find the princess and will take a stance to protect the very ground they walk on."

Leona laughed. Eleanor sighed and Ophelia frowned.

Watching the expression on her father's face as Paige told the story, Jarrett could see her as a little girl, listening to his every word. He could also see her sitting around a Christmas tree, watching him tell their children that story. The vision was so real it caused him to jerk his head up. When he did, Grand'Mere was smiling at him, then she looked away. He turned his attention back to Paige.

Horace smiled. "You remember that story?"

"Every word, Daddy." She kissed his forehead.

"Are you trying to tell me Jarrett is your hound?"

"No," she whispered in his ear. "He's my princess." Horace's laughter filled the room.

Eleanor turned to Jarrett and smiled. "You've put a light in my daughter's eyes that wasn't there before. Thank you for that."

"She's put meaning into my life. It's I who should be thanking you."

Eleanor kissed Jarrett on the cheek. "Okay you two." She stood. "It's late. You are not flying back tonight."

"We have to, Mother. I have rehearsal in the morning and a show tomorrow night." Paige stood and hugged her mother. "I love you, Mother." She then turned to her Grand'Mere, bent over and kissed her. "I'll keep you posted."

Ophelia held her granddaughter a little longer. "He loves you, remember that."

"I will."

Horace stood extending his hand to Jarrett. "Thank you for coming in person." He leaned over and whispered to Jarrett, "That's my baby. Don't hurt her."

Jarrett nodded. "I'm the hound."

Horace laughed. "She thinks you are her princess."

Jarrett gave him an incredulous look. "I can see we are going to have to have a talk on the plane."

"You do that, son."

"I'll walk you two out." Eleanor beamed as she took Paige's arm.

Jarrett took a glance over his shoulder. "Grand'Mere," he bent down to kiss her. "I look forward to seeing you again."

"We'll talk again soon. Take care of my Paige. I'm trusting you with her heart. You saw the vision. Now make it a reality."

Jarrett stared down at her, not believing she knew what was in his mind. "The Christmas tree?"

She smiled. "Two boys and one precious baby girl. Treasure them, son."

Jarrett stood, a little shaken with the notion that she could see what was in his mind. "I will," he promised.

"Mother, Grey is taking them back to the airport. Do you want to stay here tonight?"

"Do you think Harold can deal with me being under his roof?"

"Oh, I think we can find room for the old bat in the attic." Horace smirked.

"Daddy," Paige kissed his cheek. "Bye, Leona."

Leona put her hand on Jarrett's chest stopping him from walking out the door. "I'm gonna be watching you, son."

"I'm sure you will, Ms. Leona." Jarrett kissed her cheek, then smiled at the blush on her face.

She watched them for a moment then closed the door. "I'm calling it a night. Anyone want anything before I shut down the kitchen?"

"No thank you Leona," Horace replied. "Have a good night."

Horace and Ophelia waited until everyone was out of the room. He finished off his drink. "Did you arrange this?"

"No."

"This is all a coincidence?"

Ophelia shrugged her shoulders. "To some extent."

Horace stared. "Does he know?"

"No," Ophelia replied as she stood.

"What happens to my daughter when he finds out?"

Ophelia glared at him. "He will be too much in love with her to care."

Horace shook his head. "I'm your attorney. I cannot reveal anything you told me in confidence. Bryson is a very proud man. If he feels he was manipulated in any way, he will walk away. Where will that leave my child?"

"He can no more walk away from Paige than you could from Eleanor. I'm going to the guest room. Tell Eleanor good night for me."

Horace hung his head after draining his glass of brandy. He loved the women in his life, including Ophelia. He understood her reasons for setting up her will the way she did a few years ago. There was no way she could have known Jarrett Bryson and Paige would meet. Or was there?

CHAPTER THIRTEEN

Front and center on Page Six of the newspaper, on every gossip online blog, even leading on the sports channels, was the picture with all kinds of speculations on the identity of the new woman in Jarrett Bryson's life.

With his agent's help, Jarrett had been able to bypass the media for a few days. There was still no information on who had provided the picture to the media. It had taken Jarrett's team two days to track down the blogger, who as expected, refused to give his source. The blogger's popularity increased with more followers anticipating the name of the woman. Reporters gathered each day around Jarrett's condo hoping to get a glimpse of the couple and be the one to release the woman's name. Some went as far as calling Lacy to see if she knew the woman. When that did not work, they began hounding other players and their wives. Those who'd met Paige, wished they had not shunned her and had paid more attention that day in the stands. The wives who knew were told not to respond to any questions regarding Jarrett's personal life. Finally, on the day of the last game of the season the front office insisted Jarrett make himself available for the press.

The talk room, as the Knights called it, was filled with reporters. Every chair in the room was taken. The walls were lined with cameras, which began flashing the moment Jarrett arrived for the post-game interviews. The Knights had won the last game of the season 6-5 off one of Jarrett's RBIs, closing out their season with a 101 - 59 record. One of the best records in MLB history. One would think the questions would be on that. No.

"Jarrett, it's been days now. Tell us, who is the woman in the picture?"

Jarrett smiled. "It's been a long day, guys. Any questions on the game?"

"You are ending the season strong, Jarrett. Any word from the front office on the negotiations?"

Jarrett laughed. He wasn't going to get a break. The questions would either be about Paige or the negotiations.

"We've had a good season. Another double header tomorrow and the regular season comes to an end. I'm confident my actions on the field will generate interesting conversation with the front office."

"Any indications when the talks will begin?"

"That is up to the front office."

"Jarrett, what did Lacy think of the picture?"

Jarrett closed his eyes and sighed as the other reporters in the room laughed.

"I have no idea."

"So who is she, Jarrett?" another reporter asked.

Jarrett looked over to the corner where his coach and Ron stood. Ron shrugged his shoulders. Jarrett ran his hands down his face. his mind reeling on the best course of action. His public relations team was set to handle the onslaught of questions either way.

Jarrett sat up to the microphone. "Can you imagine being in the bottom of the ninth, bases loaded with your team down three zip? You're at the plate with a full count, the ball comes, and you can feel it, down in your gut. All you have to do is swing your bat at the right moment to win the game that will put your team in the World Series. Think about that feeling when you hit that ball and it goes sailing right across the center field wall. You guys know the feeling I'm talking about?"

The room of reporters all nodded their heads, laughing, acknowledging they knew exactly the feeling he was describing.

"That's exactly how I feel every time I hear her voice."

The room quieted down.

"It goes deeper when I see her smile. My entire world spins with a single kiss." He licked his lips then continued.

"I've had the honor of dating a number of women. That's not bragging, it's just what it is. This one.....I want a chance at making a life with. So when you ask me about her, I think of how the other women I've dated were treated by you guys and I don't want that for her. I'm in love with this woman. I haven't even told her that. I know it's selfish, but I want to keep her to myself for a minute. Just this once, let me have a little time to gain her love before the craziness starts. Give me until the end of the playoffs and we will sit down and talk with each of you guys for hours if that's what you want. But for now, I want to keep her to myself." He stood, then walked out of the room.

*****

The Dragon's General Manager Kurt Stack placed a call to the team Manager Ben Stanley.

"Did you see the after game interview with Bryson?"

"I did."

"They have a double header in Detroit. Should be a good time to eliminate Bryson."

"We're in the playoffs, Kurt. Have faith in the team to take us all the way. We don't have to resort to these tactics."

"Make it happen or find another job."

*****

Jolene was fed up with all the publicity Paige was receiving from her performance. All the trade rags were raving about Paige Cartwright's performance. 'Elegance personified,' one reporter wrote. 'Grace, beauty, intelligence all wrapped in one,' another said.

Jolene pushed the paper into her locker, then turned to Carin and stated, "Not one mention in the paper. All of them wrote about her."

"Calm down," Carin whispered to her roommate. "Your chest is heaving like you just completed a four mile run. You've been warned about your temper."

"All I need is one shot at the lead. I know I can out shine her."

"Remember a few weeks ago when Bryson showed up?"

"Yeah, what about it," Jolene snapped as she continued to dress for rehearsal.

Carin reached into her locker. "Take a look at this." She pushed a button on her tablet then gave it to Jolene.

Jolene looked at the picture, then back at Carin. "And?"

"Look at the picture. That looks like Paige to me."

"So?"

Carin rolled her eyes. "You need Paige distracted, right? These sport reporters are offering money for the name of the woman in the picture. They are pounding the streets trying to identify her. What do you think will happen if suddenly rehearsals are interrupted by reporters trying to get to Paige? You know how the director feels about the spotlight being on one of her performers instead of the troupe."

Jolene looked at the picture again. "Hmm, you may have something there. Let me marinade on that for a minute."

Carin shrugged. "The way I see it, you can come out a few thousand in the good and be rid of your arch nemesis all in one swoop."

Jolene gave the tablet back to Carin. "That might not be a bad idea." The two grinned, then closed their lockers.

"Did you see the latest tweet on you and Jarrett?" Victoria asked as they dressed.

"You know what my Grand'Mere says? To enjoy life you have to let all the marbles in the jar out." Paige smiled as she continued to dress. "If you don't, you just might miss the one marble that will change your life."

Victoria raised an eyebrow at her friend. "You know what my grandmother says? If you keep looking through rose colored glasses, you will miss the devil lurking beneath the soil of the roses."

"That doesn't sound very positive."

"Everything in life isn't positive, Paige. There is evil in this world." Just as she said that, Jolene and Carin walked by them. "As much as you and" Victoria looked around to be sure no one would over hear them - "you know who, want this search for you to disappear, someone is wanting the money that is being offered just as bad."

Paige closed her locker, then turned smiling brightly at her roommate. "You have to learn to smell the roses and stop digging in the dirt. What is meant to be with Jarrett and I, is going to be. All this curiosity is going to die down as soon as I'm just a girl in love with a boy."

"Some boy," Victoria teased.

"You got that right," Paige laughed.

Victoria couldn't help but join her. Her friend's happiness was contagious. It was hard not to see the love blossoming between Paige and Jarrett. However, she knew a storm was brewing even if Paige did not want to see it.

Victoria closed her locker. "Okay, let's go bust a move."

They gathered with the rest of the troupe on stage.

"Before we start rehearsals, we are distributing the holiday schedule. There are three schedules. The pink is for the New York performers, the yellow is for the US tour and finally the blue is for the European tour. Congratulations to our leads, and their backups. I know you will all give wonderful performances. Rehearsals start next week with the performances beginning Thanksgiving Day."

There was a burst of excitement from the group as they all waited to receive their copy of the schedule. Screams of joy filled the room as the assignments were read.

"You're going to Europe," Carin said to Jolene, excited for her friend.

"As a backup," Jolene groaned.

"Who cares, you are getting a free ride to Europe for six weeks."

"I want to shine, Carin, not be in a maybe role," she hissed.

"Oh no." Paige and Victoria looked at the schedule together.

"What do you mean oh no? You got the lead in the European tour?" She looked up at Paige. "What?" she questioned, not understanding her frown.

"I'll be in Europe for the holidays."

"Yes, and the problem is?"

"What about Jarrett?" she whispered.

"The man has frequent flyer miles. I'm sure he will meet you there. Look at it this way. You will be stateside for the playoffs. Then the two of you can a have a romantic getaway in Paris."

Paige smiled. "That would be wonderful. What did you get?" She glanced down at the paper then looked up in surprise to see the smug look on Victoria's face. "You got the New York lead." They both screamed and hugged each other.

"Can you believe this?"

They jumped up and started twirling along with just about everyone else on stage.

*****

As she had for the last week, Paige slipped into the private entrance of Jarrett's building, meeting his personal guard at the door. She was excited about earning the lead in the tour, but wasn't sure how Jarrett would take the news. The post season should be over before she had to leave. If they won the World Series, he would have other appearance obligations and might not be able to join her. She so hated the thought of them being separated for the holidays. But she also did not want to give up her chance to tour with the troupe.

The private elevator opened into Jarrett's foyer. Previous evenings, he was waiting for her to step off. But not tonight.

"Jarrett?" she called out. That's when she heard the music start, as a big screen began rolling down the wall at the end of the hallway. The video of JT Taylor from Kool and the Gang and Regina Belle singing, 'All I Want is Forever' from the movie Taps was playing. It was one of the best dance love songs ever. Jarrett came out of one of the back rooms with a fake microphone in his hands singing along with the music. Paige dropped her coat, flung the hat from her head and began twirling down the long hardwood hallway, then she ran and jumped in the air. He caught her, swinging her around as they sang and danced together to the song. The two danced around the condo to the music as if they were on stage doing a performance.

Their bodies moved seductively together as the music changed to Stephanie Mills singing, 'The Power of Love'. Jarrett's arm pulled her protectively against his body, slowing their moves to a sensuous sway. Her arms cradled his head as her hands followed the profile of his face. Her fingers touched his eyes, his nose, then traced an outline of his lips. Their bodies slowed, the laughter died down, the atmosphere became charged with sexual energy as her tongue trailed her fingers across his lips.

His hands that had been gently caressing her body, began to move feverishly down her back, cupping her behind, squeezing her pelvis snuggly at the junction of her thighs, as Gerald Levert's, 'Baby Hold On To Me' began to play. Her legs wrapped around him, causing his growing need to press firmly where the moisture was building inside of her. He braced her body against the wall, freed his hands, then lovingly cupped her face between them.

"I don't need a lot," he whispered. "Just your love for eternity."

Their lips met, gently once. He pulled away taking in her face as if imprinting it to memory. He parted her lips, allowing his tongue room to plunge in with a need he could not control. Her hands pulled at his sweatshirt, so she could feel the heat generating within him. Her hand clawed at his back - roaming, caressing, touching, and relishing the heat with the palm of her hand.

Her touch was driving him crazy. He slid her body down the wall, tore the top from her body, then buried his head between her breasts taking in the scent of her rising need. He pushed the lacy bra up, taking a nipple into his mouth, sucking, licking, savoring every sweet morsel of her bud. His hand caressed the other nipple, preparing it for its upcoming onslaught. Her thighs were so tight around him, he could feel her pulsating against him through the material of her leggings, causing him to swell more with need.

"Paige," he growled and forced her legs from around his waist. He pulled her boots off, the leggings down, as her lips kissed his head, his neck, and his shoulder. Every touch increased the need for him to get inside her heat. He reached into his pocket, pulled out a package, and tore it open with his teeth.

Paige took it from him, then sat up on her knees. She pulled her top and bra off throwing them behind her. Then she pushed him backwards onto the floor, pulled his sweat pants down his legs and threw them to the side. She covered his body with hers. She kissed his neck, took a nipple into her mouth, sucked, then moved to his abs, running her tongue over every indentation of his six pack.

"Paige." He reached for the condom. She closed her hand around it, and stopped his fidgeting by taking his manhood into her mouth.

The breath left his body.

When she closed her mouth around him, it literally took his breath away. She wrapped her hand around his base, pulled her mouth away, then had the nerve to smile down at him. She held him in her hand and began to lick around him as if she was eating an ice cream cone. He groaned, as she squeezed, licked and tugged him. He was going to explode. He knew it.

"Paige," he growled, "baby, please."

She sat up amazed by the size of him. She wiped her mouth, unrolled the condom then slowly slid it over him. She straddled her body over him.

Jarrett had never seen a more beautiful sight in his life. The intensity in her eyes, as she braced herself against his chest. Her hair unraveling around her face, as she gazed down at him.

"Hold on to me, Jarrett. Don't you ever let me go."

His hands circled her waist, as she slid down on him.

The sensation was intoxicating, all he could do was moan. If she never moved, his life would be complete. But she did. She moved up and down on him, tightening her muscles, building a need in him so confounding, he could not think straight.

His powerful strokes met hers, their bodies smacking, skin-to-skin. Heart rates rising with every pump, their breathing increased to a point of breathlessness, but neither could stop. The urgency to reach that peak so strong, their intensity increased to a speed causing their toes to curl, their bodies to jerk and an explosion that rocked their world.

Paige fell forward on his chest. Jarrett's body jerked repeatedly. It took Paige kissing the vein on the side of his neck to slow his heart rate down. It was moments, before either of them could speak.

"I'm in love with you, Paige." His hand lazily traced her back. He could feel her smile against his chest.

"What a beautiful thing to say. My Grand'Mere says..."

Jarrett began to laugh.

She pinched him on the waist. "No, listen. My Grand'Mere says to love is to listen. I'm lying here listening to your heart and it's telling me you love me. She says it only takes one spark of magic to hear it. Can you feel what my heart is telling you?"

Jarrett felt the rhythm of her heart beating against his chest and smiled. He had never taken the time to notice anyone's heartbeat before.

"I do feel it."

She looked up at him with her eyes beaming. "Then you know I love you too."

He brought her lips to his, kissed them, then put her head back on his chest.

They stayed there holding each other for a while before they made their way to the shower, then prepared dinner. As they ate, Paige shared her news with Jarrett.

"How long will you be touring Europe?"

"Thanksgiving through Christmas." She was waiting to see the disappointment in his eyes.

There was a touch of concern in her eyes as she looked away. He wasn't sure why, then it came to him. She was concerned about him.

"Do you think I'm upset because you have to tour?"

"It's our first Christmas together. I'll be in another country."

He reached across the table, took her hand and pulled her onto his lap. He kissed her temple.

"I know how important dancing is to you. This tour could put your name on the map and prove to you once and for all you made the right decision."

"You understand? I need to prove this to myself."

"I think your parents and my parents will be disappointed."

"Why your parents?"

"If you are going to be traveling, I'm going with you."

"What about the team?"

"The World Series should wrap up in early November. We can have an early Thanksgiving with my family then fly to Europe for your tour."

She wrapped her arms around his neck. Her eyes danced. "I think that's a wonderful plan. You just made my Christmas wish come true."

"Tell me more about this Christmas wish."

"I see us walking in the snow, horseback riding in Central Park, opening gifts around the tree with family and friends then making love at the stroke of midnight on New Year's Eve."

"Really?" He kissed her neck. "Why wait until New Year's?"

She giggled as he picked her up and carried her back to the bedroom.

CHAPTER FOURTEEN

The blissfulness of the night before ended with their cell phones ringing almost simultaneously.

Jarrett reached over to the nightstand, with Paige still wrapped around his body. He didn't bother to look at caller ID because whoever was on the line would be dead soon for disturbing him.

"It better be good."

"Please hold for Mr. Caswell," a female voice requested.

"Jarrett, Ruben Caswell calling. We need you in the front office within the hour. We are sending a car for you."

Jarrett held the phone out to see if it was indeed Ruben Caswell, the owner of the Knights. Why was he calling? Negotiations were handled by the team manager.

"Mr. Caswell?"

"Jarrett, it's important. We need you in right away."

"Yes, sir." Jarrett hung up his phone.

"What's wrong?" Paige was sitting up in the bed next to him.

"Nothing's wrong, babe." He kissed her lips. "That was the owner calling." He yawned.

"No, Jarrett, something is wrong. I can feel it."

He was half asleep, but he could see the tension in her. He pulled her body under him, kissed her with all the love he was feeling inside, then looked down into her eyes.

"There is nothing wrong. Let's take a shower and get dressed so I can get you home."

Jarrett said goodbye to Paige at the private entrance then walked to the front lobby. The moment he saw the crowd outside the door and his full security team waiting for him, he knew something was wrong.

"Mr. Bryson." Peace Newman from the Brooks-Pendleton Agency approached him. "Mr. Brooks will meet you at the Knights' main office."

"Nick is in town? What's going on?"

"Mr. Brooks will explain when we arrive." He nodded to the man at the door, who opened the door clearing a path to the waiting vehicle.

"Time to go, Mr. Bryson."

Jarrett exhaled, then followed the big man out the door. Less than a minute later, they were inside the vehicle pulling off.

Jarrett wasn't sure but he thought he heard one of the reporters call Paige's name. He looked towards the front of her building as they passed by and saw a similar crowd in front.

"What the hell?" He pulled out his cell and dialed her number. "Are you inside?"

"Yes. There's a crowd of reporters in front of my building. I think the cat is meowing loud and clear."

All Jarrett could do was laugh.

"It's not funny, Jarrett. A skunk is stinking to high heaven, I tell you."

He was leaning over laughing now. "Okay, babe. Do you have transportation to get you to the studio?"

"Yes, Carlos is here."

"Do not come out of the front door. Have him meet you in the garage. I love you." He laughed then disconnected the call.

"You okay, Mr. Bryson?" Peace asked.

"Yes, just my girl...she has this way with words," he laughed again. Then shook his head.

"That would be Paige Cartwright?" Peace asked.

Jarrett looked at him curiously. "That's right."

Peace turned his phone to Jarrett. "Not only do they have her name, they have pictures, and know where she works."

"When did that hit?"

"Last night," Peace replied.

"Is this what the front office is upset about?"

"No. There are four big guys like me in this vehicle. Do you think the Boss would send all of us for a girl?"

For the first time Jarrett looked around. "I get your point."

The front office of the Knights was in full anti-scandal mode. Every person was on the phone, or dealing with another person.

"Go right in, Mr. Bryson, they are waiting for you." The secretary opened the double door entrance to the owner's wing.

The multitude of people in the room jarred him for a moment.

"Jarrett." Nick, his agent, extended his hand.

"What's happening," Jarrett asked.

"We have a situation."

"Jarrett." Ruben Caswell extended his hand. "Thank you for coming in. I believe you know Commissioner Reid."

"Yes." Jarrett extended his hand. "Commissioner."

"Jarrett, I regret the reason for calling you in so early."

"As long as someone fills me in on the reason, I'm certain we can work it out."

"Thank you for understanding."

"There is no understanding until this situation is fully investigated and, if deemed necessary, charges filed against the appropriate parties involved."

Jarrett knew not to show any expression while Nick was talking, but he sure would like to know what in the hell had his agent so riled up.

"We understand your concerns, Mr. Brooks," the Commissioner stated then looked to Ruben. "We will get to the bottom of this."

"If any of this reveals a speck of truth, Jerry, I'm holding you accountable for the outcome."

Jarrett continued to sit expressionless, as the owner of his team threatened the Commissioner. Whatever was happening, he knew his back was covered.

One of the men with the Commissioner whispered something in his ear. The Commissioner glanced at Jarrett.

"You have no idea what this is about, do you?"

"I do not," Jarrett replied.

"Get Jarrett a drink," Mr. Caswell said to one of his men.

"Water is fine," Jarrett said as Nick stood next to him.

"Last night I received a call from one of my clients. It seems someone in the Dragons' front office approached him to 'take care of you'. Quote unquote."

"Take care of me?" Jarrett frowned. "Take care of me how and why?"

"The client is a pitcher," Nick explained. "He was offered a substantial payment to strike your knees with a fast ball."

"What?" a now surprised Jarrett asked. "Why?"

The Commissioner spoke. "We are investigating the allegation."

"They see the Knights as the main competition to the series," Mr. Caswell clarified. "If they eliminate you, they believe their chances at winning it all increases."

"We have an active roster of 25 players, not to mention the farm team. Taking out one player isn't going to lessen the value of the Knights."

Nick looked at Caswell. "It does when that player is the MVP, with a batting average of .366, with 120 RBIs, and 34 homers on the season. Those are facts."

"We are not negotiating here, Mr. Brooks," Caswell argued.

"You have a team owner who is conspiring against my client and your team. Do you seriously believe I give a damn about your negotiations? My only concern here is Jarrett's safety."

"Then we are of one accord," the Commissioner stated. "We will have security increased."

"We will cover Mr. Bryson," Peace stated from behind Jarrett with a nod.

The Commissioner recognized Peace immediately when he looked up. He'd watched the man play professional football for a number of years.

"We have a security team in place for Jarrett. What we want to see are guarantees that the owner is aware of this threat and that serious sanctions and fines will be assessed if a strand of Jarrett's hair is damaged during the games with the Dragons."

"I will second Mr. Brooks and take it a step further," Caswell said from his chair behind his desk. "If an accident of any nature, including slipping on the ice, falls upon Mr. Bryson I am holding the league financially responsible."

"The message is clear." The Commissioner stood. "I will be speaking with Dragons' management before the day is out. Good day gentlemen."

They all waited until the Commissioner and all his men were out of the room.

Nick turned to Caswell. "Do you know Kurt Stack?"

"I do."

"Do you believe the Commissioner can investigate him to the fullest?"

"No." He sat forward. "Jarrett, you are a vital part of this team. I know that, your agent knows and so do you. I have never interfered in negotiations and I will not do it now. Management needs to save face. Their delay of your negotiations puts the other players on notice. I understand what they are doing and why."

"It's a business, Mr. Caswell. I understand that. However, my agent, well, I trust him. If he states we need to look at another team, then we look at another team." Jarrett stood. "As for this situation, I believe the team's best interests are at the forefront of all of our minds. Let's find a way to keep everyone safe, not just me."

*****

Paige was wrong. The crowd outside her condo wasn't the largest she had ever seen. The one at the dancer's entrance to the theater was.

"Ms. Cartwright, do not get out of this car until I come around to open the door. Do you understand me?"

"Of course I understand you, Carlos. I can hear you very well too, so there is no need to shout."

Carlos laughed. "My bad, Ms. Cartwright. It's just sometimes you don't see danger."

"My Grand'Mere says if you go out searching for danger, that's what you are going to find."

"Yeah, well my grandmother says if you don't keep your eyes open, danger will kick you in the ass. So stay in the car until I come around."

Paige smiled at his comment, then watched as he battled with the reporters to get around the car.

They were at the door with microphones and cameras. Victoria came out the door with two male dancers, just as Carlos opened the back door. It took all four of them to battle through the reporters to get Paige inside the building.

"Oh my," Paige said in a huff as she pulled off her coat. "I can't believe they are out there like that."

"They have been pouncing on everyone as they walk in," Victoria stated. "I've been calling you all morning. Why didn't you answer your phone?"

"I turned it off last night and forgot to turn it back on." She pulled it out of her pocket and pushed the button. "I'm sorry."

"Ms. Cartwright," the director called out. "In my office, please."

Paige pulled off her coat and gloves, then gave them and her bag to Victoria.

Victoria whispered, "Good luck," as Paige ran off.

The director could be heard through the closed door.

"We do not have prima donnas in this troupe. We are all the same. This circus you have brought to our theater is unacceptable, unless they are buying tickets." She calmed down for a minute then exhaled. "Paige, you are one of the brightest talents I have come across in a very long time. I would hate to see your career ruined by your association with Jarrett Bryson. Now, I don't know anything more than what Jolene showed me online yesterday. But if this is true and you are involved with this man, it could damage your reputation. Or is this your way of getting your name known? Because if it is no one is going to take you as a serious dancer. They are going to assume you are interested in fame and nothing more. And from the circus that is outside my theater, I'm inclined to believe that too."

"Mrs. Watson, I have no need for publicity. I never cared if my name was in the paper, or on the news. I don't even read the reviews on my performances. I'm here because I love to dance. That's all. My relationship with Jarrett doesn't impact my dancing. We tried everything possible not to have my name released to the media. I did not ask the media to come here, or to my home. I don't like, nor do I need it in my life, and neither does Jarrett. He can't help that people are interested in him because of his talents on the baseball field. All Jarrett wants is to play ball. All I want is to dance. The rest is just a lot of noise."

"Then I suggest you and Mr. Bryson have a press conference. The reason they are hounding you is because you are hiding. Sit down and do an interview with the media. Let them ask their questions, do their probing into your life. Then they will leave you alone. Not completely, but it will not be as bad as it is right now." She sighed. "Go on, you're late for rehearsal."

"Thank you, Mrs. Watson." Paige walked out of the office then exhaled. She looked up to see all eyes on her. Most of them quickly turned their heads, as if they were not listening.

"So is it true? Are you dating Jarrett Bryson?" one of the dancers asked.

Paige took a deep breath. "Yes."

"Oh my God. You go, girl." Another dancer gave her a high five. "He is so fine."

Paige blushed.

"Okay, okay, okay." One of the male dancers ran over to her. "Tell the truth. Is the man hung or what?"

"David." Paige blushed more.

Victoria clapped her hands. "All right, that's enough about Paige's love life."

"More like lust life," Jolene laughed.

"Don't be jealous, Jolene," Victoria countered. "Just because a man don't want your stinky ass."

"Who the hell do you think you are talking to?" Jolene jumped up in Victoria's face like she was going to punch her.

Victoria gave her one solid pop in the chest propelling her backwards on her behind, then stood over her. "I am not Paige. You better recognize."

Victoria slowly turned away. "Now, all who are a part of the New York ensemble, come with me to stage three."

"Traveling ensemble, follow me to stage two," David called out.

"European ensemble, stay on the main stage," Paige said as she gathered her things and placed them to the side.

Carin held her hand out to help Jolene up. "I know you are not going to let that slide." She tilted her head, then walked off to stage 3.

Each group began planning their performances. As the lead, Paige had the final say on the choreography. She could feel the negative energy coming from Jolene, but she chose to ignore it. After the planning session, Paige excused the group for a fifteen minute break then they would try some of the suggested moves.

"Jolene, did I miss your suggestions?" She smiled. "I know you have some powerful moves. It would be great to incorporate them into the show."

"Why would I give you my moves so you can look good?"

"It's not about one of us excelling, it's about the team. Together we can rock Europe."

"Look, Ms. Kum Ba Yah. This is a competition. Only one of us can stand out. I don't plan on it being you."

"My Grand'Mere says...."

"I don't give a damn about your grandma."

"Grand'Mere," Paige corrected. "Disrespecting me is okay. But don't disrespect my Grand'Mere.... ever."

Jolene turned away with a smirk on her face.

"Okay, main stage break is over. Let's try some of those moves."

Jolene walked back on stage with a collection of canes. "I decided to show you one," she said to Paige as she pranced around the stage.

"It's a holiday production. How are the canes significant?"

"You can make them significant with a little imagination," Jolene replied. "Watch and learn." She demonstrated the jump, tuck and roll over the stick.

"That was pretty cool," one of the dancers exclaimed.

"You all want to try this?" Paige asked.

"You ask for my input then disregard it?" Jolene challenged.

"No. I'm just a little concerned. I don't want anyone to get injured," Paige cautioned. "Let's practice it a little more." The last thing she wanted to do was discourage Jolene. However, the cane could be a little dangerous. The first line was successful in doing the move with the cane. The second line, most of them made it through.

"Are you going to demonstrate for your team, Paige?" Jolene asked.

"Of course I will." Paige did the move with ease, but when she rolled up on her feet, Jolene tapped the cane dangerously near them. Paige jumped back. Jolene tapped the cane on the floor again close to her feet. Paige parlayed back. The taps came faster as Paige finally kicked out causing Jolene to fall backwards to get out of her range.

"You did that purposely," she huffed at Paige.

"I did," Paige acknowledged. "Did you think I would let you hit my feet?"

"Why the canes, Jolene?"

She turned to the voice of Mrs. Watson.

"It's just a prop for the performance. Paige approved them."

"I did approve the move," Paige acknowledged.

"The move, yes. The striking of your feet, no. Jolene, join me in my office."

Paige watched as the two women walked away. Jolene glared at her from over her shoulder. The look sent a chill up her spine.

"Okay, everyone, let's put this thing together."

Once practice was over, Paige thanked the ensemble then took a seat in the audience. She pulled out her phone to see she had missed a number of calls from her parents, Leona, and Jarrett. A text message came through.

Look behind you.

She turned to see Jarrett sitting in the back near the door. She smiled as he walked down the ramp towards her. He looked so good in his suit and coat.

He kissed her, the moment he reached her.

"What are you doing here?" She laughed, happy to see him.

"Some interesting developments today. I came to give you a ride home."

"I could have called Carlos," she replied as they continued to hold each other.

Victoria walked over. "You two are causing a scene," she gritted through her teeth.

Jarrett and Paige looked up to see the entire production team sitting on the main stage watching them.

Paige blushed then waved. "Sorry, guys."

She picked up her things.

"Victoria," Mrs. Watson called out. "May I have a moment?" She paused. "Hello, Mr. Bryson."

"Hello," Jarrett replied.

"Jarrett, this is our director and main sponsor Mrs. Irene Watson. Mrs. Watson, this is Jarrett Bryson."

Jarrett walked over, took her hand and kissed her fingers. "You were a dancer when I first came to New York. I saw you perform on Broadway."

"You are a charmer, Jarrett Bryson."

"Yes, ma'am, I am."

She turned away. "Victoria,"

"We'll wait for you."

"No, send Carlos to pick me up. I'll see you when I get home." She glanced at Jarrett. "Or maybe not." She smirked.

"Nonsense." Jarrett shook his head. "We'll be in the car."

Paige picked up her things, took Jarrett's hand and followed him out.

"You bitch!"

Jolene appeared from out of nowhere blocking their way to the door.

"Whoa." Jarrett pushed Paige behind him.

"Jolene. What is it?"

"You bitch," she spat out. "You had Mrs. Watson pull me from the European tour."

"No, Jolene, I didn't."

She looked Jarrett up and down. "Your ass is mine, Cartwright. I don't give a damn who you're screwing." She stomped off.

Jarrett turned to Paige. "She's a little upset with you."

"Yes, she is and I have no idea why."

"Paige!" Victoria ran up and squeezed her from behind. "Guess who's going to Europe?"

"You're going on the tour?" The two women began jumping up and down screaming.

Jarrett exhaled. "Did you take Jolene's place?"

"Jolene's not going?" Victoria looked from Jarrett to Paige.

Jarrett raised an eyebrow. "I suggest both of you watch your backs."

CHAPTER FIFTEEN

Suzette sat at her desk in her home office listening to the producer of the Queen of Knights show.

"We want to do a short run of the show to see if the numbers are there. With all the drama with Bryson, the executive producer thinks the interest is high. Do you have the wives onboard?"

"Of course, we have four wives and a fiancée onboard."

"Does that mean Valarie Weingart and Lacy Dupree will be joining the cast or do you by chance have this Paige Cartwright person on board?"

There was silence on Suzette's end.

"Suzette?"

"Lacy is willing. Valarie is a maybe."

"And the Cartwright woman?"

"I don't know her all that well."

"The show can work without the Weingarts, but the fans will wonder why they are not a part of the show. It will not work without Bryson, himself, however the hype around his love life is pulling the ratings. The possibility of him popping into the show every once in a while is what will keep people tuning in from week to week."

"We have plenty of drama going on with the queens that does not involve Jarrett or Jake."

"Listen to me, Suzette. There is no show without the possibility of Bryson appearing. People want to see the on again off again relationship between him and Lacy. Or you get the new woman involved. Either way, no Bryson or connection to Bryson, and there is no show. You have two weeks to make this happen. After that, I'm pulling the plug."

Suzette held the phone out staring at it. She wanted to throw it against the wall, but that would draw Ron's attention.

"Damn," she quietly swore as she placed her phone on the desk.

Sitting back she closed her eyes trying to clear out the anger so she could come up with a solution. Finally, here was an opportunity for her to come out of Ron's shadow. A chance for her to show everyone back in Jersey she was more than a pretty face that lucked up on a ball player. As the queen bee of the queens she could control all aspects of the show. She would be the main focus. All the other wives would have to bow at her feet. Her opportunity was being blocked by Jarrett...a man who has everything. The thought of it pissed her off.

"I'll be damned if I will let Jarrett block my chance at stardom."

Suzette sat up, then glanced at the television on the wall. It showed for the umpteenth time, Jarrett and Paige walking hand in hand, then stepping into a vehicle.

"What is the damn fascination with these two?" She picked up the phone and called Lacy. "Are you watching this?"

Lacy sighed on the other end of the phone. "It's on every channel. I can't help but watch it."

"They have an hour long press conference scheduled with Stevie Tandy, the darling of network news."

"Jarrett always goes for the best," Lacy replied.

"I could see him on ESPN, but a news show? How presumptuous is that?"

"Look, Suzette, a lot of people are interested in this. It's not just about sports. This is about the man and you know that. It's the reason the producers of the Queens show is even talking to you. They think you may be able to produce Jarrett. I know it and so do you."

"That was only used to start the conversation. We can do this without the mighty Jarrett."

"Well, you got the conversation started. Now you are going to have to find a way to keep it going. Only it will probably be without me, now that he has someone else in his life."

"You're giving up? He was with you for over a year. You're going to let some dancer take your man, without a fight?" She sat back in a huff. "Maybe I was wrong. I thought you loved the man. Far be it for me to be upset on your behalf, when it looks like you don't give a damn."

"I love Jarrett and would do anything to have him back, but...."

"No buts. I'll think of something. You just be ready when I call." Suzette hung up the phone before Lacy could change her mind again.

She needed this deal to go forward. As much as she loved Ron and the children, she was going to suffocate if she did not find an outlet. Turning to her computer, she decided to find out all she could about Paige Cartwright, then get rid of her. For that she would need Lacy and some dirt on little Ms. Paige. She turned on the computer, pulled up the Internet and began a search of the worldwide web.

*****

Paige and Jarrett discussed the situation with the media. They decided the best course of action was to do an interview. Jarrett called Nick to set it up. Since the Knights had home field advantage, the first game of the playoffs was scheduled for that Sunday in New York. Nick had the interview setup for that Saturday, to air on Sunday, an hour before the game was televised. It was great publicity for the Knights to have Jarrett's interview lead right into the game.

The ratings were off the chart. Millions tuned in to meet the woman Jarrett opened his heart to.

"It was clear to me the moment she whirled through the door, she is the light of his eyes," Stevie, said as she discussed the interview with her co-anchors. "Everyone in the room fell in love with her within minutes of her arrival. His eyes lit up. The kiss, oh my. It made me feel like I was intruding." She laughed then turned to the camera and said, "Here is another of my many favorite moments with Jarrett Bryson and Paige Cartwright."

The monitor changed to Stevie Tandy sitting in a chair with the lights of the skyline of New York beaming through the windows of Jarrett's condo as the backdrop. Jarrett and Paige were on the love seat. Her feet curled up, his arms around her as they laughed.

"So, Jarrett, tell me. How did you know Paige is the one?"

Jarrett gazed at Paige, her wavy, black, shoulder length hair, bouncing as she turned to smile up at him.

He inhaled. "The moment she smiled at me it was as if heaven had opened up. She said something funny, then laughed. It was like music to my ears. The deal was sealed the first time I held her in my arms. That was when I knew I was home."

Paige caressed his cheek, then kissed him with such passion. When she ended the kiss, she put her head on Jarrett's shoulder, looked into the camera and said, "Well, there you go."

The camera held the frame, then focused on the co-anchors.

"You can feel it, even on the screen," Stevie said. "This is the real thing for him."

"And for her," the co-anchor added. "Look at the picture."

That's exactly what the world did. Millions looked at the picture for it was replayed hundreds of times over the week of the playoffs.

*****

Kurt Stack saw the interview and placed a call to his team manager. "Are you looking at this?"

Ben held the phone wondering why in the hell he asked him the same question over and over.

"Yes, Kurt. I see them."

"The Commissioner said to stay away from Bryson. He didn't say anything about the girlfriend."

"How is the girlfriend a distraction?"

"That is a man in love. If something happens to her, believe me he will be distracted. Get it done." The call was disconnected.

Ben held the phone. "I hate this damn job." He hung up the phone.

*****

"Will you stop pacing," Carin yelled from the kitchen. "Replaying it over and over is not going to do you any good. In fact, it's pissing me off."

"The bitch has to pay." Jolene hit the play button again. The interview started from the beginning.

"Look, you were complaining about going on the European tour as a backup. Now you don't have to go at all." Carin took the stir fry from the pan and put it onto the plate. "Sit down and eat, will you?"

"You think I want to be in the chorus line?" Jolene huffed as she walked into the kitchen. "I have prepared for the lead for years...years. I don't do second."

"Good, because you're not doing anything now," Carin chuckled

The cast iron frying pan connected with Carin's head before the fork of food reached her mouth, knocking her to the floor. The second blow killed her for sure, but Jolene wasn't finished. She whaled the pan, hitting Carin again, and again and again, until her roommate's face was unrecognizable.

Jolene stopped, wiped the blood from her face and sighed. "Laugh at that."

She dropped the pan, then stood. The interview had stopped at the still picture of Jarrett and Paige. Jolene stared at the screen then proceeded to the bathroom to shower.

*****

The interview changed everything. The network called Suzette again indicating they wanted Paige Cartwright on the show. With Jarrett standing firm on a no, that meant Paige would probably follow suit. Ron was right. There was only one option left for her to follow. After discussing the roadblocks with him, he suggested she sit down with the owner. Tell him her vision for the show and how it could be a profitable venture for the organization. If she could pull it off with the head office, Jarrett's participation would be mandatory. That would mean Paige would be included whether she wanted to or not.

Suzette checked herself in the mirror. It was important that she make a good impression. She needed to come away with two things, the show and the organization's commitment to keep her as the leader of the Queens. The way it works was simple. The team captain's wife was made the leader. Since Jarrett wasn't married, the responsibility fell to Suzette. Now, if Jarrett married her, Paige would take over that duty and Suzette would again be pushed to the side. There was no way she was going to let that happen. She would do whatever it took to get the show approved through the owner.

Dressed in a navy blue power suit, hair up, with the right amount of leg and cleavage showing, Suzette stepped in the plush office after being announced, only to find Ruben Caswell, the owner of the Knights, wasn't alone.

"Suzette." Ruben stood and extended his hand. "Please come in."

"Hello, Ruben." Suzette smiled. "Thank you for making the time to see me." She glanced at the other person in the room. The older woman was impeccably dressed in a gold suit, pearl necklace and a bracelet Suzette was certain cost more than her car.

"You wanted to speak with us regarding the proposed television program concerning the Queens?"

"Yes." Suzette looked from the woman to Ruben. When it was clear he had no intention of introducing them, Suzette extended her hand. "I'm Suzette Mackenzie. It's a pleasure to meet you, Mrs...."

"Yes, I imagine it would be."

No name was given. Suzette held her smile as she pulled her hand away. There was something in the old woman's expression that warned her to proceed carefully.

"Have a seat, Suzette." Ruben pointed to one of four chairs placed around a round table. On the table were two folders. One was the package Suzette had sent. The other was unknown to her.

"We received your proposal with a request for a meeting. Needless to say, we are a bit curious as to how this program proposal came about and the impact it would have on the organization."

"Well, I'll be happy to tell you all about the show." Suzette took a seat, crossed her legs then turned her body towards Ruben who was on her right.

"It's an excellent opportunity to highlight the charitable work the Queens do each year. In addition, it will give our fans positive insight into the lives of their favorite players." She stopped then glanced at the woman. For some reason the woman assessing her was unnerving.

Ophelia nodded her head for the woman to proceed. She watched and listened as the woman who'd taken the picture that started the avalanche of press in pursuit of Paige, talked passionately about this show. As Ophelia listened, it occurred to her the woman's intention was to seduce the male owner into agreeing with the idea. How foolish, she thought. While the written proposal did have merit, it was the unwritten elements of this type of programing that raised concerns. Ophelia believed it was her responsibility to ensure that the reputation of the Knights remained above reproach for all the owners.

Yes, she was the majority owner, holding 51% of the team. It was Ophelia who allowed Ruben to be the face of the organization because she trusted his judgement and had faith he would carry out her wishes as far as the team was concerned.

When her husband died, Ophelia wanted nothing more to do with the team, but there was no way she was going to put the ownership in just anyone's hands. She'd promised her husband, she would not die until she found the right person to take over as the majority owner. While Ruben's leadership was commendable, she wanted someone whose passion for the game equaled her husband's. Ophelia believed she had found that person. Until that person was in a position to take over, it was her duty to ensure that the integrity of the Knights stayed intact. This woman sitting before her was a danger to that task.

"So what do you think?" Suzette finally concluded.

"Your presentation was certainly intriguing," Ruben commented. "I would even add passionate." He sat forward in his seat. "I have concerns with regards to the current productions that claim to show the reality of players' lives. They seem to be a bit exaggerated, in some cases forced, and laced with drama."

"Well, I understand your concerns. The organization has certainly had its share of drama lately." Suzette smirked. "This will give us an opportunity to show the world a classier side of who we are. Our wives are intelligent, caring women who do wonderful charitable work. Drama is what the public thinks we are about. I want to show the world who we really are."

"The leader of the Queens is the captain's wife," Ophelia interrupted. "Am I mistaken?"

"No, you are correct." Suzette's smile turned forced. "Our captain isn't married." She shrugged. "As the wife of the second in command, the responsibility falls on me." She sat forward. "And I take that responsibility very seriously."

"Is that so?"

"Yes," Suzette replied with a guarded glance, then turned back to Ruben. "I've had the responsibility since Ron has been with the team. If you remember, Ruben, Ron was the captain until Jarrett was voted in."

"With Ron's full support," Ruben acknowledged.

"Yes, and as was noted at the time, Jarrett had no concerns with me continuing as the leader of the Queens."

"Until now," Ophelia noted.

Suzette closed her eyes for a moment, then turned towards the woman who was beginning to get on her nerves. "Excuse me?"

Ophelia picked up the folder in front of her, opened it and pulled out a picture and held it in her hand. "I have a picture here of Jarrett Bryson and Paige Cartwright that was given to a blogger." She placed the picture face up on the table. "This is the picture that started the firestorm of press seeking information on Bryson's personal life and placing the organization in the middle of unnecessary drama." She glared up at Suzette. "I believe that picture came from your cell phone."

Suzette sat back. "You must be mistaken..."

"Let me stop you before you drift deeper into the land of untruth." Ophelia pulled out another document. "Tell me, is this your cell phone number?"

Suzette didn't want to look, but she did. "Yes, it is."

"As explained by my investigator, for I know little or nothing about these new found gadgets, this is a time stamp. Its date and time indicates it was taken very close to the time you were in the parking garage. You see dear, we know this because," -she pulled out another picture- "this picture from the parking garage security camera was taken a few minutes before this picture." She pointed to the first pictures. "Now, I could be wrong. I'm an old woman in failing health, but my mind is sharp. But it seems to me that since this picture was taken with your phone, at approximately the same time as this picture was taken, I can only conclude that you took the picture."

Suzette jumped up. "This is outrageous. Are you investigating me?"

"Sit down," Ophelia seethed.

The command was firm and not one to be questioned. Suzette slowly sat back down.

"Your husband, Ron, is a valued player to this team." Ophelia nodded. "He's a good man."

"Yes, he is." Suzette glared at the woman.

"The life he provides for you isn't enough. You want more. There is nothing wrong with that, dear. Where you've gone wrong is your willingness to do anything, or to step on anyone, to make that happen. It seems you have put your self-interests before your husband's well-being. Do you love your husband, Mrs. Mackenzie?" Ophelia held the woman's eyes without a blink.

"Of course I do."

"I loved my husband too. He passed years ago. The lessons he taught me were invaluable. You simply can't put a price on it." She smiled at the thought. "Love isn't selfish, Mrs. Mackenzie. Love is putting the other person's happiness first." Ophelia glanced at Ruben. "I think it's time to test the love you claim to have for your husband."

"Do you like living in New York, Suzette?" Ruben asked.

Reluctantly Suzette pulled her stare from the woman. "Yes, I do."

"Do you like being a part of the Knights organization?"

"Yes," Suzette answered snidely.

"Good. We like having Ron with us. However, our concern is with you. According to our view on things, you've forgotten the golden rule. The Knights do not lie, or cheat or conspire against other members of the team. We treat people with respect and hope they will respect us back. It has come to our attention that you treat the ladies as if they are your personal puppets to use at your beck and call. This is your notice that your time as the leader of the Queens has come to an end. Jake Weingart's wife will take over as leader of the Queens until our captain marries, or we get a new captain."

"You can't do that," Suzette growled.

"It's done, my dear," Ophelia all but yawned.

"She won't do it. The ladies will not follow her."

"Yes, dear, they will. You are going to bow out as gracefully as the woman you proclaim to be. Your actions concerning these pictures demonstrates your lack of respect for Mr. Bryson's privacy. I'm going to do for you what you did not do for Paige Cartwright. I'm going to allow you to control your own destiny."

"You're going to allow me?" she snarled.

Ophelia stood, then glared down at Suzette.

"Tomorrow you will call a meeting of the Queens. You will tell them your children need quality time with their mother and you've decided to relinquish your role as their leader. You will then nominate Mrs. Weingart as the new leader. Then you are going to ensure a smooth transition into the role."

"And if I don't?"

Ophelia shook her head "Mrs. Mackenzie, you need to learn when to quit." She walked towards the door. "If you do not do exactly what I requested, your husband will be traded to the worst team that is as far away from New York as I can find."

"Ron is great at his job. You would not jeopardize the overall well-being of the team."

"Mr. Mackenzie is good." Ophelia nodded in acknowledgment. "There is always someone younger and better. However, we respect your husband's abilities. It's you with whom we have issues." Ophelia glanced at Ruben. He stood then walked towards the door. He opened the door and waited.

It took Suzette a moment to realize she had been dismissed. She stood, then walked over to the door and stopped.

"Why are you doing this," she cried.

"You said it yourself. It's time to bring some class to the organization."

"I will tell my husband about your threat," she huffed. "He will not be happy."

"Better pissed off than pissed on. Good day Mrs. Mackenzie."

Ruben held the door open.

"Ruben..."

"It's done, Suzette."

"You would let her trade Ron?"

"No, I wouldn't. It will be your actions that will set the wheels in motion. I suggest you proceed cautiously."

Suzette looked down, shaking her head. "Ruben, don't do this to Ron, please, I'm begging you."

"I'm not doing anything to Ron. That power is in your hands. One last thing. Do not disrupt my playoffs with any antics you come up with to tell Ron. If you do, the rejection of your show will be the least of your worries." He tilted his head, stepped back then closed the door.

Suzette stood there watching the closed door for the longest time. She could not believe the turn of events. Just like that, she was no longer the leader of the Queens, no show and Ron's career with the Knights was in jeopardy.

In the twenty minutes it took for her to drive home, she'd received a call from Valarie advising her of a call from the front office regarding the Queens. She responded by telling Val she had to call her back once she dealt with a situation at home. She wasn't anywhere near ready to concede to the old woman or Ruben. It then dawned on her she never got the woman's name.

"Who in the hell is she?" The question caused Suzette to calm down and think. Whoever she was, the woman had clout. Ruben was in the meeting, but other than the part on Ron, the old woman ran things. "Why?" Why would Ruben take second chair to the old woman? Suzette continued to try to clear her mind. She had seen the woman before. Was it at a function with the organization? No, she shook her head. "It was a picture, but where?" Her phone rang again. It was Ron. She couldn't talk to him right now. She was too pissed and he'd know something was up. "Concentrate, Suzette, concentrate." She pulled into the garage of her home, then ran to her office. She went to her browser's history and proceeded to search through all the pages she'd pulled up on Paige the week before. About ten minutes in, Suzette slumped back into her chair. She had found it.

"Holy shit," she proclaimed. She remembered Val telling her Paige was going to sit in her family's VIP box when they were at the game.

"Damn! Damn! Damn!" she screamed out. Pissed with herself for not thinking before opening her mouth to Paige.

"Okay, calm down. What is Ophelia Hylton's connection to the team? It had to be high up. Could she be one of the owners?" She keyed back into the computer. This time she googled everything she could on Ophelia Hylton.

"Wow." Suzette began to read. "The old bag is loaded." The article explained how Ophelia Hylton had become one of the richest women in the world when her husband passed away, leaving her assets around the world, totaling over a hundred billion dollars. Of those major assets, she now had part ownership of the Knights, a Major League Baseball team. The article was old, they speculated on what the widow would do as far as the team goes.

"She owns the damn team. Mother lover," Suzette exclaimed as she sat back, almost in tears. This could backfire on Ron. That was the last thing she wanted to happen. All of this because Jarrett picked Paige Cartwright, of all the women in the world, to fall in love with. She sat up. "Does he know?" she wondered. "Does Jarrett know Paige is the granddaughter to the owner of the team?" She had to find out.

How? she thought, then picked up the phone.

"Lacy, darling, do I have news for you?"

CHAPTER SIXTEEN

"It's' game six in the Championship round of the World Series. The Knights are leading the series against the Dragons, 3 games to 2. The Knights stadium is rocking with excitement, hoping their team will bring home the American League title," the sports news anchor stated.

"On the other side of the field, we have the Dragons fans, praying for another chance to get to the World Series with a win here tonight. The gates opened at noon, for the six o'clock start time, moved up an hour for the weather. We're all praying the weather will hold out, with a call for rain, possible snow later tonight," the co-anchor stated as Victoria turned phone off.

Paige stretched from the split position on the stage. Leaning to the right, and then to the left, then forward, getting all the kinks out before the matinee performance.

"What time are you leaving for the game?" Victoria asked as she stretched in front of Paige.

"Right after curtain call, if Mrs. Watson approves it."

"She will," Victoria replied as she stretched towards the front, just about kissing the floor. "This could be it. Your man could be in the World Series next week."

"It would be great if they could close it out tonight. That would give them a few down days as they wait on the outcome of the National League."

"Excuse me, ladies," Mrs. Watson interrupted them. "Have any of you heard from Carin?"

Victoria and Paige glanced at each other shaking their heads. "No," Victoria replied. "Have you checked with Jolene?"

"Yes, I spoke with her earlier today. She said Carin left for the theater."

"Traffic could be holding her up," Paige suggested. "She will be here in time for the performance."

"If not, Victoria you will have to take her solo, since Ms. Front Page over here needs to leave early," Mrs. Watson teased.

"Thank you Mrs. Watson. You know my Grand'Mere says that sunshine fills the heart of those who make others happy."

"Really? Ask your Grand'Mere if she could fill my pockets next time." She laughed, then walked off.

"Carin didn't show yesterday," Victoria told Paige. "I hope she is not holding out because Jolene was suspended."

"I feel responsible for that happening." Paige sighed.

"What were you supposed to do? Let her hit your feet with the damn stick? I think not," Victoria replied. "Jolene had this coming. It wasn't just the stick incident, it was her entire attitude. I'm just happy Mrs. Watson recognized it before somebody got hurt."

"Well, she is very passionate about her dancing. That can't be all bad."

"It's not." Victoria stopped and looked at Paige. "Your passion has to meet your talent. Then you have to respect others' talents as well. She is good, there is no denying that. Her problem is, she is not the best. That happens to be you."

"I think she wants it more," Paige said just as music from her cell phone played.

"The unmistakable voice of Stephanie Mills and Power of Love." Victoria laughed. "I wonder who that could be?"

Paige laughed as she answered the call. "Hi."

"Hi yourself. The game was moved up an hour. We won't be able to ride in together. I'll send a car to pick you up out front. The family will be in the box. Are your parents and Grand'Mere there yet?"

"Not yet. Thank you for your thoughtfulness. My father is so excited about the game."

"I'm looking forward to both families being together. We'll do dinner immediately after the game."

"I think it's wonderful to see everyone before we leave for Europe. I'm going to miss spending Christmas with them. We'll make this our celebration."

"I think we are going to have a number of celebrations before we leave. I'll see you at the game."

"Remember, stay off the first pitch and enjoy the game."

*****

Jarrett hung up the phone, and looked out the window. The sky was blue, no signs of clouds, yet the weather man was calling for rain. The vehicle stopped and Sergio climbed in.

"Do you have it?"

"No," Sergio growled. "They said it will be ready before the game starts. They will deliver it to the box."

Jarrett growled. "Are you serious?"

Sergio laughed, then pulled the box from his pocket. "You should have seen the look on your face."

Jarrett grabbed the box from him. "That's not funny, Serg." He opened the blue box to examine the single solitaire sitting inside a J and a P.

"Hold on, man." Peace pulled out his sunshades and put them on. "I have to protect my eyes from all that bling."

Jarrett smiled at the vision, then closed the box and put it inside his coat pocket.

"When are you planning to do this?" Serg asked.

"All the family is here tonight. I think that will be the perfect time."

"Mama Connie is here? She cooking?"

Peace and Jarrett laughed. "Yes, Serg. Give us an hour after postgame. Call Victoria and invite her to join us."

Peace cleared his throat, then looked out the window.

Jarrett laughed. "Yes, you too."

"You know, man, I didn't want to be presumptuous or anything. But I do like the little lady."

"She is easy to love. Speaking of Paige, she has a matinee that should end around 4 pm. Will you pick her up and bring her to the stadium?"

"You got it."

*****

"Darling, we have seen you dance before, but tonight you were simply radiant." Eleanor hugged her daughter.

"I think you need more clothes on," Horace said.

"Oh, Harold, she has a beautiful body."

"Sir, I am so sorry, I thought your name was Horace," Victoria apologized.

"It is," Horace replied. "The old woman is losing her memory." Everyone laughed except Ophelia.

"While you are laughing traffic is building up," Ophelia stated. "I suggest we get going. Tinker Belle we'll see you at the stadium."

"See," Horace laughed. "She doesn't remember Paige's name either."

"Stop, you two." Eleanor kissed Paige's cheek. "See you at the stadium. Be sure to dress warm. There's going to be a storm tonight."

Ophelia stopped dead in her tracks. She turned back to look at Paige. Something passed through them.

Paige shook the feeling of dread off. "Go on, Grand'Mere. I'll be fine."

"What is it Mother? Are you feeling okay?" Eleanor asked as they entered the car.

Ophelia looked out the window. The sky was blue, no clouds anywhere. "Why do you think a storm is coming?" She turned to her daughter.

"I can feel it," Eleanor replied.

"The sky is clear," Horace said looking around. "But if you say it's going to storm, I believe you." He kissed her cheek.

As the car pulled off, Ophelia looked back. That's when she saw what she feared. A black cloud. Only one, hanging over the theater. "How is Paige getting to the field?"

"Jarrett is sending his security team for her," Horace replied.

The further the vehicle traveled, the more the feeling of dread grew for Ophelia.

CHAPTER SEVENTEEN

Paige was getting dressed when Victoria stepped out of the shower. "Looks like we are going to get that rain after all. It's getting a little dark outside."

"No. I refuse to believe that. It's going to be a wonderful day for a game."

"Only you would think a baseball game in November is a good thing," Victoria teased.

"It's not just good, it's great. If you're playing ball in November, you are the best there is. That's what my grandfather says." The statement made Paige pause. It was as if she heard her grandfather, whom she had never met, say that in her head.

"I thought your grandfather was dead," Victoria said as she continued to dress.

"Yes, he is." Paige shook the thought away. "It's a beautiful day for a game anytime. I'm out of here. My ride is meeting me out front." She gave Victoria a hug.

"Have fun at the game. I'll be listening," she yelled after the running Paige.

The moment Paige pushed the front door open she realized she had left her coat. Seeing the black sedan out front, she decided to just run to the car. The driver opened the back door. Paige ran out the door just as a loud clap of thunder sounded. It frightened Paige. As she jumped in the backseat, something slammed into her head. Her purse fell and the world went black.

*****

Victoria walked out of the performance entrance door with Paige's long white coat on. Peace stepped out of the vehicle. "Paige," he called out when she turned to walk away from where he was parked.

Victoria turned. "Hi Peace. You're looking for Paige?"

"Yes, we're here to pick her up for the game."

"She said she was meeting you out front about five minutes ago."

"Thank you. We'll get her."

"Okay, have fun." She waved them off and kept walking until something grabbed her and pulled her into the alley.

Peace pulled the vehicle to the front. There was no sign of Paige or anyone near the entrance. He got out to check the front door. It was locked. As he walked back to the vehicle, he saw the strap of a purse on the ground. "Oh hell. This ain't good." He picked the purse up and looked inside. "Damn."

He pulled out his cell and pushed a button. "I think we might have a problem."

*****

"It's the bottom of the ninth, two outs and The Knights are down by 1," the excited voice of the commentator spoke. "Every person in the stadium is on their feet, as Jarrett Bryson, Mr. Clutch walks up to the plate. The noise is deafening as they wait on the first pitch."

Stay off that first pitch. Jarrett could hear Paige's voice in his mind. "I hear you babe," Jarrett said, then stepped into the batter's box.

"Here comes the first pitch." The commentator held his breath. "He takes a ball. You can hear the collective sigh as the crowd quiets down. That is different. Bryson is usually all over the first pitch. Let's see what happens next. "

Jarrett steps back up to the plate. *Enjoy the game.* There was her voice in his head again. He smiled, raised his bat. Took his stance.

The crowd started to chant, "Bryson, Bryson, Bryson."

"Here's the pitch. The swing ....."

Crack.

"And that ball is going.....going.....gone. The Knights are going to the World Series." The crowd erupted. The dug out cleared. Jarrett dropped the bat, clapped his hands then began to take the bases one at a time.

"There you go," he said as he stomped on the plate.

He was mobbed by his teammates. Reporters surrounded him. The crowd was in a frenzy, jumping, cheering, and then he saw Nick. He searched the crowd for Paige.

Nick walked towards him with the security team.

"Paige," escaped from his lips as his heart stopped.

They surrounded him without a word, then escorted him to the dugout.

"What happened? Where is Paige?"

"At this point, she's missing."

"What in the hell do you mean she's missing?" Jarrett asked as he tried to remain calm.

"We don't know where she is," Nick replied. "Peace found her purse in front of the theater."

"Did you call her roommate Victoria?"

"We've been calling her for hours," Nick replied. "No answer."

"Get Sergio to call her number," Jarrett suggested.

"Peace spoke with Victoria at the theater. She was wearing Paige's coat so he thought it was Paige. She told him Paige was meeting him out front. He went to the front. That's where he found her purse."

"The theater has security cameras, right?" Jarrett inquired as he nodded acknowledging Nick's words.

"The police are checking on it now," Nick replied.

"Where are Paige's parents?" Jarrett began walking towards the locker room.

The Commissioner stopped his progress. "Jarrett, great game. They brought me up to date on what's happening. There is something you need to know."

"Our investigation did not clear the Dragons organization. We believe they were conspiring to distract you from the game."

"I'm getting dressed." Jarrett continued walking through the tunnel. "I want to see their management, now."

"Jarrett, you can't do that," the Commissioner stated.

Jarrett stopped walking and turned back to the Commissioner. "I talk to them or the media. Which do you prefer?" He glowered at the man.

The Commissioner conceded. "I'll have them detained in the visitors' box."

Jarrett turned and walked off.

The moment the locker room door opened, the celebration was on. Champagne was pouring all around, but none of it deterred Jarrett.

"The man of the hour. Mr. Clutch," Ron yelled. The room exploded with applause. Players reached out for his hand.

Jarrett kept walking.

"Hey," Serg called out. "What's wrong?" He held a bottle of champagne in his hand.

"Paige is missing."

"What?" Serg put the bottle down.

Jarrett grabbed a pair of jeans, a sweater and his phone from his locker. "Call Victoria and meet me in the box."

"You got it," Serg replied as Jarrett pushed by the other teammates.

"What's going on?" Ron asked as he watched Jarrett's back.

"Paige is missing."

"What?" Ron turned and glared at Serg, then turned back to see Jarrett struggling with the reporters.

"Hey!" Ron ran over. "Let him go." He freed Jarrett by distracting the reporters.

Jarrett turned grateful eyes on him then left the room.

*****

The police filled the family box along with Jarrett and Paige's family.

"Jarrett." His mother took him into her arms the moment he walked in. "Have you heard anything?"

"No." Jarrett saw the disappointment on the faces of every one of them. He walked over to Paige's family. "You all were at the theater, was anything off? Anything that caught your attention?"

"The black cloud," Ophelia said.

"What?" Jarrett knelt down next to Grand'Mere who looked as if twenty years had been added to her life since he'd seen her a few hours ago.

She took Jarrett's hand in hers, then lowered her head. "The black cloud was over the building. I should have turned back." The tears poured down her face.

Eleanor turned into her husband's arms at the sight of her mother in tears. Horace held his wife, and reached down to take Ophelia's hand in his. "We are going to find her." Horace exhaled. "We're going to find her."

Jarrett stood, nodding at Horace's words. "I am going to find Paige," he declared.

Nick walked in and motioned to Jarrett.

"Excuse me." Jarrett walked over.

"The Commissioner has the Dragons' management team, interrogating them. I thought you should be there."

Jarrett nodded. "Nick, will you take the family to my place. Make sure they are comfortable. I want to speak to the police."

Sergio and Ron walked in just as Jarrett reached the officers in the room.

"Mr. Bryson, I'm Detective Sanders." The man dressed in a suit spoke. "The Commissioner asked me to volunteer to work this case. Technically this isn't a missing person's. She's an adult. It could be as simple as she's out with friends."

"Detective I respect your theory," Jarrett said. "But I debunk it. Paige would be here if she was able. Something has happened to her and I'm going to find out what. You can work with me or I'll do it on my own. Either way I'm finding Paige." He walked out the door with Sergio and Ron trailing him.

"Where are we starting?" Sergio asked. "I'm not getting an answer from Victoria."

"Keep trying." Jarrett stopped, took a deep breath. He looked up at his friends to speak, but the words wouldn't come out. He wiped his hands down his face, to cover the tears. "She is every good thing in my life." He exhaled. "I feel it in my soul, something is wrong."

"Don't think that way," Ron encouraged. "We are going to find her."

The Commissioner stepped into the hallway. "Jarrett." He motioned for him to come.

Jarrett stepped into the room to see Kirk Stack and his team manager Ben standing on opposite sides of the room.

"Bryson, what do you mean having us delayed?" Kirk challenged.

"Mr. Stack, my girlfriend Paige is missing. If there is anything you know about where she might be, I would appreciate you telling the authorities."

"Missing?" Ben pushed away from the wall as he confronted his boss. "What did you do?"

"Shut up, Ben," Kirk Stack demanded.

"Mr. Stack, if you know anything about this situation, I strongly urge you to tell us now."

Jarrett turned to see Detective Sanders behind him.

"I don't know what you are talking about and I resent the implications."

"Ben," Jarrett pleaded. "If you know anything, please."

"Look," Ben sighed. "He asked me to look at doing something to your girl to distract you. I couldn't do it."

"Shut up, Ben, or you're fired."

"Don't bother, I quit," he yelled at the man, then turned back to Jarrett. "Look, Bryson. I wanted us to win fair and square, so I didn't do it. I've been monitoring his calls, so to be honest, I don't think he had a chance to contact anyone either. I'll be happy to make a few calls to verify one way or another."

Jarrett's heart sank. Dejected, he nodded to Ben. "Thanks, Ben, I would appreciate that."

"I'll handle Stack," the Commissioner said. "Keep me posted, Jarrett. If there is anything I can do, don't hesitate to let me know."

*****

Jarrett walked out the door to find Sergio on his cell phone.

"Where are you?"

"In jail."

"Is Paige with you?"

"No, you moron. Isn't she at the game?"

"Who are you talking to?" Jarrett asked.

"Victoria..."

Before Sergio could get her name out Jarrett grabbed the phone.

"Victoria, have you heard from Paige?"

"No. What's going on?"

"She's missing."

"What do you mean missing?" an agitated Victoria asked.

"No one has seen her since she left the theater."

"I should have killed her ass."

"Who?"

"Jolene."

"Jolene the dancer?"

"Full name," the Detective asked overhearing the conversation.

"What's her full name?" Jarrett asked.

"Jolene Cadet," Victoria replied. "She jumped me in the alley thinking I was Paige. I whipped her ass and the police arrested me."

"Where is she now?"

"I don't know," she yelled. "I'm in jail."

"We know where you are. Paige is still out there some damn where and we have to find her. Do you know where Jolene lives?" Jarrett repeated what the Detective was asking him.

"No. I have Mrs. Watson's number, you can ask her. Do you think she did something to Paige too?"

Jarrett watched as the detective made a call, then began walking towards the elevator.

"We don't know." Jarrett gave the phone to Sergio. "Tell Victoria to send the info to my phone." He ran down the hall following the Detective.

"Will one of you come and get me the hell out of here?" was the last thing Jarrett heard as the elevator doors closed.

"Where are we going?" He faced the detective.

"To find this Jolene Cadet," Detective Sanders replied. "What is the situation with her and Paige Cartwright?"

'They are both dancers with the same troupe. They constantly compete with each other. Paige has gotten the lead on a tour and this Jolene person was suspended. She blames Paige."

"Enough to harm her?" Sanders didn't seem convinced.

Jarrett's phone buzzed, he showed the message to Sanders. "This is Mrs. Watson's contact information."

Sanders took the phone and sent the message to himself. "Bryson, go home. We will contact you as soon as we know something."

"No. Hell no." He exhaled. "Look, this woman is my life. I have to find her."

"I understand that, but at this moment you are hindering my investigation."

"I can help," Jarrett countered. "I know Mrs. Watson and I've met Jolene Cadet. If you see her on the street you won't know who she is, I will."

The detective hesitated. "We'll talk to Mrs. Watson. After that you are out."

CHAPTER EIGHTEEN

The doorman at Mrs. Watson's apartment indicated she was there. "She said the police had already questioned her about the break-in."

"What break-in?" Sanders asked.

"Someone broke in and ransacked Mrs. Watson's apartment earlier today."

Jarrett was on his phone. "Mrs. Watson, this is Jarrett Bryson. I'm in your lobby with Detective Sanders. May we come up?" He started walking towards the elevator as he looked back and nodded to Sanders. "Thank you."

"Great game tonight, Jarrett," the doorman called out after him.

Mrs. Watson met them at the door. "It's late, gentlemen, but come in." There was an older gentleman standing in the hallway. "This is my husband, Grady."

Jarrett extended his hand. "How do you do, sir? This is Detective Sanders. I apologize for disturbing you, but Paige is missing."

Mrs. Watson gasped. "What?" Her hand went to her chest then she looked at her husband. "Not another one."

"What do you mean another one?" Detective Sanders asked.

Her husband took her hand. "One of her other dancers has been missing for two days."

"Not a word from her." Mrs. Watson sighed. "Now Paige. Oh my word, not Paige."

"Who is the other missing young lady?" Sanders asked.

"Carin Tomey," she replied. "I've been calling her for two days now. I spoke with her roommate Jolene, but she hasn't heard from her either."

"Jolene Cadet?" Sanders asked.

"Yes." The woman looked up. "Why do you ask?'

"That's who we wanted to talk with you about," Sanders replied.

"She attacked Victoria sometime today," Jarrett added.

"Victoria?" Irene turned to her husband, distraught. "Oh my goodness."

Sanders gave Jarrett a look that indicated not to say any more. Jarrett stepped back.

"What can you tell me about her?" Sanders asked Mrs. Watson.

"Jolene." Mrs. Watson's demeanor changed. "She's talented, but she has a mean streak in her. I had to suspend her for just being an all-around bitch."

"When did you suspend her?"

"Three days ago."

"And have you seen Ms. Cadet or Ms. Tomey since?"

Mrs. Watson thought about it, then shook her head. "Come to think of it, no, I haven't."

The woman was looking hurt over the news.

"Do you have her contact information?" Sanders asked.

"It may be in my phone." She looked around. Her husband picked up her purse. "My journal with all the girls' personal information is missing. Whoever broke in here must have taken it." The woman talked as she dug into her bag. "Though I have no idea why anyone would want that."

Jarrett was trying to be patient as the woman searched, but his nerves got the best of him.

"Could your phone be in your coat pocket or jacket?"

She stopped digging and nodded. "I think it is," she said as she walked over to the closet, reached inside, then came out with the phone. "Thank you, Mr. Bryson. You're an impatient one."

"Paige is missing, ma'am, every minute counts," he said unapologetically.

"I'm sorry, I understand." She opened the contacts in her phone, found Jolene's information then showed it to the detective.

Sanders took the phone and sent the info to his own, the same as he had with Jarrett's phone. "Thank you, Mrs. Watson. We will be in touch."

"Please let me know about Paige," she yelled as the two men ran out the door.

Sanders called dispatch. "Send a car to this address." He relayed the address. "Proceed with caution. We have two missing women, maybe three."

"Who's the third," Jarrett asked when he finished the call.

"Jolene Cadet."

"She attacked Victoria. Why do you think she's missing?"

"At the moment, we don't know where she is. This Victoria woman is in jail. Where is the Cadet woman?"

"If she is a victim, then who has Paige?"

"Who has any of them?" Sanders asked as they got into the car. "Now that there is a possibility of more than one missing woman, I might have a lot more help on this."

Jarrett's phone buzzed. "Anything, Ron?"

"No," Ron replied. "Where are you?"

"We are going to Jolene Cadet's place."

"Sergio and I will meet you there. Send us the address."

"I need Jolene's address."

Sanders shook his head. "Not a good idea."

"We need all the help we can get. Come on."

Sanders hesitated, then gave Jarrett his phone. Jarrett sent the address to Ron.

Sanders glanced over at the man sitting next to him. This was supposed to be his night. He'd gotten his team to the World Series. A feat not many can boast on. Yet, he had spent the last few hours trying to find his missing girlfriend. The chances of this going the wrong way were strong.

"You know there is a chance that this may not turn out good for these women. Are you going to be able to handle that?"

"We'll know when we find Paige. But I'm not giving up on her."

"Dead or alive?" Sanders asked.

"She's alive," Jarrett declared, even though he couldn't shake the thought that Paige was in danger.

The detective's phone rang.

"Sanders," he answered, then listened. He did not ask any questions or make any comments. He listened then hung up the phone. "There are times I hate this job."

"Was that a call about Paige?"

He shook his head. "I don't know."

When they turned the corner, police cars were parked in front of a brownstone. Officers were putting up yellow tape, people had started gathering around a outside.

"What's going on?" Jarrett asked as they slowly stepped out of the car.

People from the crowd started pointing as they recognized Jarrett stepping out.

"It may be better if you stay inside the car," he said as Ron and Sergio joined them.

"No, I'm going inside," Jarrett declared.

"No, you are staying here until I know what's going on inside."

Sanders nodded to two officers, then walked into the building.

"What going on, Jarrett?" Sergio asked.

"I don't know," Jarrett replied as his hands began to shake. "I have to get inside that building." His heart began racing. "Something's not right," he said as it became more difficult for him to breathe. "I've got to get in that building." He rushed past the officers, Ron and Sergio blocking their path as he ran. Once inside, there were two doors on the first floor. He stepped inside the open door and was immediately blocked from entering.

Another officer came over to assist. "Jarrett Bryson?" He looked at the other officer as if questioning what to do.

"Hold up, let him go." He still blocked Jarrett's view. "What are you doing here, Jarrett? Why aren't you out celebrating?"

"Is there a woman in there?" Jarrett stretched to get a better view. "Is she alive?"

The officer looked around. "Is this your place?"

"No," Jarrett replied, exasperated. "I need to see if that's my lady. Man, I need to see."

The officer nodded, "Let him in."

"Us too, man," Ron begged.

The officer recognized the catcher and first baseman. "The detective is going to have my ass for this."

"We won't tell him," Sergio swore. "I swear we won't. We just want to be there for Jarrett if this goes bad." The officer nodded, then opened the next door.

There was a living room with a sofa and chair, a coffee table, television on the stand, a few items of clothes. Next to the door was a bag like Paige's with the dance troupe's logo on the front. Jarrett began to hyperventilate. He breathed in then out, in then out. After a brief moment he turned towards the kitchen. There was a body wrapped in plastic sitting up in a corner beyond the table.

The sound of Jarrett's knees hitting the floor as they unraveled the plastic, caused Detective Sanders and officers in the room to turn.

His head fell into his hands. Ron grabbed his shoulders and stood at his side.

"It's not Paige," he moaned into his hands as he shook his head. "It's not Paige." He took deeper breaths. The stress of the search was getting to him. He wasn't sure how much more he could take.

Detective Sanders shook his head, then stepped in front of Jarrett blocking his view. "This is the end of the road for you, Bryson." He bent to where Jarrett knelt. His head down as if defeated.

"This is my job. I give my word as a man who loves my wife dearly. I will not sleep until I find Ms. Cartwright." He helped Jarrett up. "Take him home," he said to Ron and Sergio.

"Is it Jolene?" Jarrett exhaled.

"No. It looks like it could be Carin Tomey," Sanders replied.

Sergio and Ron took Jarrett out the door as Sanders ordered an APB on Jolene Cadet.

The rain was now falling, but Jarrett never felt a drop. He strolled down the sidewalk away from the vehicle and the crowd of people standing around. They were taking pictures while he was trying to get the image of the dead woman out of his head. He bent over, clutching his knees when her voice called out to him as clear as daylight.

"Jarrett, my Grand'Mere says there is no connection like the one to your heart. The Queens are the hearts of the Knights." He stood suddenly, looking one way then the other into the crowd expecting to see her. But she wasn't there.

"She's alive," he said more to himself than anyone else. In that moment, he didn't know how he knew it or why, but he knew she was alive. She was connecting to him in some way.

The detective came out the door. Ron and Sergio were standing near their car.

"Where's Bryson?"

Ron and Sergio stood straight from leaning against the vehicle. "Over there." They pointed towards the yellow tape.

"Bryson," he called out.

"She's alive," Jarrett said to the detective with a bit of relief.

"She called you?"

"No, but I know." He exhaled, "She's alive.

"Well, we found Jolene Cadet."

"Where?"

"She's in the hospital. It seems Victoria Gaye rendered her unconscious."

"Then where is Paige?"

Sanders shook his head. "I have no idea, but I damn sure hope we find her before we find another dead body." He turned and walked back towards the building."

Jarrett's cell phone buzzed. He answered it without checking the number. "Paige."

"She's alive, son." Ophelia's strong voice came through the phone. "Find the queen of hearts."

"What?" a confused Jarrett asked.

"Find Suzette Mackenzie. She is the queen of hearts. I don't know why, but she is the key to finding Paige."

Jarrett hung up the phone, then walked purposely towards the car. "Take me to your house," he said to Ron without breaking his stride.

"Okay." A confused Ron nodded, then jumped in the driver's seat. Sergio opened the back door for Jarrett and he jumped in the passenger seat. "I'll call Suzette to let her know we're coming."

"No," Jarrett replied. He had no idea why, but he believed if he did, he would never find Paige.

"All right, man." Ron glanced at Sergio who shrugged.

CHAPTER NINETEEN

They walked into the family room of the multi-million dollar home. Ron dropped his jacket on the sofa as Sergio slumped down into a chair.

"Man, this unbelievable," Sergio shook his head.

"Where's Suzette?" Jarrett asked a little too calmly.

There was something in the way he asked that caused Ron to be on alert.

"It's late. I'm sure she's upstairs with the kids."

"Call her," Jarrett demanded.

"What's going on, Jarrett? Why do you need to talk to Suzette?"

"Does she know Paige is missing?"

"The whole team knows. Management put the celebration on hold until we know Paige's outcome," Suzette said from the staircase leading into the adjoining kitchen. She walked over, kissed Ron then turned to Jarrett.

"How are you holding up, Jarrett?" Her voice was filled with what Jarrett took as false concern.

"Where's Paige, Suzette?"

Suzette frowned as she assessed him. "How would I know where Paige is, Jarrett? She's your woman not mine. I do know Lacy would have never pulled this kind of stunt."

"Stunt?"

"Yes. All the attention is on her, not the fact that the Knights won the playoffs," she huffed.

"You never liked her." Jarrett walked towards Suzette.

"Hey, hold up, Jarrett." Ron stood in front of his wife. "Look man, I know you are having a rough night. I understand. But I can't let you take that out on my wife."

"I'm not taking anything out on your wife, Ron. I'm just asking a few questions. Driving over, a few things cleared up for me." He shook his head as his voice remained dangerously calm. "We've been riding around for hours following one dead end after another. I have to admit." He smirked. "I almost lost it at the dead body."

"What?" Suzette glanced at her husband then back at Jarrett. "What dead body?"

"Jarrett, what are you getting at?" Sergio sat up looking concerned.

"It all started with the picture. You took that picture, Suzette. You started this whole chain of events." He walked towards her, as she stepped behind her husband, but didn't deny what he was saying. "Did you give her name to the media too?" he asked as he continued to stalk towards her.

"Jarrett," Ron cautioned him.

"What else did you do, Suzette?"

Sergio stood. "Suzette did you have Paige taken?"

"No, of course not. What's wrong with you?"

"The celebration was cancelled around eleven," Sergio stated. "It's close to three in the morning. Why are you still dressed?"

Ron stopped then looked back at his wife. She was dressed in an off the shoulder black dress with stockings and heels. He frowned. "Why are you dressed?"

"I had a drink with Lacy."

"Lacy?" Ron frowned. "When did you meet up with Lacy?"

"What's with the hundred questions, honey? You are going to the World Series, we celebrated with a drink before Lacy had to leave."

"Leave? Where is Lacy going?" Jarrett asked.

"Oh, now you want to know about Lacy? For the last month or two, it's been like she never existed. But now that she has beef with your precious Paige you want to know."

There was silence in the room.

Ron faced his wife. "What beef does Lacy have with Paige?"

"She took her man, what do you think? You can't just walk in and step to one of the Queen's men and think there would not be consequences to pay."

Jarrett couldn't believe what he was hearing. Was this payback for him breaking up with Lacy? Had Lacy and Suzette done something to Paige? No, he didn't want to believe that.

He spoke softly. "Suzette, did you say that to Lacy? Did you tell Lacy that Paige had to pay the consequences?"

Suzette paused before she answered. She looked to Ron then back to Jarrett. "No," she replied defiantly.

Ron stayed between Jarrett and Suzette. He knew his wife. She was lying. His problem was he had no idea how deep she was involved in this...whatever it was.

Jarrett sat hard on the seat. "Suzette." He shook his head. "Please tell me you did not provoke her about Paige. Please tell me you didn't do that."

"You ditched her for another woman," Suzette taunted him. "Yes, we talked about it."

"Suzette." Jarrett looked up at her with sad eyes. "Lacy and I broke up long before I met Paige. Did you ever wonder why?"

"Because you are a womanizer, Jarrett. You jump from on to the other. Lacy is a good person and you thought so too until Ms. Paige came into the picture."

"No." Ron shook his head. "Jarrett was done with Lacy before."

"Why?" Suzette angrily folded her arms across her chest. "Tell me that...Mr. Bryson?"

"Did you know Lacy has a mental condition?"

Sergio and Ron glanced at each other, then at Jarrett. The look on his face was one of fear. It seemed he wanted to say more, but couldn't.

"What is the consequence?" Sergio asked.

Suzette looked away. "I have no idea what you are talking about."

Jarrett's phone buzzed. He quickly answered. "Paige?"

"No, it's Sanders. But we may have something. The security camera captured the vehicle Paige got into and the driver. It's a female. I'm texting you a picture now."

Jarrett's head dropped and he exhaled. He knew it would be a picture of Lacy. He replied without looking at the text. "Yeah," he exhaled. "I'm at Ron Mackenzie's house. I think you'd better get over here."

*****

The police knocked on the door. Ron answered and escorted Sanders and two uniformed police officers into the family room.

"Mrs. Mackenzie, I understand you may have some information on the whereabouts of Paige Cartwright?"

"No, I do not," she replied.

"Okay." Sanders nodded. "I ran a background check on Lacy Dupree on my way over. Were you aware she spent a number of years in a mental facility?"

"No," Suzette replied, then looked at Jarrett.

"Did you know she purchased a weapon two days ago?"

Suzette gasped. That was the day she told Lacy about Ophelia Hylton. She quickly scanned through her mind trying to remember everything she said to Lacy that day.

"Suzette?" Ron called out to her, his voice filled with concern "What is it?"

"You mean a gun?" She looked up at her husband. "I didn't know about a gun." She turned to Jarrett filled with the realization that she may have initiated all of this. "Jarrett, I swear. I had no idea."

"Suzette, did you ever once stop to think I had a reason for leaving Lacy?" Jarrett glared at Suzette.

"Where did Lacy go when you left her tonight?" Ron asked.

"You were with Ms. Dupree tonight?" Detective Sanders asked.

Suzette nodded. "She took a cab."

"To where?" Sanders asked.

"I don't know, I don't know."

"Think, damn it." Jarrett jumped up.

"Jarrett, man, chill." Ron stepped between them.

"I'll chill when I find Paige. Where in the hell is she, Suzette?" he yelled.

"I don't....." Suzette stopped. "Wait, wait, wait. The day we talked she said something about taking Paige to her brother's warehouse for target practice. But I thought it was just talk. I had no idea she was serious."

The police did an immediate search for Lacy's brother's information. "He has a warehouse in the garment district," the officer reported.

"Let's move," Sanders ordered. "Send cars to that address. Hold the lights. We don't want to spook her."

Jarrett ran out the door with the police.

"Jarrett, hold up," Ron called out. "I'm driving." He grabbed his keys, turned to his wife with clenched jaws and scowling eyes.

"I didn't know, Ron," Suzette yelled as he ran out the door.

*****

"She's in there," an officer confirmed.

"Is she alive?" Sanders asked holding his breath.

Jarrett jumped from the vehicle. "Is Paige inside?"

Sanders nodded. "Yes." He then motioned to the officer to continue.

"Yes, but I don't know for how long. The woman with the gun is losing it," the officer explained.

"Give me something to work with," Sanders asked half relived. "What is this all about?"

The officer shrugged. "From this distance, I could not make out all of it, but is it possible that she killed her mother."

"It was ruled an accidental death," Jarrett offered.

Sanders turned to Jarrett. "You know about this?"

"Her brother told me she accidentally shot her mother when she was nine. He thought I should know because it seemed we were getting close."

"Now your ex-girlfriend is holding your current girlfriend hostage." Sanders shook his head and sighed. "This shit is not good."

"Let me talk to her," Jarrett pleaded. "I don't want either of them to be hurt."

"No." Sanders shook his head. "I'm not letting you go in there."

"That is my life in there, I have to get Paige out."

"I let you go in and something happens to you that puts my life in jeopardy." Sanders turned to the SWAT team commander who had just arrived. "Is the area secured?"

"Yes, and we have our men in place. The room they are in makes a clean shot difficult. We need to try negotiations."

"Let me talk to her," Jarrett asked again. "Just let me talk to her."

Sanders sighed looking up towards the heavens as if waiting for an answer. He shook his head again. "I can't do it."

"She has an emotional connection to him. Put a vest on him and send him in with my men," the SWAT Commander suggested. "She twitches the wrong way towards him and I'll give the order."

*****

Paige awakened in pain. The bruise to her temple was throbbing. She moaned. Blurry eyes saw the rope that bound her hands. It was thick, like the ropes backstage that they used for lifts. The pain was too much. She closed her eyes again and exhaled.

"You're awake."

Paige heard the voice. She opened her eyes, then looked around. She saw a figure. No, that was a mannequin. She closed her eyes again, then opened them. This time she saw someone walking towards her.

"I was concerned I'd hit you too hard." The voice laughed. "I don't want you to die, yet."

A hand reached out to shake her. Her head vibrated. "Please, stop." Her voice was low.

The hand jerked on the rope. "I need to make sure your circulation isn't cut off. Sometimes I don't know my own strength. Some people just don't understand the dedication it takes to be in entertainment. The torture we put our bodies through to be beautiful." She grabbed Paige's face. "But you don't understand that do you. For you and my mother, it all came naturally. But for me, I had to work at it. It took years, to have a body like mine." She laughed then released Paige's face. "Now look at me. I'm as beautiful as my mother was. Oh, she was beautiful. She would look in the mirror and say only the beautiful people matter in this world, then turn and laugh at me. Well," she chuckled. "She's not laughing now. I sent her to hell for taking my boyfriend. Oh I know she thought he was there to see her, but he wasn't. That man was mine. Now, here I am again. "

Paige opened her eyes, watched the figure walk away, but it was still too blurry to make out who it was.

The person sighed. "I thought my looks, my talent, my body." -she posed, running her hands down her waist to her thighs- "would be enough." She sighed. "For a while it was. I had people's attention." She smiled. "I was America's sweetheart. Yes, I was." She brushed her hair back from her face, then turned angrily towards Paige.

"Then you came along. Suddenly, I found myself in the background. And you in the forefront." She slowly walked towards Paige. She still couldn't make out who the person was, but she knew exactly what the person held in her hand.

She waved the gun in Paige's face. "Nobody saw me once you came. I was back to being a nobody. You know how humiliating that is after months of being in the spotlight," she screamed.

"I'm sorry," Paige moaned only half hearing what was being said.

"I don't want your pity." She slammed the gun across Paige's face rendering her unconscious again. "Damn you."

"Lacy," Jarrett called out.

Lacy swung around.

"Jarrett?" She looked around at the police officers walking into the room then stammered out, "What are you doing here?"

"I came to get you, Lacy." He walked slowly into the room.

She turned. "Jarrett." A surprised look appeared on her face. "You remembered?"

"I did," Jarrett agreed as he continued to walk towards her. "This is where we met. You were doing a fashion show for your brother."

"Yes." She beamed. But then an officer kicked something. The sound alerted her that something wasn't right.

"Why are you here?" Then she frowned, looking from him to Paige then angrily back at him. "You came for her." She pointed the gun at Paige.

His heart dropped. "No, no, Lacy." He stepped forward. "I came here for you. I knew you would be here." He pleaded, "I came for you."

"You did?" Lacy sounded more like a confused child. "How did you know I would be here?"

He stepped closer. "It's where we would meet after every game."

Her full attention turned back to Jarrett. "Yes, we did." She smiled at him. "This was the place where I told you I love you. Do you remember?"

"Yes, Lacy, I remember."

"I do, you know. I love you, Jarrett."

"I know." Jarrett nodded his head. "I know you do."

"Suzette was right. I have to get rid of her. It's the only way I can have you again. Suzette told me about her plan to use you and I couldn't let that happen," she shouted. "You know I had to show her the place where real love existed for me and you. Because, Jarrett," -Lacy shook her head back and forth- "She doesn't love you." She pumped the gun up and down still pointing it in Paige's direction. "All she wants is for you to run the team for her grandmother."

"What team, Lacy?"

"The Knights, Jarrett...Don't you know? Her grandmother owns the Knights." She laughed. "Isn't that funny. Yeah. If you marry her, they will have you. The perfect man to take over the team. There will be no approval needed from the league, no legal hassles, no long drawn out process. This was all a game her grandmother put into motion to get you to take over the Knights. Suzette told me everything." She shook her head. "I could take you leaving me for her, if she loved you, Jarrett, but she doesn't."

Jarrett had no idea what Lacy was talking about. All he knew was he had to get her to put the gun down.

"Lacy, I don't want you to get hurt. Do you see the officers in the room? They think you are going to shoot them or me."

"Jarrett, no. I would never hurt you."

"I know, Lacy, but the officers don't know that. Will you give me the gun?"

"No, Jarrett, she's playing you for a fool." She turned back to where Paige lay on the floor. "She has to pay."

"If you hurt her, you will be hurting me, Lacy," he said as he continued to walk around her to get closer to Paige.

"I don't want to hurt you, Jarrett."

"Then please, Lacy, give me the gun." He was now standing between her and Paige. He looked over her shoulder to see the officers approaching her from behind. She glanced back and in that split second multiple shots rang out as Jarrett yelled, "NO!"

CHAPTER TWENTY

The sun was rising as the double doors to the emergency room burst open. "Gunshot victim, female...." the EMT's voice trailed off as they rushed the gurney into the trauma room.

Another gurney burst through the door. "Unconscious female," another EMT called out vitals as the gurney was pushed into another trauma room.

Sanders rushed in with officers. "I want two guards on trauma room 1 and a guard on the second room." He then turned to see Jarrett standing to the side as emergency room personnel began working on Paige. The woman was alive. He looked upwards giving thanks above.

Ron and Sergio ran through the doors.

"How is Paige?" Sergio asked.

"Still alive," Sanders replied.

"And Lacy?" Ron asked.

Sanders shook his head. "Not looking good, but she is still breathing."

Sergio pulled out his phone and dialed a number. "Nick, we found Paige."

"She wasn't the dead body they found?" he asked.

"No." Sergio heard Nick call out to Horace. "It's not Paige. Paige is alive. Where are you, Sergio?" he said into the phone.

"We're at Manhattan First on the upper east side."

"We'll be right there."

"Hey, Nick, there's a lot going on. You're going to need security. I'll fill you in when you get here."

A group of ten reporters burst through the doors. Cameras and microphones were pushed into Ron and Sergio's faces.

"Why did Bryson leave the game in a hurry?"

"Who's in the emergency room?"

"Does this have anything to do with the body found earlier tonight?"

The questions kept coming. Sanders pulled two officers and ordered them to push the press back out the door. He then asked the head nurse, who was trying to keep order, to call the hospital administrator.

"Already done," she called out.

Sanders pulled Ron and Sergio away from the crowd.

"This is going to be a media disaster," Ron huffed.

"Yeah, and we have your wife to thank for it." Sergio gave Ron a look. "What are you going to do about it?"

Ron put his hands on his hips and exhaled.

*****

Thirty minutes later Jarrett was taken to a private waiting room. Horace and Eleanor jumped up immediately.

"Paige? Where's Paige?" Eleanor cried with Horace at her side.

"Paige is alive. She is still unconscious, but she is alive." Jarrett wanted to reassure her parents. "They are doing a scan to assess the extent of the brain damage, if any." Eleanor fell into her husband's chest, thankful.

"Can we see her?" Horace asked.

Jarrett shook his head. "They are still running tests. That's why they put me out."

Horace nodded. "Thank you, Jarrett. Thank you for finding her."

Eleanor reached out and hugged him, doing all she could to reassure him all was well. Jarrett stepped out of her embrace, then smiled at Ophelia, who was sitting quietly by the door.

"You were right. Suzette was the key to finding Paige." He kissed her. "Thank you for being the wise woman you are."

"You would have figured it out, son." Ophelia touched his cheek. "You would have figured it out."

His parents stood. His mother opened her arms and Jarrett walked right into them.

Connie held her son, giving him all the love and encouragement only a mother could give. "We were so worried about you."

His father patted him on the shoulder. "What happened, son?"

Jarrett relayed the events of the night to his parents. While he spoke, Victoria ran into the room.

"How is she?" she asked looking like she had spent the night in jail.

"She's alive," Sergio replied.

An audible cry of relief sounded around the room. Sergio reached for her. Victoria swung at him.

"Don't you talk to me. You left me in jail all night."

"You beat a woman to within an inch of her life."

"That woman attacked me. What did you think I was going to do, play with her?"

"How did you get out?" Sergio asked.

"No thanks to you, some Detective Sanders had me released and told me to come here."

Eleanor stood. "Paige is holding her own, Victoria. Why don't we get you home so you can change, get some rest and then come back when Paige wakes up."

"I think that's a good idea." Horace turned to Ophelia. "You need to get some rest too."

"You two go on. I'll stay here with Paige until you return."

Horace nodded, then walked over to Jarrett. "Son, you've had a hell of a night. Is there anything I can do for you?"

"Take my parents back to my place. I'll stay here."

Horace nodded. "I'll bring you a change of clothes when I return. Call me if anything changes."

*****

"How's Paige?" Nick asked as he walked back into the private waiting room after dealing with the press.

"No change. I spoke with the doctors. They think it's just a matter of when she wants to open her eyes now. The tests came back negative for any serious damage."

The anxiety of the last twenty four hours had Jarrett on edge. With Paige still unconscious and Lacy's fate unknown, the guilt was eating him alive. All of this happened because of him.

"Don't do that," Nick said as he handed him a cup of coffee. "Don't blame yourself for this."

Jarrett took the cup, then exhaled. "Paige hasn't awakened. She has no idea why any of this happened to her. I feel like I should have seen it coming."

"How?" Nick asked. "You could no more see this coming than I could see the plane crash I was in. Do you remember what you told me when you visited me in the hospital?"

"Nick, really?" Jarrett gave him an incredulous look.

"This is important. You said, only you can be in a plane crash and come out alive. Appreciate the moment and live the rest of your life with no regrets."

"I said that?"

"You did." Nick nodded. "I thought it was pretty deep even for you."

Jarrett smiled. "That was pretty deep." He took a sip of coffee. "What in the hell does that have to do with what's happening with me?"

"I'm glad you asked. This was your plane crash. Don't question what could have been...it's a waste of time. Appreciate the outcome and use that time to be with Paige."

The loud snores of Sergio filled the private waiting room. The two men looked over to see Sergio asleep on the sofa.

"This has been a hell of a night," Jarrett sighed.

"You took your team to the World Series. Lacy lost her mind. Paige is fighting to come back to us and Victoria captured a killer." Nick inhaled. "Only you, Jarrett Bryson...only you."

"Yeah, Victoria whipped that ass of a killer."

Jarrett and Nick thought for a long moment then suddenly fell out laughing uncontrollably. Just as suddenly, they both sobered.

"What are you going to do about Suzette Mackenzie?" Nick glanced at Jarrett.

It took Jarrett a moment to respond. The vein in the side of his neck looked like it was about to explode. The woman who set the chain of events in motion, was considered one of his closest friends a few months ago.

"To think all of this is over a television show is just unreal to me. Lacy is fighting for her life because Suzette used her as a pawn in her plans." The anger was seeping out with each word.

"You mentioned earlier something about Ophelia owning the Knights. Are you sure about that?"

Jarrett shrugged his shoulders. "Lacy was ranting about it. I have no idea what that was all about."

"It is possible. There are silent owners," Nick said. "We know Ruben Caswell owned the team."

"He is one of the owners."

"Yes. Is it possible Ophelia Hylton is one of the silent owners?"

Jarrett and Nick stared at each other.

"There is only one way to find out." Jarrett stood, then walked into Paige's room.

*****

"Is it true?" Jarrett asked. "Are you one of the owners of the Knights?"

Ophelia sat beside Paige's bed. She didn't bother to turn when she heard the voice. The conversation needed to be had. It had been five years ago when she made the decision to change Jarrett Bryson's life. It was time.

"I met Edward Hylton during a Knights baseball game. I was cleaning a bathroom stall when he walked in." She smiled at the memory. "Lord, he had to pee so badly, he ignored the closed sign and walked right in. For a while he danced in the middle of the floor, shocked to see me there cleaning. He said, excuse me, ma'am, I really need to go.' Well that surprised me on two fronts. He called me ma'am and waited for me to leave before he relieved himself."

Jarrett took a seat next to her and listened as they both watched Paige for signs of movement.

"Back then, the tone of your skin color mattered. The light skin of my ancestors opened a few doors for me. You see, instead of cleaning the urinals in the common areas of the lower seats, I was assigned to the VIP urinals. One would laugh, what an honor, but you see to this day I thank the powers that be for it's how I found true love."

Jarrett smiled.

"He would accidentally keep running into me in that same restroom, at just about the same time, when there were day games. I didn't work at night. I can't tell you how many times I told that man no, when he asked me to have dinner with him. He eventually wore me down. Promised me no one would know. He sent a car to pick me up. Had me delivered to his front door. That was when I knew he was serious. Any other man would have had me taken to the back door and sneaked in. Not Edward. When I asked him why, he said a queen should be revered, not hidden in the back somewhere. I was a goner then. No one would have ever thought a White man could love a Black woman, but my Edward did. We married in his home, with only my mother and his parents as witnesses. You see, back then if you had money you could keep your life private. While all knew Edward was married, they did not know his wife was Black. We didn't have all that Internet foolishness. We just had cameras with film that had to be developed. By the time that happened, whatever they had pictures of, was old news." She laughed then continued.

"Edward loved baseball. He loved the game, the atmosphere of the stadium and the idea of it being the all American game. The Knights held a special place in his heart from the moment he met me. There was no other team for him after that. When financial troubles began for the team, it was my Edward who bailed them out. Other teams were still digging themselves out of the hole, while the Knights seemed to have an unending bank account. He was granted 51% of the team. He didn't want or need the publicity so he became and remained a silent partner of the Knights. He never interfered with daily operations or negotiations, but he stayed on top of things until the day he died. On that day, we talked and laughed as much as we could. The cancer was eating him alive you know. They didn't have the comforts that they do now to help with the pain. My Edward suffered, but I kept laughter in his life those last days. Anyway," she exhaled.

"That last day he told me to keep love and laughter in my heart. Teach Eleanor to love without blinders." She laughed. "The last thing was to not let his baseball team get in the wrong hands. Wait for the right man to turn it over to. I told him that was sexist, it could be a woman. He said only if that woman is you. You understand the joy of the game, the importance of integrity, and the love of a well-earned win. The league had changed a lot by then, and a number of owners tried to pressure me into selling Edward's shares. I'll never forget the day they tried to challenge my marriage because they could not believe Edward had married a colored woman. Well, my Edward must have been a mind reader. He had the top attorneys in the country handling his affairs. There was nothing those owners could do to take the Knights away from me. Ruben's father was the only one who stood up to the group of owners. They shunned him, Lord they shunned him. But it didn't matter. I made sure Ruben had whatever he needed to keep that team thriving. You see, Edward left me a very wealthy woman. To this day they tell me I'm one of the top ten wealthiest people in the world. I don't keep up with it because I don't care. I care about the love of my family. It was young Ruben who brought you to my attention. You were young, playing high school ball, but there was something about you that captured young Ruben's eyes. He asked me to come see one of your games and I did. I had Horace, Eleanor and Paige with me when your team won the state championship. You won the MVP that day. When you stepped up to the podium, you said, there is something about the integrity and the pureness of the game of baseball that summons you."

Jarrett nodded his head remembering the day. "It takes a genuine love of the game and pure athletic ability to play through the cold and heat for months. May the integrity of the game of baseball live on."

Ophelia nodded her head and smiled. "I've been watching you since then. You love this game. It's not about the money, or fame for you. You simply love the game. When the Knights drafted you, I had an amendment made to my will. While everything else will go to my family, the ownership of the Knights goes to you."

Jarrett's head snapped up. "You did what?"

"When I close my eyes, you become the majority owner of the Knights. Ruben is the only person in the organization who knows."

"Ruben Caswell knows this?"

"Yes, he does. He's known for a while."

"Does Paige know this?"

"No, her father knows, because he is one of my attorneys. But no one else knows."

Lacy's words came back to him. *They used you to run her team.* "Did you encourage Paige to be with me?"

"Of course I did. You're a good man."

"No." Jarrett stood then walked around to face her. "Did you set it up for us to meet?"

"Yes."

"You tried to buy me with your granddaughter?"

"No." Ophelia was trying to understand how he came to that conclusion. "You can't buy anyone's love, Jarrett. I knew you were going to be on that plane. I made sure Paige was there too. What happened next between you two, I had nothing to do with."

"But you did. You set it all up just as Lacy said."

There was a knock at the door. "Mr. Bryson, you asked to be informed when Ms. Dupree was out of surgery."

Jarrett's eyes hardened as he glared at Ophelia. "Yes, I did," he said then walked out of the room.

Paige could feel Jarrett's anger. But she could also feel her grandmother's fear for her. She hadn't heard the entire story, but she did hear what her Grand'Mere said about the will. Jarrett was a proud man. It would kill him if the world thought he was with her because her grandmother owned the Knights. That would make him a man bought and paid for by the front office. It was a distinction he would have a difficult time living with.

"The heartbreak begins," Paige murmured.

"Paige." Her grandmother stood next to her bed. "Paige, are you awake?"

"Yes, Grand'Mere, I'm awake," she replied but did not move. "Will he forgive me?"

Tears filled Ophelia's eyes. "There is nothing for him to forgive. You had no part in this." She pushed Paige's hair away from her face.

"It's going to take him a while to see that."

"Yes, but he will see the rightness of you and him." She kissed her temple. "For now, you, my darling, remember to love him as if that is all that matters in this world."

"That will be easy, for it's true. Jarrett is all that matters." Paige closed her eyes then traveled back into the darkness in the recesses of her mind. She wasn't ready to deal with the heartbreak.

CHAPTER TWENTY-ONE

Jarrett had been sitting by Paige's side for the last twenty-four hours. She hadn't moved. The doctors were concerned. Her vitals were good, but she just hadn't opened her eyes. Her parents left the hospital around midnight, but Jarrett didn't want to leave.

The media was wild with the stories of that night. Many were supportive of him and Paige, but somewhere along the way Suzette's involvement in the situation came to light. She took to the airwaves as a way to clear her good name, as she told the reporters. She told the media that Ophelia Hylton, Paige Cartwright's grandmother, is the majority owner of the Knights. When she discovered that the family was conspiring to make Jarrett a permanent part of the team by marrying her granddaughter, Ophelia threatened to trade Ron and force them out of New York. That generated a media frenzy for the front office. In a way he was glad Paige wasn't awake to have to deal with the negative press that was directed at her. The PR firm hired by the front office had dispensed of the conspiracy story fabricated by Suzette. Contrary to what Suzette thought would happen, the public began to turn on her, as did Ron. Last time he and Ron had talked, Ron was sleeping in the guest room.

There was a bright spot in all the drama from that night. Victoria had been given the lead in the European tour. Even if Paige opened her eyes today, the doctors would not release her to go back to work until well after the holidays. Jolene had been charged with the murder of Carin Tomey. It was funny how the two major events of that night had only one connection. Jealousy and a chance at the limelight were at the core of both. *Everybody wants to shine,* Jarrett thought, as he opened his eyes. He needed to get away from it all.

He checked his watch. It was almost three in the morning. He pushed the blanket aside and walked over to the bed. The area on her face where Paige had been hit, was now turning blue. It was not as red as it had been. She still looked pale, almost ghost like to him. He pushed her hair away from her face. His finger traced her profile. She wasn't cold, but the warm fuzzy feeling he always felt was missing. Thoughts of his conversation with Ophelia came to his mind. He pulled his hand away. *She's making a fool out of you* were Lacy's words. He closed his eyes willing the doubt that was seeping into his heart to go away. He opened his eyes, then looked out the window. He blinked. Yes, it was lightly snowing.

It's a spark of magic.

He jerked around thinking he would see her eyes open. They weren't, but he knew it was her voice he heard. The same thing happened the night he found her. He walked back over to the side of the bed. He took her hand.

"Paige, open your eyes for me."

Nothing.

He tried again. "Paige, you can hear me. Please open your eyes."

Her hands tightened around his. "Paige," he called her again.

Her eyes blinked.

He turned the bedside light on.

"No." She closed her eyes as if in pain.

"The light?" He turned it off. "I'm sorry. Paige, it's off." He pushed the button for the nurse.

The pain shot through her like a knife to her eye. It was such a shock to her system she screamed out.

The nurse ran into the room.

Jarrett stepped aside. "She opened her eyes. I turned on the light, but she screamed out in pain. Is she okay?"

"Step outside. Let me look her over."

Jarrett reluctantly stepped outside. He pulled out his phone to call Horace. "Sorry to wake you. Paige is awake. She opened her eyes." He didn't know until the moment he said it, just how relieved he was. "Yes," he replied to something her father said as tears streamed down his face.

"Everything okay, Mr. Bryson?" Peace asked from the chair outside the door.

Jarrett quickly wiped his face. "Yes, Paige just opened her eyes."

The elevator chimed. A few people stepped off. They all ran into Paige's room. "Something's wrong." He hung up the phone. He walked to the door and looked inside. They were leaning over her with a light. He heard her call his name.

He ran inside. "I'm right here Paige," he called out from behind the people around her.

"Jarrett," she cried out again. "I need to see Jarrett."

He ran to the bed and took her hand. "I'm right here."

She turned her head towards him. She blinked twice, then he came into view. She began to cry. He gathered her into his arms.

"I thought she shot you."

"No." He held her tight and rocked her until she settled down.

"We need to finish examining her."

"Please don't leave, please," she begged.

"I'm not leaving. I'm going to stay right here while they examine you."

*****

As it turned out Paige was sensitive to light. Later in the day she was able to tolerate it with dark sunshades.

That was an easy fix. What wasn't easy was the uneasiness that had developed between her and Jarrett. Oh he said all the right things. Did the right things, sent flowers, visited each day, even stayed each night he was in town; made sure she had everything she needed. That was everything except him. While family and friends were around, he was perfect. Once they were alone, the conversations turned polite.

"Jarrett, tell me what happened?" she asked once.

"Not now, let's talk about it when you are better."

That was it. Paige received most of what happened that night from Sergio and Victoria when they visited. The piece she was missing was what actually happened inside that warehouse. The detective did not want to taint her memory in case there was a trial.

The only other people who knew were Jarrett and Lacy. Neither of them was talking.

The nights he was at away games he would call and she would end each call the same way. "Enjoy the game." Afterward Paige would hang up the phone and cry. The only excitement was that the Knights were up in the series three games to one.

"Okay, enough is enough." Victoria threw the paper across the bed. "I knew he was going to eventually hurt you."

"What is it?"

"The general consensus on the internet is that you, like every other woman in the world, were attempting to trap Jarrett."

"It's not him, Vic."

"No, he's not saying it. In fact, he's not saying anything to the press. He's not standing up for you."

"He has never been a press person, you know that," Paige defended him.

"Jarrett needs to step outside himself and think about how all of this is impacting you. I'm worried about you."

"What I'm going through is not his fault. It's everything that's happened in the last month. It's you leaving. It's my chance at proving I made the right decision to dance being taken away. It's Jolene, Carin and Suzette. It's like my life is not my own," she cried. "I don't feel a song in my heart."

Victoria hugged her friend. "Look, I'm not leaving for a few days. Why don't I bust you out of here? We can go to the park and just sit if you like." Angry tears were filling her eyes. This just wasn't right. This gentle heart was hurting through no fault of her own. The only thing Paige had ever done was try to bring smiles and joy to every person she met. While people like Jolene and Suzette got away with murder.

One Spark of Magic 219

Paige put a smile on her face as she wiped away the tears escaping from beneath the rim of her glasses. "My Grand'Mere wants me to recuperate at home."

"Good heads up. I'll clean the place."

"I'm going to Virginia."

Victoria pulled away and assessed her friend. "Oh, have you told Jarrett?"

"No. Their plane is coming in tonight after the game. I'll stop by his place before I leave."

"You're going to tell him before the game tomorrow?"

She nodded. "We're flying out before the game. I want to tell him in person."

"How long are you going to be gone?

"Until I feel a song in my heart again."

*****

The elevator to Jarrett's apartment opened. He stepped out, dropping his bag next to the door. It was well after midnight as he spoke on the phone with his mother.

"I can't. I want to go see Paige tonight. I'm going to grab a shower then go to the hospital."

"Jarrett, honey, you need to get some sleep. I'm sure Paige is fine. I spoke to her earlier today."

"I slept on the plane. Mother, stop worrying. I'll sleep once the series is over and I know Paige is okay."

"Have you told her about Florida?"

"No, I haven't told her yet," he said as he took a bottle of water out of the refrigerator, opened it then took a drink. He turned to see Paige standing in the hallway.

"Mother, let me call you back."

"Paige." He walked over and hugged her. "What are you doing here? Should you be up?"

"I'm fine." She forced a smile on her face. "How are you?"

He took a step back, somewhat confused by her question. "I'm good."

"Are you? What happened at the game last night?'

"We won." He glanced away from her. "Live to fight another day." He took her hand. "I'd feel better if you were sitting." He took her hand and guided her to the sofa.

"When was the last time you slept?"

He smiled. "My mother just asked me the same question. I slept on the plane."

Paige nodded. "Jarrett, tell me about that night. I know bits and pieces, but I don't know what happened inside the room."

He sighed, then stood. "It's better to wait."

Paige turned away. "Do you feel it?"

"What?"

"The tension in the air. It's all around us. You don't feel it?"

Jarrett knew, he'd been feeling it since that night.

"This isn't us, Jarrett." She inhaled. "You know my Grand'Mere..."

Jarrett turned away. "I don't want to hear what your Grand'Mere has to say right now, Paige."

Paige inhaled and stood. "All right." She inhaled. "Then let's talk about Lacy."

"Paige, not now." His voice was a little rougher than he intended. "We shouldn't, not now. We'll talk after you are better."

"Will we? If we don't air out what's inside your soul, you will never be free. Which will impact my soul. Until we do, the healing process will not begin."

"Paige." He turned away in frustration.

"Jarrett, you are not responsible for her death and neither am I."

He jerked back around. "I don't blame you, Paige." He reached out to her, but she stepped back.

She shook her head. "You would never say it. But it's in the room, in every look, in the way you don't touch me. It's there in everything you do. Being here, at this moment, it feels like you're talking to me out of guilt not love."

"What do you want from me, Paige? You weren't the only one impacted by that night. I'm still trying to work through all that happened. Lacy died trying to protect me in her own way."

Paige inhaled from the blow she'd just received. "From me?" She spoke softly. "Since I was the person she threatened to kill, I can only surmise, it was me she was trying to protect you from." She looked directly into his eyes. "Please tell me how I was a threat?"

"Paige, let's not."

She couldn't let it go. They had to have the conversation no matter how much it hurt. "How was I a threat? What did she say?"

Jarrett was tired. He hadn't been to sleep since she was taken from him. She was right and he couldn't deny Lacy was between them. It wasn't about her death, though he did feel guilty; but he held Suzette responsible for all that happened. What concerned him was exactly where Paige was heading in her sweet elegant way.

"Lacy believed you didn't love me. She was told you and I were setup by your Grand'Mere."

"And you, Jarrett. What do you think?"

"I don't know what to think." The anger was more apparent now. "Your Grand'Mere admitted she knew I was on that flight to Virginia. She insisted you catch that plane that day. You told me that yourself. All of it was her doing for whatever reason. It's just like every other woman who put together schemes to be with me."

"God must hold you in high favor to be loved by so many."

"That's not the point, Paige. You came into my life under false pretenses. I have to believe you weren't a part of that. I have to believe that."

There it was. That's what he was struggling with. She knew there was nothing she could do or say to get him to believe her love was real. All she could do was state her claim and let him come to his own conclusions.

"That is how we met." She nodded trying hard to keep the tears at bay. "What about the rest? The question you need to ask yourself is do you believe the love I shared with you was faked. That would make me a very good actress. I would say I went far and above the call of duty by sharing myself with you." She smiled as she removed her glasses to wipe the tears that were now flowing freely.

"As much as it breaks my heart that you would question that, I feel sadder for you for not being able to tell the difference."

"Paige, I just need time to work everything out in my mind." He exhaled.

She nodded her head as she put her glasses back on. "I understand. You are a very proud man, Jarrett. You think my Grand'Mere is manipulating you in some way. What a devil she must be to want you in the front office or to have put me in your life."

"That's not it, Paige."

"That's how I see it." She stepped closer to him. "Time is precious." Her lips trembled as she spoke, but she had to get it out. "You can savor it by forgiving quickly and loving longer. It gives you more time for nice slow kisses." She kissed him on the cheek. Then walked towards the elevator.

"Paige, it's late. Where are you going?"

"I'm going home with my parents," she said as tears streamed down. "You're going to win tomorrow. It will be the last game of the season. Enjoy the game and stay off that first pitch." She pointed at him teasingly. She hit the down button, then looked up. "Goodbye, Jarrett."

He felt his heart breaking as the elevator doors closed. His heart wanted to go after her, but his feet wouldn't move.

*****

Paige's prediction was dead on. The next day the Knights won the World Series. The town and the team were celebrating the victory. The media was in full force. Champagne was overflowing around the locker room and Jarrett was doing one interview after another. Whenever the question of Paige and that night came up, he gave his patent answer, "We are blessed. She's healing." Then he would politely change the subject.

The celebration didn't end until the next morning. By the time he made it to his place, the sun was rising. He laid across the bed and slept.

*****

Who in the hell was at the door? The front desk hadn't called up. There was a knock again.

"I'm coming," Victoria yelled out. "It's eight in the morning, most people are asleep." She yanked the door open. "Serg. What are you doing here?" She pulled him inside. "Congratulations." She hugged him.

"It's been crazy all night. I haven't been to sleep. Man, it's been wild." He was beaming.

"I bet. You want some coffee?"

"Yes," he declared in desperation. He followed her into the kitchen. "What time are you leaving for the airport?"

"The troupe is meeting at the theater at eleven," she said as she pulled cups out and turned the coffee machine on.

"Are you packed?"

"I've been packed for a week."

"Excited huh?" He smiled.

"Yes," she said with excitement. "The only thing that could have made this better is if Paige was still going."

"Yeah. That's a bummer. But if she was going, you wouldn't have the lead."

"You know, she is the one person I would have no problem giving it up for."

"What happened to her was just bad luck. Now, with Jarrett leaving, I'm afraid they won't work things out."

"Jarrett is leaving?"

"Yes, he's leaving for Florida today. And get this, Ron's going with him."

"What? He's leaving Suzette?"

"No. He will never do that. But he's going to give her something to think about for a few weeks."

"Well, I don't want to see anyone split up but all of this happened to Paige because of her. Lacy Dupree is dead because of her," she said as she put a cup of coffee in front of him "It would serve her right if he left her for good. Since he's not, it's still going to sting, him leaving right at the holidays. Will he be back before Thanksgiving?"

"That's two weeks away. What can I say? He loves her and funny as it may sound I believe she loves him too. As for me, I will have the pleasure of being the wing man to the two brooding lovesick men while in Florida, the land of white beaches and women with too few clothes on."

"I'm sure you will find a way to enjoy yourself. In the meantime try to remind Jarrett what he has. Paige was the one who was kidnapped and almost killed, all because she fell in love with him. She can't help that her Grand'Mere owns the team. Like that's such a bad thing."

'To Jarrett it is. All through the series, players were calling him a bought man."

"Bought by who?" She sipped from her cup.

"The front office. Now that it's out that Paige is an owner's granddaughter, he's being treated differently."

"That's just stupid."

"I agree, Jarrett is a good guy who is hurting. He loves Paige, I have no doubt about that. But his pride, and to some extent, he feels his integrity is in question."

"When your pride is bigger than your heart you are destined to live your life alone."

"You sound like Paige."

"Yeah, well I think some of her sweetness is rubbing off on me."

"It certainly rubbed off on Jarrett. You should have seen him with the ring."

"Ring?" Victoria sat up. "What ring?"

Sergio sat his cup down. "Holy crap, he never got a chance to give it to her. All hell broke out that night."

"Jarrett brought Paige a ring? Is it an engagement ring?"

"Seven figures. Had it specially made for her."

"Oh my God. How do we get them back to that point?"

*****

Ron walked back into the bedroom. "I told you, after my obligations to the team I was leaving. The parade was yesterday. You've had your fifteen minutes of fame."

"You can't do this, Ron. What am I supposed to tell everybody? How is this going to look to people?" Suzette screamed.

"That's the problem, Suzette. You are more concerned with people, not your family or me. You jeopardized my career, our livelihood, over a maybe reality show. You played with someone's life. All so that you could be in the spotlight. Being my wife and a mother wasn't enough for you. You put a woman's life in jeopardy because she was blocking your way. Your friend, if that's what she ever was, you used her and she died." He picked up his packed bag. "I'm leaving before I get in the way of something you want and you have me killed."

"Ron, don't you walk out that door," Suzette screamed.

Sergio was waiting in the car when the door swung open. Ron came out, then Suzette ran out behind him. She didn't look happy.

"Where are you going?" she screamed.

"Away from you." Ron put his bag in the back.

"Ron, don't do this," she cried out.

"You didn't tell her where you were going?" Sergio asked as Ron climbed in.

"No, let her wonder for a while. She tore Jarrett's life apart. The least I can do is help him put it back together."

The driver pulled off.

Sergio nodded in agreement. "Did you know he got a ring for Paige?"

"No, when?"

"The same day she went missing. I don't think he ever had the chance to ask her."

"Damn, man, we got to make this right."

*****

Jarrett walked along the strip of private beach connected to his property. Ron and Sergio had made the trip with him. They were a week in and there were times when he wished the guys were gone, and others when he would have gone crazy without them. Not a day passed without Paige entering his mind. They hadn't talked much since the night she left his place. A text here and there, just to see how the other was doing. So many times when he heard her voice he could hear the hurt. Knowing he had caused it didn't help, so the calls turned into text messages.

This was the time for all of the Knights to bask in the media celebration of their accomplishment, but for him, that was difficult. They had won the World Series, yet with every mention of his name, Lacy Dupree and Paige Cartwright were mentioned. The fact that Paige's grandmother owned the Knights, raised questions as to whether or not Jarrett had been receiving preferential treatment during contract negotiations in the past. The commentators were speculating whether all the publicity had been sent in his direction to help build his off field endorsements. It was as if everyone had forgotten about his ten years of living right, staying clear of controversy and negativity. Now, for all of that to be in question, was more than he could take.

He reached inside his pocket and pulled out the small object he had been fumbling around with each time he took a walk. The diamond sparkled at him even in the daylight. It was a symbol of all that had happened because he opened his heart. It was time for him to close it out. This chapter had to end. He threw the ring into the ocean then walked back into his house.

*****

The morning started with a phone call from Nick. "The front office is ready to talk. Are you ready?"

"You're the agent. Are we?"

"As your agent, I think we should have a sit down before we set a date with them. I'm at the airport. Ask Sergio to stick around, I have a few things to discuss with him."

"Will do," Jarrett replied as he disconnected the call. He looked around the multi-million dollar home that he'd built planning to fill it with a family. He walked to the media room to find Sergio.

"Hey," he called out.

They turned to him and quickly turned the newscast off.

"Hey, what's up? Sergio replied.

"Nick is on his way here. We're going to start negotiations with the front office and he wants to talk to you too."

"Did he mention me?" Ron asked.

"No." Jarrett walked into the room taking one of the seats and putting his feet up. "He's not your agent." Jarrett grabbed the remote. "Why would he want to talk to you?"

Serg and Ron glanced at each other, then back to Jarrett.

"Give." Jarrett looked at the two suspiciously.

"There are rumors of a trade involving Ron."

Jarrett sat up. "You're joking?"

"Afraid not." Ron walked over to the bar and fixed himself a drink. "Looks like old lady Hylton is sticking to her word."

"What are you talking about?"

"Ron didn't tell you?"

"Tell me what?"

Sergio laughed. "You're going to love this." He shrugged at Ron. "Tell him."

"Tell me what?"

Ron chuckled. "Another disaster of my wife's making." He sat with his drink. "According to Suzette, Ophelia Hylton threatened to trade me if she did one more thing to interfere with you and Paige. That's when she decided to use Lacy to get back at Paige."

Jarrett sat there just staring at him in disbelief. If either of them knew the telltale signs, they wouldn't have said what came out next, not even in joking.

"Since you have a connection to the front office, you think you can work something out for him," Sergio laughed.

A second later, Ron and Sergio were jumping out of their seats. The table their feet had been resting on, went flying across the room, crashing into the television they had just been admiring. The screen shattered as did the table.

"Jarrett!" Ron yelled. "What the hell?"

"Will that damn night never end?" All the anger Jarrett had been keeping inside suddenly exploded. "She's dead. Lacy is dead. Paige is lost to me forever, and you're telling me now the Knights are impacted too. What in the hell is wrong with your wife? Why didn't she just leave Paige alone? Why?"

Nick walked in. "Your front door was open. What do we have here?" He looked around at the damage to the room.

"Jarrett had a human moment," Ron replied as he fixed a drink.

Nick had seen worse from clients. Frankly he was happy to see Jarrett releasing some of that pent up anger he'd been carrying since that night. Only a few people knew he'd planned to win the playoff game, propose to Paige and marry her on Christmas Eve. The night was supposed to be special and it ended up being the night from hell.

"Gentlemen, will you give Jarrett and me the room?"

"Sure," Sergio replied for both of them.

Jarrett held up his hand, as he shook his head. "I'm okay. Just another blow from that night."

Nick went behind the bar, poured Jarrett a drink and one for himself.

"It's the gift that keeps on giving." He smiled.

"Humph, that's one way to look at it."

"What bombshell brought this on?" Nick pointed around the room. They took a seat at the bar.

"Ophelia Hylton threatened to have Ron traded if his wife interfered in her plans for me and Paige."

Nick shrugged. "Does he have a 'do not trade' clause in his contract?"

Jarrett glared at him. "I don't know."

"Ask him. If not, it's an easy fix. As for Mrs. Hylton, she didn't have plans for you and Paige. She had plans for you." He took a drink. "Speaking of that, I've been thinking on this since you told me. From what I gather, she admires your integrity for the game so much so that she wants to entrust you with her team. Explain to me what is so wrong with that?"

"She tried to manipulate me."

"I see." He cleared his throat. "Have I ever told you how I met my wife?"

Jarrett shook his head. "Ericka? No."

"It's actually a funny story if you were on the outside looking in."

"Nick, I don't mean any disrespect but listening to a love story is not what I need right now."

"Would it change your mind to know I was a mark?"

"A what?"

"Ericka was a con artist who was hired to con me out of a good deal of money."

Jarrett raised an eyebrow. "Ericka is a con artist?"

"Was," Nick corrected.

"Did she succeed?"

"Yes, in fact, she did."

"Why did you marry her?"

"I fell in love with her. You see, I believe when you are blessed with the gift of love, and believe me it is a blessing, you get down on your knees and thank God every minute of the day. It doesn't matter how that love comes into your life. If you are one of the lucky ones, you grab it and hold on to it for dear life."

"It's not that simple."

"Do you love her? Wait, don't answer that. Answer this for yourself." He turned to look at his friend. "Have you ever heard her voice in your mind so clearly that you turn to see if she's in the room? If your answer is yes, you are wasting time. If that night did not teach you anything, it should have taught you that life is short. Paige could have been the one who did not open her eyes."

*****

That night Jarrett called Ophelia Hylton. "Mrs. Hylton, it's Jarrett Bryson."

"How are you, son?"

"I've had better days." There was silence. "I miss her."

Ophelia exhaled. "She misses you."

"I'm angry at you for putting us in this situation."

"I'll take the blame for putting you and Paige on that plane, son. However, my responsibility ends there."

"Did you threaten to trade Ron Mackenzie?"

"I did and would have, to get his wife out of the Knights' organization. You don't keep a rat once you trap it."

Jarrett smiled. "You sound like Paige."

"No, darling, Paige sounds like me." Silence again. "You're young and have so much ahead of you. What I did wasn't done to harm you or manipulate you as the news reports indicate. I gave you two of my most valued gifts, my husband's team and the love of my granddaughter. It was done because I believe you are a good man. One who will keep the team honest and love Paige like my Edward loved me. Take my advice. Live this life with as much laughter as possible and find a love that lasts for an eternity. Jarrett, you love Paige. Paige loves you. Everything else is noise."

"I do love her, but, there is a lot of noise."

"Well, darling, put on some earplugs and tell the world to go to hell."

Jarrett laughed. It seemed like it had been ages since he laughed. It felt good.

"There's something I need you to answer for me." He sobered. "The night Paige and I made love, how did you know?"

Ophelia laughed. "Victoria told me you had spent the night. What? Do you think I can read minds?"

The two laughed.

"You get one spark of magic. Paige is yours. Now let's talk baseball."

*****

The next morning, after talking with Ophelia most of the night, there were a number of decisions Jarrett had to make. Taking his morning walk on the beach, Paige filled his mind. He wanted her in his life. Not partially, or as a girlfriend, he wanted her as his wife. He didn't care about the talk on the internet or talk shows. He was in love with Paige. Part of the reason for the negative vibe she was getting was because he did not stand by her when the story broke about the ownership of the Knights. He allowed his pride to interfere with their lives. It was time to change that. It was time to go get his woman. The decision made him feel free. He had no idea why, but he took off his flip flops and threw them in the air to celebrate. A wave came in and took them away. He laughed.

"That was stupid." He stepped back to avoid the next wave and stepped on something hard in the sand.

"Ouch, damn it."

He picked up the item with the intention of throwing it all the way to Cuba if he could. But, he stopped. He could not believe what was in his hand. He blinked again, then chuckled. He dropped to the sand and laughed. It was the only thing he could do.

He walked back into the house.

"Where is Ron?" he asked Sergio who was sitting at the kitchen table eating.

"He's in his room still moping about Suzette. We have to fix that. "

"We are going to take him home."

"When?"

"Now. I'm taking Ron back to his wife, then I'm going to get Paige."

"Well it's about damn time."

CHAPTER TWENTY-TWO

"Judge Cartwright." His clerk stood in the doorway to his office. "You have a visitor." The usually unexcitable clerk was damn near giddy.

Horace stared at the young woman, a bit agitated by her demeanor. "Are you going to tell me who it is?"

"Yes," she exclaimed, then walked in and closed the door.

Horace raised one eyebrow. "Well?"

"It's Jarrett Bryson....The Jarrett Bryson."

Horace was somewhat surprised. Jarrett had called to check on them and on Paige's progress over the last month, but had not indicated he was coming for a visit.

"Will you show him in?"

"Sir, would it be inappropriate to ask for his autograph and a picture?"

"Yes."

"Oh." She settled down. "Yes, sir, I would just like to say he is so fine," she squealed.

"Casey, let the man in."

"Yes, sir." She stood, exhaled, then composed herself. She opened the door. "Mr. Bryson, Judge Cartwright will see you now."

Horace was relieved to see she was back to the promising, reserved clerk he had hired.

"Hello, Jarrett." Horace stood and extended his hand. "It's good to see you, son."

Jarrett extended his hand. "Thank you, it's good to be here."

"I would prefer that your visit was at the house. There is someone there who needs to see you."

"Yes, sir. I know. I need to see her as well."

"Have a seat." Horace pointed to a chair in front of his desk.

"I prefer to stand for this first part."

Horace noticed the nervousness in his stance. It stood out in such a confident man. "Very well," he said, then listened.

"Judge Cartwright, I want to marry once in my lifetime. I love your daughter and would love to have your permission to marry her."

Horace sat back. His heart filled with relief. "Let me think on that. How do you plan to support my child? She's spoiled you know."

Jarrett laughed, "Yes sir, I know and I promise to spoil her with the same love you do."

"Well, then you have my permission."

Jarrett exhaled. "Thank you, sir." He smiled. "There's a few things I need to do before I ask Paige." He took off his coat, then took a seat. "I spoke with Grand'Mere at length last night. She advised me you are her counsel on all matters concerning her will."

"I am," Horace acknowledged.

"That surprised me, since it seems she didn't know your real name."

Horace laughed. "Well, we had a rocky start. She loved her daughter and so did I. We had a difference of opinion on who loves her more. We came to a meeting point where neither of us was willing to bend. We had to find a way to live in harmony, if we both wanted to be in Eleanor's life. The compromise was her calling me Harold and me calling her an old bat. Hence, the fire you see between us when we are in the same room. But have no doubt, I love and respect Ophelia."

"And she does you, sir," Jarrett, replied, then sat up. "It's taken me a minute to come to terms with her plans for me. I plan to play for another five years, at least. I'm concerned there may be a conflict of interest. I'd like to turn control of the team over to Caswell, by proxy, until I retire. At that time, I'd like to have the controlling interest go to Paige and me. That way it would still be in Edward Hylton's family. Is that possible?"

The more Horace learned about Jarrett Bryson, the more he admired and liked him. "It is possible and the honorable thing to do."

Jarrett physically relaxed. "That's good sir. That is what I would like to do." He exhaled. "That will give me a few years to get used to the idea."

Horace didn't reply.

"Let's talk about Paige." Jarrett sat up. "I know it's short notice, but will you invite my family to Thanksgiving dinner on Thursday?"

Horace picked up his cell phone, then pushed a button. "Honey, guess who's coming to Thanksgiving dinner." He smiled.

*****

Her cell phone chimed at seven fifteen am. She didn't have to look at the number, she knew who it was.

"Good morning, Grand'Mere." She sat up in bed.

"I spoke with Mrs. Watson this morning," Ophelia said. "It's time for you to prepare to return to the stage."

Paige sighed. "I'm not sure I'm ready."

"You are."

Paige giggled as she threw the comforter to the side. "Grand'Mere, everything doesn't happen on your timetable."

"Of course it does, darling. Now what are your plans for today?"

Standing, she stretched. "I think I'll start my morning with a dance."

"That's my girl. Have you heard from Jarrett?"

"No," Paige sighed. Then there was silence. "I've been thinking a lot about us. The time, the distance, it may all be a good thing."

"Why do you say that, dear?"

Paige closed her eyes as she sat on the bed and exhaled. "Everything happened so fast. We met, fell in love and just didn't think about the people around us or how our two worlds would collide. With everything that happened, it seems we should have been more cautious."

"You don't have a cautious bone in your body." Ophelia laughed. "You are a free spirit, Paige. You came into this world your own unique way. You've lived your life with abandonment of the conditional way of life. You stepped into love the same way."

Paige smiled. "Maybe if I hadn't been so free and open, someone would not have lost their life."

"Neither of you could have anticipated the turn of events. You can't allow others' actions to change your course of life. Remember what I told you. Don't waste time on the noise. Live this life with as much laughter as possible and find love that will last for an eternity."

"Yes, Grand'Mere. I remember." Paige stood. "It's just that I so wanted to spend my holidays with Jarrett. But it doesn't seem that will happen."

"Christmas is a time when the air is filled with magic. It only takes one."

"I love you, Grand'Mere."

"I love you more, sweet pea."

Paige hung up the call feeling better, but then she always did after talking with her Grand'Mere. She missed Jarrett so much, her heart ached, but she believed in her love for him and his love for her. The universe would work it out, she thought, as she jumped into the shower.

*****

Paige ran downstairs after her workout. The kitchen had groceries all over the counter top, breakfast bar and table.

"Why all the food?" she asked Leona.

The woman turned and almost dropped the container she was putting away. "Thanksgiving is tomorrow. I have to prepare, child."

Paige looked around. "You have enough food here for an army."

"Good morning, darling," Eleanor said as she walked into the kitchen. She kissed her daughter on the temple, then examined the scar that remained on her face. "How are you feeling? Any headaches? Dizziness?"

"Only in certain lights," Paige replied. "It's getting better."

"Wear your glasses like the doctor told you and you won't have that problem," Leona scowled.

"I do, sometimes." Paige shrugged.

"I heard music." Eleanor smiled. "Were you dancing this morning?"

"I was." Paige sat at the table where Leona had placed a cup of tea. "Grand'Mere said it would make me feel more like myself and she was right. It felt good. I spoke with Victoria last night. She is flying on a cloud. Her reviews are wonderful."

"That should have been you," Leona huffed.

"It wasn't in the cards for me this time. But, I'll dance again."

"Of course you will," Eleanor encouraged her with a hug, then sat at the table next to her. "Have you spoken with Jarrett?"

"No, not since he left for Florida." Paige shrugged. "Do you think..."

"Do I think what, darling?"

"Do you think he has forgotten about me? Could he have moved on?"

Eleanor hated seeing her daughter doubt herself even for a minute. "How could he? You are unforgettable."

"And move on to what?" Leona asked. "As your Grand'Mere says, he is your destiny."

Eleanor and Leona glanced at each other over Paige's head and smiled.

"You know, you are both right. No more negative thoughts. I love him and he loves me. It will work out."

"Of course it will. Tomorrow the whole family will be together and this room will be filled with love.

*****

It only takes one spark of magic.

Paige sat straight up in bed at the sound of her Grand'Mere's voice. She looked around the room. Of course her Grand'Mere wasn't there she chastised herself. She looked out the window, it was still dark. She heard the house phone ring and her heart stopped beating for a second.

"Something's wrong." She jumped out of the bed and ran down the hallway to her parents' suite. She heard her mother gasp. She pushed the door open to see her father holding her mother in his arms.

*****

His cell phone chimed early Thanksgiving morning. Seeing it was Paige brought an immediate smile to Jarrett's face, then he frowned. Had she found out his plans? Had her parents sold him out?

No. She's calling to say happy Thanksgiving, he thought as he answered the phone.

"Jarrett."

He was on instant alert. He could hear her hurt through the phone. "Paige. What's wrong?"

"Grand'Mere transitioned this morning."

It took him a moment to take in what she had said. "Where are you, Paige?"

"At my parents' house."

"I'll be right there."

It didn't take long since he and his family were already in Virginia. They'd had dinner the night before with her parents. Ophelia had kept Paige busy to keep her from knowing they were in town. His only thought was to get to Paige. To hold her, to comfort her.

Leona opened the door when he arrived.

"Hello, Ms. Leona. Where is Paige?"

"She's upstairs in her room."

"Her parents?"

"They are at Mrs. Ophelia's house."

He hugged the distraught woman. "I am so sorry. This is a loss for all of us." He held her at arms' length. "Are you going to be all right to set things up for the house?"

She nodded.

"All right. I'm going to check on Paige. Which way is her room?"

Leona pointed as tears flowed. "Up the stairs to the right. The room at the end of the hallway."

"Thank you."

Jarrett found his way, then lightly knocked on the closed double door.

"Yes." He heard her quiet voice.

He opened the door. She was sitting on her window seat looking out. She turned towards him and it was as if a ray of sunshine brightened the room.

"Jarrett."

The sight of him standing in the doorway filled her heart. In that moment, she didn't care why he was there. She'd deal with that later. Right now she needed his arms around her. She needed him to take the hurt away. Paige stood and walked right into his arms. He wrapped them around her. All the hurt of losing her grandmother, the hurt of that night, the hurt of not having him, all poured out of her. Her tears ran down his neck, soaking his shirt, dripping down to his heart as he held her.

He picked her up, carried her to the bed and laid there holding her until her tears were all spent and she rested.

A few hours later there was a knock on the door. It opened to reveal Horace in the doorway.

Jarrett eased out of the bed, covered Paige then joined her father in the hallway.

"How is Mrs. Cartwright?"

"The doctor gave her a small sedative so she could sleep for a while. Where is your family?"

"At the hotel."

"Have them brought over. I don't want their day marred by this. Ophelia wouldn't want that. How is Paige?"

"Hurt."

Horace nodded. "I'm glad you are here to help her through this."

"I wouldn't be anywhere else."

*****

The funeral was held that Saturday. Jarrett watched her from a distance as Paige placed white roses on the casket of Ophelia Hylton. He could feel the sadness in her eyes even with the sunshades on. It stabbed at his heart with each beat. He hurt for her, and the family. The love they had for each other was remarkable to watch. He felt fortunate to be a part of it for a short period. Paige hadn't said much over the last few days. He was by her side day and night. They talked mostly about her Grand'Mere as he held her each night. There was distance between them, but neither of them acknowledged it or allowed it to keep them from supporting each other during the week of visits from other family members, friends, associates including Ruben Caswell, and different players.

It wasn't until Sunday morning when they walked around the estate that they had a chance to talk about them. They walked out the back of the house towards the gardens. The air had turned cold, unlike the day before.

"Virginia weather is a little interesting," Jarrett said as he pulled up the collar to his coat.

"That's why you always stay prepared." She pulled a pair of gloves and earmuffs from her pocket.

"Should you have something on your head?"

"I have a scarf." She put it over her head and around her neck. "Better?"

"Yes." He kissed her then took her gloved hand in his and began walking down the path. "What are the doctors saying about your headaches?"

"The headaches are fading. They should go away permanently soon. Grand'Mere says they will disappear once my life settles down."

A sadness filled the moment. "You're going to miss her," Jarrett said, "but I'm sure she has given you a lifetime of sayings for you to share with our children."

"Our children?"

He looked down at her. "I certainly hope so." He bent over, kissed her gently on the lips, then continued walking.

She took his arm, snuggling closer as they walked.

"We never talked about that night," Jarrett began. "I had to find my way through all the noise that surrounded us. Searching for you that night damn near killed me inside. Our first mistake was accusing the Dragons' management of being involved in your disappearance. As it turned out, they had indeed discussed injuring me to improve their chances in the playoffs. When that was uncovered, they discussed targeting you." He exhaled. "Then we found out about the incident between you and Jolene Cadet. So we went to her place." He stopped, remembering the feeling of doom he'd felt walking into the apartment.

She squeezed his arm. "Let's sit in the gazebo. We can light the fire pit for a little heat. And hold each other as we talk."

Jarrett loved that she knew he was struggling. It was a conversation they had to have in order to move forward, but it was still hard.

Once lit, the heat from the fireplace took the nip off the night air.

"I know this isn't easy." Paige exhaled. "But it's better to bring things to the light before the dark bites you in the behind."

Jarrett smiled, then pulled her close on the bench. They sat there with her head on his shoulder and his arm around hers.

"There was a body wrapped in plastic inside the apartment. For a minute, I thought it was you. My heart broke in that moment, Paige." He shook his head. "I literally stopped breathing until the face was revealed. It was so mangled, there was no way to tell who it was. I only knew it wasn't you because of the hair color." He shook his head trying to get the vision from his mind. "I thought I had lost you, right there, Paige."

Paige reached up to wipe the tears away from his cheeks, then turned his face towards hers. She kissed his lips. "You didn't lose me, Jarrett. I'm right here."

He put his hand over hers. "I didn't know that at the time. I couldn't breathe, I couldn't think. All I knew was that I had to find you."

"And you did."

"Yes." He sniffed. "I did." He put her head on his shoulder and continued. "That's when the problems really began. I felt the guilt of Lacy's death, the guilt of what happened to you, but there was something more." He took a moment, because he wasn't sure how she would take what he was about to say. "It frightened me to think you had that kind of impact on my life. That meant you could walk away and my life would be devastated. I know this sounds crazy, but I needed to step away before I could put my life in somebody else's hands." There, he said it. "When Lacy said your Grand'Mere planned all of it, even meeting you, I lost it. Here I was putting my life into the hands of a woman who was manipulating me. I was angry and hurt. I didn't trust myself or my judgment when it came to you. It took a really good friend and your Grand'Mere to help me see my life wasn't worth a damn without you." He sighed. "I doubted you, and I am so sorry for that."

Paige nodded her head. "I know." She shrugged. "I wish you had shared your fears with me. I had no idea what happened that night, other than getting into that car and waking up in the hospital. You suffered much more than I did. You went through an ordeal and I am sorry for that. I could feel the torment as you talked about it."

"You were taken hostage, pistol whipped and you are sorry for me?"

"Yes, because I have no memory of any of it. I was safe by the time I knew something was wrong." She sat up, then took his hand in hers. "There's so much mistrust." She shook her head. "The players in the league questioning your position with the front office. The fans questioning my love for you. Your fans' reaction to all that happened. There were some cruel things said about you. Some of it was frightening. It's just that I fear for you." She looked away, then back at him. "In game four during the eighth inning, the catcher said something to you that made you angry. What did he say?"

"How do you know that?" Jarrett remembered the catcher saying 'the great Jarrett Bryson got taken by a big ass and a pretty face.' It pissed him off.

"I saw your body's reaction. I could feel your anger. I said a quick prayer that you would let it pass. I prayed that you would take it out on the ball."

He smiled for that very saying came to his mind. Jarrett pushed her hair away from her face, then kissed her scar. "It wasn't nice, but I ignored it and did just what you said. I took it out on the ball."

"That's what scares me. This whole journey is a test, Jarrett. We have to make sure we are strong enough to make it through the rest. There are still going to be questions and people who wonder if I did try to manipulate you. There will still be people like Suzette who are going to try to come between us for their own personal gain. I'm disappointed you thought for one moment, I was involved in a plot of any kind against you. But I know the reason it hurt is because my love for you is so deep. Your fear of someone having control over your heart is real. I have that same fear. The difference between you and I, is I refuse to let that fear stop me from experiencing the love of my life."

"You are an amazing woman, Paige Cartwright. Come home with me."

Paige smiled at him, then looked away. "I need time, Jarrett. I know that sounds crazy after us being apart for a month. But I need to clear some things from my mind."

Jarrett was disappointed, but a lot had happened in the last month, not to mention the last week. He took her in his arms.

"I love you, Paige. No matter how much time you take, that is not going to change."

"Are you going back to Florida?"

"No, I'll be in New York having bagels with Jake, waiting for you to join me." He took her hand in his and they began walking back towards the house. "You owe me a horseback ride in the snow."

She snuggled close to him. "Can we walk across the Brooklyn Bridge too?"

"In the snow?" He gave her a sideways glance.

"Of course."

"Only you, Paige," he laughed. "Only you."

*****

It was the week of Christmas. For a man who had everything, it sure felt like Santa had forgotten him. They had won the World Series. He was named MVP and it all meant nothing. The one thing he wanted, wasn't there. Paige. They had talked every night before they closed their eyes and first thing every morning. But, he was missing her some kind of terrible.

The balcony was covered with snow from the night before. But it did not deter him from doing what he had done every morning for the last three weeks. He walked out on the balcony, sat in his designated chair with his coffee and bagel from Jake's and watched Paige's condo. He knew she would appear one day. He had to believe it would be before Christmas, but if it wasn't it didn't matter. He would wait. His cell phone rang, but he had left it on the kitchen table. He ran back inside and picked it up.

"Have you ever dreamt about a slow kiss?"

He closed his eyes at the sound of her voice. His heart rate began to increase as it nearly burst with joy.

"I have." He nodded as he walked back to the balcony with his head down.

"You know the kind where your lips linger, because the taste is so sweet you just don't want to let it go."

With his eyes closed, he nodded as he leaned against the balcony door frame. "Yes, I know exactly the kiss you are talking about."

"If you meet me in front of Jake's, I'll give you one."

Jarrett's eyes popped open. Across the street, on the balcony he had watched for days, weeks even, there she stood. He couldn't take his eyes from her for fear she would disappear. "I've missed you so..."

"Then you better hurry, because I'm already dressed. I double dare you to beat me there."

He watched as she disconnected the call and ran back into her condo. He ran into his room, threw a sweater on and a pair of jeans. He ran to the elevator, then turned back. "Shit, shoes."

He ran back into the bedroom, jumped into a pair of boots then ran back to the elevator. He ran out the front entrance, not caring that a few reporters were there. He ran around the corner and looked across the street. There she was, standing in front of Jake's Bistro, playing in the snow. He started to run across the street but stopped at the car horns blowing. He willed the cars to go by, then dashed to where she was.

His heart was pumping fast, but he slowed down. He took slow steady steps towards her. She smiled and his heart melted, right then and there. The snow falling around her face made her look like an angel.

His hands cupped her face. The scar now dull from the passage of time. His lips met hers as he slowly applied pressure to the softness of them. Her arms circled his waist, pulling him closer. Her body blended together with his, as his tongue parted her lips. He took it slow, tasting every corner of her mouth. Relishing every drop of her sweetness. Allowing his heart to fill with the love she had for him. He pulled the hat from her head, allowing his fingers to run through her hair, as he held their lips together.

He took a breath. "I love, Paige Cartwright. I'll love you until the day the baseball gods call me home." He got down on one knee in the snow, reached into his pocket, then took her hand.

"You are the spark of magic I need in my life. Paige, will you marry me?"

Tears welled in her eyes, then began to fall. She wiped one away and said, "Yes."

Jarrett pushed the ring on her finger then stood, pulling her close.

Her smile was radiant, her laughter music to his ears. She caressed his chest with the ring sparkling in their faces and said, "Well, there you go."

His laughter could be heard inside the bistro as cheers from patrons exploded. The reporters around them put down the cameras and microphones and joined in the cheering. It was a Christmas kiss to remember.

Epilogue

Eleanor looked at her daughter through the full-length mirror. "I wish your Grand'Mere was here to see you tonight."

"She's with us, Mother." Paige lowered her head as Leona pinned the veil into her hair.

"Yes, she is." Leona nodded. "Only she and you would want a winter wedding, outside, in Central Park in the dead of winter on New Year's Eve."

"It's not that cold, Leona." Eleanor shook her head. "The tent is heated and will be sealed the moment we walk in."

"I'm with Ms. Leona on this," Victoria chimed in. "Don't get me wrong, the red cape with the hood is to die for. I really feel like little red riding hood in some freaking fairy tale or something."

"Will Sergio be your prince charming?" Paige smiled at her friend.

"Could be, we'll have to see if he can handle all of this." She smirked then looked out the door of the restaurant towards the tent across the lawn. She jerked her head back when she saw the couple getting out of the vehicle. "Did you invite Suzette to your wedding?"

Paige turned towards her friend. "I have had this discussion with Jarrett. Yes, I invited Suzette. She is Ron's wife for goodness sake. Why is everyone so up in arms about this?"

"Cause she should be in jail," Leona mumbled.

"I second that." Victoria walked over to where Paige stood near the mirror.

"We have to find ways to love our enemies despite our differences. Isn't that right, Mother?"

Eleanor raised an eyebrow. "You love your enemies from afar. You don't have to invite them to your dinner table."

"Thank you," Victoria replied.

Paige sighed. "She has been banned from the Queens, shunned by the front office and ridiculed by the public. I think she has suffered enough."

"Here, try these." Eleanor gave her daughter a pair of diamond earrings.

Paige gasped when she looked inside the box. Then she looked up at her mother.

"Nothing says love like a sweet pair of diamond studs." The two laughed.

"Your Grand'Mere gave them to me when I married your father. That was the first of many times I heard her say that."

Paige touched her heart. "I will cherish them and pass them on to my daughter on her wedding day."

Eleanor smiled as she stood back to watch Paige put them on.

"Oh my."

They all turned to see Horace standing in the doorway.

"You are too beautiful to give away."

"I'm afraid that ship has sailed, Daddy," Paige laughed, then whirled around in the middle of the floor. "Do you think Jarrett will like it?"

"No, he's going to want to tear it off of you."

"Horace." Eleanor kissed him on his cheek. "Stop teasing your daughter."

He closed the distance between them. Then smiled down at her. "I wish the old bat was here to see you. She loved you so much."

Paige tilted her head to the side. "Not enough to tell me she was ill." She looked away, acting as if she needed to adjust something on the perfect dress she was wearing.

Horace glanced at his wife. "Would you all give us a minute?"

"Sure." Victoria waited for Leona then stepped out of the room. Eleanor patted her husband on the shoulder, then closed the door behind her.

Horace inhaled. "The day your grandmother was diagnosed she called me." He took Paige's hand, led her to the small sofa and sat, then pulled her onto his lap. "She asked for three things. First and foremost she did not want any treatment. No chemo, no exploratory treatments...nothing. She wanted to go on her own terms. Second she asked me to handle the team ownership transfer to Jarrett Bryson. I thought she was crazy to turn the team over to a stranger. I should have known that Ophelia Hylton never left anything to chance. She knew once he met you he would fall in love with you." He shook his head. "How she knew it, I will never know. But over the years, I've learned not to question your Grand'Mere." He turned her face to look at him. "The last thing she requested was that I never tell you or your mother that she was ill. She did not want to spend her last days seeing sadness in your eyes. That's why it was so important that you found Jarrett before that day came. She wanted to see you happy and settled with the kind of love she'd had with your grandfather and that I have with your mother."

"If I had known, I could have said goodbye that day."

"You did." Horace smiled. "When you left you said, good bye. That was all she needed."

Paige inhaled and smiled at her father. "I miss her."

"I know you do. But she is here with us and she will always be in our hearts."

She kissed him on the cheek. "Are you ready to give me away?"

"No."

Paige smiled, then stood. "Well, I'm ready."

Horace sighed. "Oh all right. If I have to."

*****

Jarrett was standing near the entrance greeting guests as they arrived. A few key members of the team, their wives and members of the front office were among the guests. He froze when he saw Ron and Suzette approaching.

"Adjust your face," Jarrett warned Sergio as the couple approached.

"You invited her to your wedding that almost did not occur because of her?" Sergio hissed.

"You got all of that out in one breath."

"I'm a little bothered that she is here."

"Me too, but this is what Paige wanted to do."

"Jake." Jarrett extended his hand, then hugged Val.

She whispered, "What is Suzette doing here?"

"Paige," he replied as she stepped back from their hug.

"You don't invite a wolf to your feast," Jake warned.

Jarrett raised an eyebrow in understanding. "If I can get through her being here, so can you."

"Me, why would I have to?"

"She's going to be sitting at the table with you."

Val rolled her eyes. "You have the nerve to smile when you say that."

Jarrett nodded then greeted Mr. and Mrs. Weingart.

"I knew this day would come." Mrs. Weingart kissed him on the cheek.

"Thank you for coming." Jarrett smiled.

Sergio cleared his throat. "Ron." He nodded to his teammate, then turned from Suzette.

Ron noticed the slight, but continued on.

Suzette huffed, "Ron, you're going to let Sergio disrespect me like that?"

He looked back at her. "It's no more than what you deserve." He shook Jarrett's hand as Suzette gawked at him.

"Close your mouth, Suzette. Someone may fly in and choke you," Jarrett said as all eyes in the room discreetly watched the exchange.

"I didn't come here to be disrespected."

"The only reason you are here is because you are my wife, for now," Ron spoke. "That can change by tomorrow."

Jarrett stopped them from proceeding. "There is something Paige asked me to do." He took Suzette's arm, then stepped away from the receiving line. His voice changed to a warning. "Smile and listen carefully. Make no mistake. If it was up to me, you would meet the same fate you setup for Lacy."

Suzette glared at him.

"Smile, or I'll walk away with everyone looking."

Suzette glanced around, people were indeed watching. "I'm having Ron's contract renegotiated to include a no trade clause with the Knights. He loves you so to have him I have to deal with you. With that said, this is what you will do. You will not interfere in any activities with the Queens. Don't call them, don't go to lunch with them. Keep your distance. The Queen of Knights pilot has been approved. Val will choose the participants. You will not be one. Your name will not be attached. You will be affiliated in no way."

"It was my idea. I sent the proposal in. It was mine."

"No, it is the Knights. You will be watching it from home." Jarrett hugged her. "Paige asked me to give you a hug in front of people so they can think we are past our differences and you will not be shunned here at the wedding." He smiled then walked back to the line.

Ron walked over to Suzette with a glass of champagne. "Are you okay?"

She took the glass. "No, he took my show and gave it to Val."

Ron exhaled. "You know, I'm sick of hearing about that show. It was that show that cost Lacy her life. You haven't acknowledged your role in all that happened, have you?"

"How was I supposed to know Lacy wasn't all there?"

Ron showed no expression. He looked over her shoulder as he spoke. "Enjoy the wedding, Suzette." He glared into her eyes. "When we return home. I'll be moving out." He held out his arm. "Shall we?"

"I don't know what has gotten into you."

Ron lowered his arm, then motioned for one of the security guards. "Will you escort my wife to the car? She isn't feeling well."

"What?"

"Go or I will let them carry you out," he whispered in her ear.

She huffed, then stomped off.

Jarrett stepped over. "What happened?"

"We had a difference of opinion. She wanted to stay and I didn't want her anywhere near me."

Jarrett shrugged. "About time you grew some balls when it comes to your wife."

Ron shoved Jarrett in a playful way, however, the new security guard did not realize that. One kick and Ron found himself flat on his back with a spike heel boot in his chest and a gun pointed at his head.

"No," Jarrett said a second too late.

"Hey, Ron, she laid you out like a blanket on a horse's back," Sergio laughed, then turned to the guests who were gawking at the scene. "Nothing major. Just a little fall," Sergio announced.

Rod started to speak as his eyes saw the spiked boot, solid thick thighs, a short black dress, voluptuous breasts, red-bone, with her hair slicked back into a ponytail. Her eyes were coal black and ready to strike.

"What in the..."

The heel of the boot dug deeper in his chest.

Jarrett bent down next to Ron trying hard not to laugh. "This is Karess Parker, ex-military, and part of Paige's new security detail."

Ron didn't dare take his eyes from the woman staring down at him. "Yeah? Well can you tell her I'm a good guy?"

Jarrett smiled. "Let him up."

Karess secured her weapon back into her thigh

holster, stepped from Ron's chest, then held her hand down to him. Ron reluctantly accepted it. The woman pulled him up as if he was a rag doll. Then she had the nerve to smile.

"What woman in her right mind let you out unprotected?"

"A crazy, selfish witch," Sergio jested.

"Feel free to put a b at the beginning of the last word," Jarrett added, then turned to Ron. "Are you okay?"

Ron's eyes were still on the woman, who was walking away to join the other security guard he knew was Peace.

"Yeah, yeah, I'm straight," Ron replied as he dusted off his suit.

Jarrett and Sergio watched the look between Ron and Karess.

Sergio leaned over to Jarrett's ear and whispered, "Talk about a spark of lightning. Whew. Did you see that look?"

Jarrett was still watching. "I'd like to see Suzette go up against that one."

The two stopped laughing when Ron turned to them. "What's so funny?"

The music began playing at that moment and the men stepped back.

Everyone took their seats at the tables, which were covered in white tablecloths and had gold place settings, stemware and goblets. The centerpieces were dark burgundy roses with candles in the center. As the lights in the enclosed tent dimmed, the candles brightened. The setup allowed premium viewing of the ceremony for everyone.

The song Forever Mine by the O'Jays began to play. Jarrett's parents walked in and took a seat at a table near the front. Eleanor walked in escorted by

Sergio. He sat her next to Jarrett's parents, then stood next to Jarrett and waited.

Victoria stood in the opening of the tent dressed in a red, form-fitting gown with a mini train in the back. The tent doors closed behind her. She took the fifth position, bent to the floor, then did a pirouette down the aisle. She stopped at Sergio, curtsied, then stood next to him.

The doors opened. Jarrett's eyes could not believe the sight standing there. She was exquisite.

Dressed in a white fur trimmed cloak with matching hand mittens, Paige stepped inside on her father's arm. Horace removed her cloak, revealing an elegant, sleeveless, lace wedding gown. It had a fitted bodice and a flared bottom with lace trim. The dress was made in the old school elegance of Grace Kelly. Her hair was in an up do with a diamond crown.

To Jarrett, she looked like a snow princess. His princess. It was as if she was floating down the aisle. She gave her mittens to Victoria then kissed Jarrett on the lips. The guests laughed.

"It seems like you needed a kiss." She smiled then took his hand in hers.

Horace stepped in front of them. "Are you ready?"

"Yes." Paige smiled and Jarrett laughed as he shook his head.

"Good evening, family and friends. We've gathered here in this beautiful setting to witness the union of Jarrett Deon Bryson to Paige Simone Cartwright. They decided on their own vows, so all I have to do is seal it with the powers vested in me." The guests laughed. "Paige."

Holding his hands Paige gazed into Jarrett's eyes. "I was on a cloud the day I met you. I still haven't come down. You look at me and my heart wants to dance. You say my name and birds begin to sing. You smile and the sun shines so bright it's almost blinding. I promise to dance, sing and shine with you every day of my life."

Horace composed himself from his daughter's declaration of love. "Jarrett. Make it good." He smiled.

Jarrett pulled Paige a little closer. "We go through life looking for love before we begin to walk. I believe the day I was born my steps were directed towards you. If a genie granted me one gift, it would be for you to see yourself through my eyes. You would see that you are my sun, my stars, my everything. You made me realize love grows, it never dies. For that I will love, cherish and protect you all the days of my life and beyond. When we leave these bodies to ascend to heaven, I pray God will grant me eternity with you."

Paige palmed his face and kissed him again.

"Paige, wait."

"Well hurry up, Daddy."

Horace cleared his throat then looked at Jarrett. "That was good."

Jarrett smiled. "Thank you. Can you hurry up?"

"By the powers vested in me, I pronounce you husband and wife."

He barely got the words out of his mouth before Jarrett pulled Paige to him and gave her a long, slow, deep kiss to seal their union.

The guests cheered and clapped as the couple paid them no mind.

For the next few hours they danced, celebrating the love they had for each other and their guests until it was time to leave. Sergio and Victoria performed their toasts to the bride and groom.

"It's snowing." Paige beamed as she ran to the opening in the tent. She held her hands out to catch the flakes. "What a perfect way to start our life."

Jarrett wrapped her white cloak around her

shoulders. "Close your eyes."

"Why?"

The light in her eyes filled his heart with so much joy, he was as giddy as she. "I want to surprise you."

"Okay." Paige closed her eyes.

Jarrett took her hand as he signaled Sergio.

"Aww," some of the guests began to sigh.

He turned to them with his finger to his lips for them to be quiet.

"Jarrett?"

"Keep them closed." He led her to the end of the walkway. When they were in position, he said, "Okay, you can open them now."

Paige opened her eyes to a beautiful, white horse drawn carriage, with velvet seats. The driver was dressed in a tuxedo with tails and the horse had a harness with white feathers.

"I promised you a carriage ride in Central Pack. The snow is a plus."

"Oh, Jarrett, it's beautiful." Paige went directly to the horse.

"Let's take a ride," Jarrett said as he held his hand out to her.

He helped her into the carriage, tucking her dress around her. He gathered the blanket across their laps, then gazed into her eyes.

"Your spirit touched my heart the first day I met you." She beamed, gazing into his eyes.

Jarrett gently kissed her cheek. "It's a good thing it did, for you touched my soul."

My job is done.

The two turned, looking into the night as if someone was standing there speaking to them.

"Did you hear that?" Jarrett asked.

Paige snuggled close to him. "Yes, it was Grand'mere saying goodbye."

They gazed at each other and said, "*Well, there you go.*" Their laughter rang throughout the park causing those inside the big white tent to turn their way as they kissed.

It was the love of a lifetime that only took one spark of magic.

The End

The Heart Series
Streaming on Amazon Video

Scan with your phone.

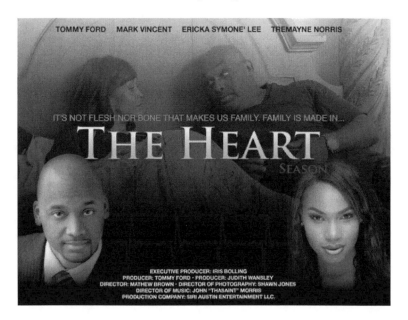

Made in the USA
Middletown, DE
09 April 2024

52769400R00148